T0285222

# FORGOTTEN ON SUNDAY

ALSO BY

VALÉRIE PERRIN

*Fresh Water for Flowers*
*Three*

Valérie Perrin

# FORGOTTEN ON SUNDAY

*Translated from the French
by Hildegarde Serle*

Europa
*editions*

Europa Editions
27 Union Square West, Suite 302
New York NY 10003
www.europaeditions.com
info@europaeditions.com

Copyright © Editions Albin Michel - Paris 2015
First publication 2024 by Europa Editions

Translation by Hildegarde Serle
Original title: *Les Oubliés du dimanche*
Translation copyright © 2023 by Europa Editions

Library of Congress Cataloging in Publication Data is available
ISBN 979-8-88966-018-7

Perrin, Valérie
Forgotten on Sunday

Cover photo: Allan Cash Picture Library / Alamy Stock Photo

Cover design by Ginevra Rapisardi

Prepress by Grafica Punto Print – Rome

Printed in Italy

To Valentin, Tess, Emma, and Gabrielle

Being old is just being young for longer than others.
—PHILIPPE GELUCK

# FORGOTTEN ON SUNDAY

1

I went to buy a notebook at old Prost's store. I chose a blue one. I didn't want to write *Helen's Story* on a computer because I want to carry her story around in my smock pocket. I went back home. On the cover I wrote, "The Beach Lady." And on the first page:

*Hélène Hel was born twice. On April 20, 1917 in Clermain, Burgundy, and on the day she met Lucien Perrin in 1933, just before summer.*

Then I slid the blue notebook between my mattress and bed, like in those black-and-white movies Gramps watches on *Cinéma de minuit* on Sunday evenings.

And then I went back off to work because I was on duty.

My name is Justine Neige. I'm twenty-one years old. I've been working at a retirement home called The Hydrangeas for three years. I'm a nursing assistant. Generally, retirement homes are named after trees, like The Lindens, or The Sweet Chestnuts. But mine was built upon banks of hydrangeas. So no one considered trees, despite the home being on the edge of a forest.

I love two things in life: music and the elderly. I go dancing one Saturday in three, pretty much, at the Paradise club, about thirty kilometers from The Hydrangeas. My Paradise is a kind of reinforced-concrete cube stuck in the middle of a field, with a makeshift car park where, sometimes, I drunkenly kiss people of the opposite sex at around five in the morning.

Of course, I also love my brother Jules (who's actually my cousin) and my grandparents—my late father's parents. Jules is the only young person I spent time with at home during my childhood. I grew up with the elderly. I skipped a generation.

I divide my life into three: caring by day, interpreting the old folks' voices at night, and dancing on Saturday evenings to get back that carefree feeling I lost in 1996 because of grown-ups.

Those grown-ups were my parents and Jules's parents. They had the terrible idea of dying together in a car accident one Sunday morning. I saw the article that Gran cut out from the newspaper. An article that's supposed to be hidden away, but not if you rummage. And I saw the photo of the car, too.

Because of them, Jules and I spent every other Sunday at the village cemetery, placing fresh flowers on their tomb. A wide tomb featuring two photographs, framed by two cherubs, of my father's wedding and my uncle's wedding. As for the two brides, one's a blonde, the other a brunette. The brunette's my mother. The blonde, she's Jules's. On the photos, the husband of the blonde and the husband of the brunette are the same man. Same suit, same tie, same smile. My father and my uncle were twins. How could the same man, seemingly, have fallen in love with two different women? And how could two women be in love with the same man? Those are the eternal questions I still ask myself as I enter the cemetery gates. And I have no one to answer me. Perhaps that's why I lost that carefree feeling: because I'm missing answers from Christian, Sandrine, Alain, and Annette Neige.

At the cemetery, while the long dead lie down below, the recent dead are contained in small enclosures, all somewhat on the periphery. As if they'd arrived late. My family lies at the top of the village. Half a kilometer from my grandparents' house.

My village is called Milly. Some four hundred inhabitants. You need a magnifying glass to find it on a map. There's one commercial street: that's Rue Jean-Jaurès. At the center, a small Romanesque church with its square. When it comes to stores, apart from old Prost's grocery, there's a betting office, a garage, and a hair salon, whose owner shut up shop last year because he'd had enough of doing just tints and sets. The clothes stores and florists have been replaced by banks and a medical analysis lab. Otherwise, windows have been lined with newspaper, or, if the stores are now homes, white curtains hang there instead of slacks.

There are almost as many "For Sale" signs as there are houses. But since the nearest highway is more than seventy kilometers away, and the nearest station fifty, no one's buying.

There's still a grade school. The one I went to with Jules.

To get to middle school, high school, the doctor's, the chemist's, or to buy some socks, you have to catch a bus.

Since the hairdresser's departure, it's me who does Gran's sets. She sits in the kitchen with wet hair and passes me the curlers, one by one, as I wind her white strands around them and then skewer them with a plastic pin to hold them in place. When I've finished, I pop on a hairnet and put her under the dryer, where she drops off after about five minutes, and then, once the hair's dry, I unroll it, and it lasts until the following week.

Since my parents died, I have no memory of being cold. At home, it's never less than a hundred degrees. And I can't remember a thing from before they died. But that I'll talk about later.

My brother and I grew up in old-fashioned but comfortable, softener-washed clothes. Without smacks or slaps, and with a mixing desk and LPs in the cellar for making a racket when we'd had enough of the silence of polishing-slippers sliding on parquet.

I would have loved to go to bed late, have grubby fingernails, and hang around empty lots, grazing my knees and cycling down hills with eyes closed. I would have loved to feel pain or wet my bed. But with my grandmother, no chance. She always had a bottle of antiseptic to hand.

Aside from Gran cleaning inside our ears with Q-tips throughout our childhood, and washing us twice a day with a cloth, and forbidding anything that could be dangerous, like crossing the road alone, I think that, since the death of her twins, she had waited for the day when Jules or I would finally look like our fathers. But it never happened. Jules has Annette's face. As for me, I don't look like anyone.

Despite being called Gran and Gramps, my grandparents are younger than most Hydrangeas' residents. But I don't know when one starts to be old. Madame Le Camus, my boss, says it's when you can't look after your home on your own anymore. That it starts when the car must stay in the garage because you're becoming a danger to the public and ends when you break a hip. Personally, I think it starts with loneliness. When the other person has left. For heaven, or for someone else.

My colleague Jo says that you become old when you start to ramble on, and it's an illness that can be caught very young. Maria, my other colleague, that it comes when you lose your hearing, and your keys, having to search for them ten times a day.

I'm twenty-one, and I search for my keys ten times a day.

1924

Hélène works by candlelight in her parents' tailoring and dressmaking atelier, late into the night.
She grows up alone, in the midst of suits and dresses. Without a brother or sister.

On a wall of the atelier she makes shadows. Always the same ones. She joins her palms to form a bird that eats from her hand. The beak she outlines with her right index finger. The bird resembles a seagull. When it wants to fly off, the little girl links her thumbs and flaps her fanned-finger wings. But before letting it go, she entrusts it with a prayer—always the same one—which the seagull must carry up to heaven, God's home.

G ran?"

"Mmm."

"Where were they going, Mom and Dad, the morning they got killed?"

"To a baptism."

"Whose baptism?"

"The son of a childhood friend of your father's."

"Gran?"

"Yes."

"Why did they have that accident?"

"I've already told you a hundred times. There was black ice. They must have skidded. And then . . . there was that tree. If there hadn't been that tree . . . they would never . . . anyhow, let's not talk about it anymore."

"Why?"

"Why what?"

"Why d'you never want to talk about it?"

My love of old people began when my French teacher, Madame Petit, took my seventh-grade class to spend an afternoon at The Three Pines (before The Hydrangeas existed in Milly). After lunch, we all got into a bus for a drive of almost an hour. I remember throwing up twice into a brown paper bag.

At The Three Pines, the old people were waiting for us in the dining room. It smelt of soup and ether. Made me want to throw up again. When we had to greet them, I stopped breathing through my nose. And they were prickly. When it came to facial hair, it was anarchy.

My class had prepared a show: we were supposed to sing ABBA's "Gimme! Gimme! Gimme!" We wore white Lycra costumes and wigs borrowed from our school's theater club.

After the show, we sat down with them to eat pancakes. Not one of them let go of the paper handkerchiefs gripped firmly in their ice-cold fists. But for me, it was there that everything began: they told us stories. And old folks, since that's all they have left to do, can tell the past like no one else. Don't bother searching in books or movies: like no one else.

On that day, I understood that, with the elderly, it's enough just to touch them, to hold their hand, for them to talk. Like when you dig a hole in dry sand at the seaside, and the water instantly rises up under your fingers.

I have my own favorite story at The Hydrangeas. She's called Hélène. Hélène is the lady in room 19. She's the only one who offers me a real vacation. And given the day-to-day of a nursing assistant in geriatrics, that sure is a luxury.

The staff call her "the beach lady."

When I started working there, I was told that "she spends her days on a beach, under a parasol." And that, since her arrival, a seagull had set up home on the establishment's roof.

Around here, there are no seagulls. This is the center of France. Blackbirds, sparrows, crows, starlings, plenty of them, but not seagulls. Apart from the one that lives above our heads.

Hélène is the only resident I call by her first name.

Every morning, after her ablutions, we settle her into her armchair facing the window. And I swear, what she gazes at isn't Milly's rooftops, but something fabulously beautiful, like a blue smile. And yet her light eyes are like those of the other residents here: they're the color of a faded sheet. All the same, when I'm feeling down, I pray for life to give me a parasol like hers. Her parasol is called Lucien; he was her husband. Well, her almost-husband, since he never married her. Hélène told me her whole life. But in jigsaw-puzzle form. As if she'd given me the finest object in her home but had broken it into a thousand pieces first, without meaning to.

For a few months now, she's been speaking less, as if the song of her life were playing at the end of a record and the volume reducing.

Whenever I leave her room, I cover her legs, and she says to me, "I'm going to have some sunlight therapy." Hélène never feels cold. Even in the middle of winter, she treats herself to warming up in the sun, while we're all pressing our backsides to the Hydrangeas' dodgy radiators.

The only family of Hélène's that I know is her daughter, Rose. She's a painter, and does drawings, too. She's done many portraits of her parents in charcoal, some seascapes, harbors, a few gardens, and bunches of flowers. Hélène's walls are covered in them. Rose lives in Paris. Every Thursday, she arrives at the station and hires a car to come to Milly. On every visit, it's the same routine. Hélène looks at her from a distance, or rather, from where she seems to live.

"Who are you?"

"It's me, Mom."

"I don't understand, *madame*."

"It's me, Mom, Rose."

"No it isn't . . . my daughter's only seven, she's gone for a swim with her father."

"Oh, right . . . she's gone for a swim . . ."

"Yes. With her father."

"And do you know when they'll be back?"

"Later. I'm waiting for them."

And then Rose opens a novel and reads passages to her mother. Often love stories. When she's finished reading, she leaves me the books. It's her way of thanking me. Thanking me for caring for her mother as if she were mine.

The craziest chapter of my life began last Thursday, at around three in the afternoon. I opened door 19 and saw him, sitting beside Hélène's armchair. Those portraits of Lucien hanging on the walls. It was him. I just stood there, like a fool, looking at the two of them, not daring to move: Lucien was holding Hélène's hand. And as for her, the expression on her face was one I'd never seen before. As if she'd just discovered something amazing. He smiled at me. And said:

"Hello, are you Justine?"

So, I thought, Lucien knows my name. That must be normal. Ghosts must know the names of the living. They must know plenty of things we don't know. And above all, I thought: I understand why Hélène waited for him on a beach. I understand why she stopped time. Everything can suddenly make sense; with a guy like him, it's as if life were delivering everything. His eyes . . . I'd never seen anything as blue. Even when scouring Gran's mail-order catalogs.

I stammered:

"You've come to collect her?"

He didn't reply. Neither did Hélène. It's crazy how she was looking at him. Her eyes, the faded sheets, all that, it had gone.

I approached them and kissed Hélène on her forehead. Her skin was even warmer than usual. I was in the same state as the sky when they say the devil's beating his wife: in my head, it was rainy and sunny all at once. It was the last time I would see her: Lucien had finally come out of the water to lead her to their paradise.

I took Hélène's hand in mine.

"Are you taking the seagull with you?" I asked Lucien, with a lump in my throat.

From the way he looked at me, I could see he didn't understand. The man before me was no ghost.

It's then that I got the fright of my life. This guy existed, in real life. I turned tail and left room 19 like a thief.

Lucien Perrin was born in Milly on November 25, 1911. In his family, blindness is passed down from father to son—a hereditary condition that only affects the men. They're not born blind, they become so. The sight problems begin in infancy and, for generations, not one of them has seen the flames of his twenty candles dancing on his birthday cake.

Lucien's father, Étienne Perrin, met his wife Emma when she was still but a child. He knew her when he could still see. But, little by little, Emma disappeared from his field of vision, as if a veil of mist had settled over her face. He loves her from memory.

Étienne tried everything to save his eyes. He poured all sorts into them: elixirs, spring water from France and beyond, magic powders, infusions of nettles and chamomile, rose and cornflower water, iced water, warm water, salt, tea, holy water.

Lucien was born by accident. His father didn't want to have children. He didn't want to risk perpetuating the curse. And when he learned that it was a son, not a daughter, who had just been born, he was in despair.

Emma describes the child to him: black hair and big blue eyes.

In the Perrin family, no one has ever had blue eyes. At birth, they are black. The pupil can't be distinguished from the iris. Then, as the years go by, they lighten, ending up gray, like unrefined salt.

Étienne starts to hope that Lucien's blue eyes will protect him from the curse.

Just like his father, grandfather, and great-grandfather, Étienne is an organist and organ tuner. He is called upon to play Johann

*Sebastian Bach at church services, and also to tune the region's organs.*

*In addition, on weekdays, Étienne teaches Braille. His books are made by a first cousin, himself visually impaired, in a small workshop in Paris's fifth arrondissement.*

*One morning in 1923, Emma leaves Étienne. He doesn't hear her closing the door, very gently, behind her. He's busy with a pupil. Nor does he hear the voice of the man who is waiting for his wife on the sidewalk opposite. But Lucien does see her leave.*

*He doesn't try to stop his mother. He thinks that she'll be back later. That, understandably, she's gone for a drive in the gentleman's fine car. That his father could never offer her such an outing. That she surely has the right to have a little fun.*

Before, Gran had the suicide sickness. She would seem fine for a month or so, and then, suddenly, she would swallow three packs of tablets, or stick her head in the oven, or throw herself from the second floor, or try to hang herself in the junk room. She would say, "Good night, my dears," to us, and two hours later, from our room, Jules and I would hear the ambulance or fire engine come screeching up to the house.

Her suicide attempts would take place during the night, as if she waited for everyone to be asleep to end it all. Forgetting, no doubt, that Gramps loses sleep as often as he loses his glasses.

The last attempt was seven years ago. She had managed to get a prescription for two packs of tranquilizers from a replacement doctor, who hadn't read the note, despite it being written in red felt-tip, on Gran's medical file: "Chronic depression, prone to suicide attempts." At all the region's pharmacies, everyone knows not to give Gran the drugs on her prescription if Gramps isn't with her.

Old Prost also knows not to sell her rat poison, caustic drain cleaner, or any other corrosive products. Gran cleans the entire house with white vinegar, not for ecological reasons, but because everyone's terrified she'll end up swallowing the liquid dish soap or the oven cleaner.

The last time, she very nearly did die. But when she saw Jules's tears (I was too shocked to cry), she promised never to do it again. All the same, there are no bottles of surgical spirit or razor blades in our bathroom cabinet.

She did see a psychiatrist a few times. But since the nearest one's office is fifty kilometers from Milly, and you have to wait months for an appointment, she says it'll be easier to consult one in heaven, when she's dead, and in the meantime, she swears, truly, she won't do it again. "It's a promise, my dears, I swear to you, I'll die a natural death, if such a thing exists." She never promises a thing to Gramps, but always to us, her grandchildren.

In the tenth year after my parents' death, she jumped from a bit higher than usual and crushed her hip bone. Which left her with a slight limp and a walking stick forever hooked on her hand.

I've just set her hair. Jules is beside us in the kitchen, polishing off a jar of Nutella, spread on baguette. Gramps, seated at the end of the table, is flicking through *Paris Match* magazine. In the dining room, the TV is screaming at the empty sofa, screaming things we no longer even hear.

"Gramps, did you know Hélène Hel?" I ask.

"Who?"

"Hélène Hel. The lady who ran old Louis's café, until 1978."

My sad and taciturn granddad closes his magazine, clicks his tongue, and utters these few words, rolling his "r"s the way folk around here do:

"I've neverr frrequented bistrros."

"You still had to go past it every day to reach the factory."

Gramps grumbles. Whereas Gran has waited, since the twins' death, to see her sons again in Jules's face and mine, while occasionally trying to do herself in, Gramps has stopped waiting for anything at all since the day they died. I've never seen him smile, and yet, on the childhood photos of my father and Uncle Alain, he wears colorful tops and often seems to be larking around. He may not have much left now, but he had a fine head of hair when the three of them climbed Milly's big hill, one Sunday in July. At the back of my favorite photo it says "July 1974." My granddad is thirty-nine years old. He has thick, dark hair, and is wearing a red T-shirt and an ad-worthy smile.

When my granddad was a dad, he was very handsome. All that remains of his youth is his height: 1.93 meters. He's so tall, he looks like a diving board.

He's turning the pages of *Paris Match* again. What on earth can he make of the stories inside it? And more to the point, what on earth can he care? He who's so distant from the world, from us, from himself. Could he tell the difference between an earthquake in China and one in his kitchen?

"I rememberr her dog. Looked like a wolf."

Louve . . . Gramps remembers Louve.

"You remember Louve! Well then, you must remember Hélène!"

He stands up and leaves the kitchen. He hates me asking him questions. He hates his memory. His memory is his children, he hurled it into their coffins the day he buried them.

I'd like to ask him if he remembers a seagull that lived in the village when he was small. But I already know he'd say to me: "A seagull? How could I rememberr a seagull . . . Ain't none arround here."

8

On the Sabbath, Bijou, the old mare, takes Lucien and his father to Tournus, Mâcon, Autun, Saint-Vincent-des-Prés, or Chalon-sur-Saône. The destinations change with the seasons. There are more deaths and fewer weddings in winter.

Lucien accompanies his father to the great organs of the region. He has become his white stick, directing him and settling him in front of the keyboards. It's what Emma did, before. His mother who never returned from her car ride.

Lucien is present at Masses, weddings, baptisms, and funerals.

While Étienne plays or tunes, Lucien remains by his side and watches the congregation praying and singing.

Lucien isn't a believer. He thinks that religion is just the beauty of the music. A ruse to subjugate people. He's never dared tell his father that, and says grace every evening without flinching.

Étienne has never wanted to teach Braille or music to his son. He always feared it would bring him bad luck. He implored Lucien to do everything a blind person is deprived of doing, as if to exorcize the threat of blindness. As if to chase it away. To reassure his father, Lucien goes cycling, running, and swimming.

He attends the local school, where he learns to read and write like the other children. But unlike Étienne, Lucien has the feeling that, one day, this will no longer be of any use to him. So he learned Braille on his own, secretly, while listening to Étienne's lessons with his pupils.

When nearly thirteen, Lucien accompanies his father to Paris. Étienne wants to stock up on new books from his cousin's workshop. During this visit, Lucien is seen by a specialist, who takes a *long look at the back of his eyes. The doctor is categorical: Lucien doesn't carry the gene of his father's affliction. He has inherited his mother's eyes. Étienne is overjoyed. Lucien pretends to be overjoyed.*

*One day it will be his turn to walk with a white stick, and that's why his mother had left. One day, the others won't call him "the blind man's son" anymore, but just "the blind man." He, in turn, will become dependent on someone to do everything for him. That's why he'd learned Braille without telling anyone.*

*Since his mother's departure, Lucien can do everything with his eyes closed. Scouring the pans and the floor, bringing water up from the well, weeding, going to the vegetable garden, cutting logs, carrying bottles, going up and down the stairs. The house he and his father live in is forever plunged in darkness. Lucien intentionally draws the curtains without making a noise, so his father doesn't hear him. That's why all the plants die. Lack of light.*

*Back from Paris, with trunks full of new Braille books that he'll sneak, one by one, from his father, Lucien won't be changing his habits.*

"Tell me a story."

"I thought you didn't like my old folks' stories."

Jules makes a face. Takes a drag and blows smoke rings onto my wallpaper. He's making me listen to "Subzero" by Ben Klock, resident DJ at Berghain in Berlin, so he tells me. I often feel as if I'm living with an extraterrestrial.

When I found my job at The Hydrangeas, Jules screamed. It was the first time that had happened. At our house, no one ever screamed. Except the TV.

I think what bothered him most was my working five hundred meters from home. For Jules, succeeding in life means leaving Milly. In September, after his baccalauréat, he'll be off to Paris. That's all he ever talks about: Paris.

"Open the window. I can't stand the smell of your tobacco."

He unfolds his 1.87 meters and half-opens the window in my room. I love him. Even if, occasionally, I suspect him of being ashamed of us, his family, I love him. And whenever he moves, I love him even more. He's like a dancer with the hands of a pianist. It's like he fell from the sky and Gramps picked him up in his garden. Like he isn't from Milly but from a big capital city, where he'd have grown up between an astronomer father and a French-teacher mother. He's so graceful that it's objects that dance around him. He's more than my brother. Maybe because he isn't my brother. And yet he makes a racket when he walks, puts nothing away, is selfish, moody, pretentious, and has his head in the clouds. And he smokes like a chimney, particularly in my room.

Even if I never had a kid, I don't think I'd give a damn because

I have him. He's ridiculously handsome. I often tell him that being that good-looking shouldn't be allowed. I'm forever kissing him. As though making up for all the kisses our grandparents never gave him. At our house, kisses are given reluctantly, in exchange for a gift, on a birthday or at Christmas. Never for free. And all that because of a damn resemblance that never appeared. I also think that Gran and Gramps couldn't stand Annette, Jules's mother. Gran doesn't like blondes; when she sees one on TV, she grimaces. A grimace that's invisible to the naked eye, but when it comes to this family, my eye is fully clothed.

Jules lost his parents when he was two. He thinks his father was richer than mine, that the studies he'll do in Paris are thanks to the money Uncle Alain, his imaginary hero, had in his bank account when he died. The truth is that Uncle Alain was broke. And that it's the money I've saved, cent by cent, since working at The Hydrangeas that will pay for his studies. But I'd rather die than let him know that. I earn 1,480 euros a month. A bit more when I'm on call. I put 600 euros into an account every month. I've already saved 13,800 euros for him. I give 500 euros to Gran and Gramps to help them out. And my bonus I spend at the Paradise club.

Jules wants to be an architect, and I'm sure that, in time, when he's building palaces, he won't visit us anymore. And that, if he does return here once a year, it will be for himself, not for us. I know how he operates off by heart. I could even recite it.

Jules doesn't get attached because he lives in the present. He couldn't care less about yesterday. And tomorrow doesn't yet interest him. As soon as he goes out the door in the morning, off to school, he stops thinking about us. And when he comes home in the evening, he's happy to see us but hasn't missed us.

We've never known which of our two fathers was driving the car; for the emergency services, the two men were impossible to tell apart. We've never known what malfunctioned that Sunday. And since they shared the car, we've never known which of our fathers killed the other one.

Jules is sprawled on my bed again and looking at me as if to say: go on, tell the story. So I tell it:

"Madame Epting decided to come to The Hydrangeas the day her little dog died. Because, on that day, she told herself that she'd never be of any use ever again. She told me that she'd experienced all sorts in life. That she'd known war, hardship, the fear of the Boches, and even a broken heart. But the death of her little dog, that was the last straw. He was called Van Gogh because his previous owners had cut off his ear to remove his identification chip."

"Bastards," says Jules, lighting a cigarette.

"That's today's story."

"And it's already finished?" he asks.

"No. It's not really finished. I then said to her: 'Will you tell me about your broken heart, Madame Epting?' She laughed so hard, she had to keep her dentures in with her thumb. 'He was called Michel.' 'Nice name, Michel,' I said, 'but I've got to go, I'm really pushed.' She looked at me strangely and said, 'Really *what*?' 'Really pushed. It means I'm running late this morning, so you can tell me about Michel at the end of the afternoon.' She nodded, and I left her behind door 45, with her broken heart and her little dog. When I dropped by that evening, her armchair and bed were empty. She'd had a stroke. You see, that's my daily reality. Listening has to take priority, because silence is never far away."

"Shit, how depressing."

"But you know, I still get the giggles almost every day."

"Between changing diapers and pushing wheelchairs?"

I start laughing. Jules says nothing more. He stands up and, like any self-respecting prince, is unaware that he lives in a principality that's his alone. He leans out of the window to throw his cigarette into the garden, and I shout at him because it's freezing outside.

1926

The good Lord didn't answer her prayers. Hélène still doesn't know how to read.

This evening, she has decided to die. She's already heard about suicide. Last year, in the village, a man poisoned himself by swallowing tablets. For Hélène, it's the big blackboard that's poisonous.

After class, she hid in the storeroom, where the chalks, ink, paper, and dunce's cap are kept. With heart pounding, she listened to the other children leaving and her teacher, Monsieur Tribout, coughing, putting away his things, fastening his big briefcase, stepping down from the dais, and closing the door behind him.

Once the corridors and yard are silent, Hélène stuffs the dunce's cap in her pocket and returns to her empty classroom. It feels strange. And yet she's very familiar with this empty classroom: at recess, she's always in it, as punishment or to finish off her work. But usually she can hear the cries of the other children outdoors. This evening, she's surrounded by silence.

She looks at the books neatly lined up near the teacher's big desk. She has a burning desire to rip out every one of their pages, tear them to pieces, hurl them at the walls, for being so pretentiously lined up. But she'd never dare.

She's facing the blackboard. With a remnant of hope, she attempts to read the first sentence of a paragraph Monsieur Tribout has written out in several colors of chalk, underlining certain words: SHE HAS BROKEN THE LITTLE MILK JUG.

SHASBROKELITHETLEMIKUG.

*This is what Hélène reads.*

*Monsieur Tribout doesn't try to change her perception of letters anymore. At first, he tried to help her by stressing each syllable. By making her write the same word ten times, but it's as if Hélène can't retain a thing. As if her words were forever being tossed around by the wind.*

*This year, he sat her at the back of the class. On her own. Who'd want to sit next to a pupil you can't even copy from? Before, the teacher would take out the dunce's cap. Now, it's worse. She senses he pities her and has given up hope. As long as he was punishing her, it meant he had faith, had hope.*

*SHASBROKELITHETLEMIKUG.*

*No tears well in her eyes. Her grief ran dry ages ago. During her first year of school, she cried herself out.*

*She presses her mouth to the blackboard and starts licking, like some small creature. She begins on tiptoe. Then, realizing that the first sentence is far too high, she perches on the teacher's chair. She licks each letter, whether red, blue, or green. She swallows them, wants to poison herself with their kind of poison. She spits on them so they slide better down her throat. She rubs her lips over the capital letters, the periods, the commas.*

*When the blackboard is clean and Hélène's mouth every color of the rainbow, she goes to sit in her place. At the back of the class. On the opposite side to the wood-burning stove. And she waits for death. Sitting quietly there, she waits for the swallowed words to kill her forever. For them to finish the task begun on that first day she entered the school.*

*She is wearing a pretty red dress. Like Little Red Riding Hood's dress, she'd said to her mother in front of the sewing machine. What she didn't know was that the big bad wolf would appear to her in the guise of a big black board.*

*But death doesn't come. SHASBROKELITHETLEMIKUG doesn't have the magic powers of a lethal pill. And yet she'd thought it would finish her off as fast as the pig the neighbors kill once a year with a blow to the back of the head.*

*She won't leave the classroom before she's dead.*

*She decides to swallow the ink in all the pots on the class's little desks, and finish off with the teacher's. That way it's certain she will die. And if that's not enough, she'll swallow the sewing needles she always keeps in her pocket to prick her thigh when the pain in her tummy becomes unbearable.*

*She gets up and opens the ink pot on the first little desk. It's Francine Perrier's, the best pupil. Top of the class. The girl who succeeds at everything and never crosses anything out. The girl whom Monsieur Tribout always addresses with a smile. The girl whose handwriting looks like a bird on the wing, and whose voice sounds like music when she reads aloud, never making a mistake or stumbling at the first comma.*

*Just as Hélène is taking a sip from Francine Perrier's ink pot, and thinking that there are another twenty-seven to go, a noise makes her jump. Something has just struck one of the classroom windows. As if someone had thrown a stone in her direction. Someone's watching her. Hélène's heart races. She puts down Francine's ink pot and hides under the teacher's desk.*

*Ten minutes go by. Not another sound.*

*She finally comes out of her hiding place and goes up to the window. She can see nothing outside. The yard is empty. The big oak tree is losing its last leaves. Hélène's eyes follow one in particular. Falling to the ground along with the night. The leaf flutters over a small white puddle. Hélène stares at it for a few seconds. It isn't a puddle, it's a bird that's fallen to the ground. It's still moving. Hélène rushes out to the yard. Through the corridor with its empty coat racks. She'd not worn her cape this morning so no one would notice she was still there after school.*

*Under the oak tree, she stops at first a few centimeters away from the bird. It's a seagull. Her seagull! The one that's followed her like a shadow since she was small. The one she watches in the sky to cleanse her eyes of the sentences she can't read. The one she depicts with the shadows of her fingers on the atelier wall. It really does exist. She hasn't just imagined it.*

*The seagull is wounded, but alive. It stares at Hélène, its beak half-opened, its breathing erratic, as if its heart were beating too hard. It seems to be suffering. Hélène suddenly understands that it threw itself against the window so she'd get out of that accursed school. Or perhaps it wanted to die at the same time as her.*

*The bird and the child observe each other. Kneeling beside the seagull, Hélène daren't touch it. She fears hurting it even more. But she can't abandon it. Hélène has no brother or sister. She can't abandon her double.*

*Finally, gently, she cradles it with her hands, and slips it into the big inside pocket of her smock, against her heart.*

Room 19.
The blue-eyed ghost is there. Sitting beside Hélène. He closes the book he was just reading to her.

"Sorry about last time, I thought you were Lucien."

"I've been known to mix people up myself."

It doesn't seem odd to him that I could mistake him for a man who would be almost a hundred-and-twenty years old. He runs his hand through his hair. It's the first time I see him doing what I presume is a habit.

"How do you know whether it's day or night on her beach? Because today, she hasn't said a word to me. I'm convinced she's asleep."

"There's no morning at Hélène's beach. It's always daytime."

"Has she been there for long? I mean, on . . ."

"Vacation? For as long as I've known her. I believe it's the beach she went to with Lucien, in 1936."

He gazes at her for a long time. Then turns his blueness on me. I'd stake my life on the blue of Hélène's sea being exactly the blue of his eyes, and that's why she'll never come back.

"How do you know that?"

"She talks a good deal to me."

"What else has she told you?"

"On her beach . . . fathers chase after balls and mothers sip cool drinks. Older kids press their ears to the pop charts, or re-wind cassettes . . . Sometimes she stubs her toes on pebbles and I hear her murmuring: 'Ouch, the pebbles are hot today.' Or then: 'Oh no, I've just swallowed some sand.' Sometimes she talks out loud with passers by, the ice-cream seller, or a woman spreading a towel near hers. Hélène says, 'Do you come here often?' She does the questions, but rarely the answers."

The ghost remains silent for a long time while I fill the carafe with fresh water.

"It shouldn't be us reading novels to her, but the other way around," he says.

His remark makes me want to laugh. But I don't. Because of his blueness. Its effect on me is intensifying. Usually, you'd get used to it. But with him, it's different: the more he turns it on me, the more disturbed I feel.

"But . . . what does she do, on this beach?"

"She reads love stories while waiting for Lucien and the little girl; they went off for a swim earlier."

He looks stunned by my reply. He wasn't actually expecting me to give him one. I think he just asked in an offhand way, as if thinking aloud.

"The little girl?"

"Rose. Your mother. I mean, Rose, she is your mother?"

"Yes."

I make Hélène drink little sips of water. I think to myself that he must see us as two crazy women.

"Which love stories?"

"The ones your mother reads her at every visit."

"It's as if you've just read me a poetic instruction manual."

Him saying that to me means he's from the same world as us, the one in which you don't believe only what you can see. The world of idiots, the naive, optimists.

When Hélène pushes open the door to her parents' boutique, there's a woman in the fitting room with her mother kneeling in front of her, marking the hem of her dress. Her father is behind the cash register and stifles a cry when he sees his daughter.

Hélène lies to him. Dunces lie. Lies are their second skin. That's why they have more imagination than others. She tells her father that some pupils blindfolded her and forced her to eat chalks. That she never wants to go back to school again, that everyone's cruel, and there's no point forcing her. She'll work in the atelier. She'll be good. And if he refuses, she'll kill herself.

She leaves her parents to discuss it behind her back, make a decision. She knows very well what they'll say to each other. She's already overheard whispered conversations:

"Monsieur Tribout says she'll never pass her exams . . . Even if she does the year again . . . She'll never manage to . . . She can't even tell the time . . . at nine years old . . ."

As she goes up the stairs to her room, Hélène feels the seagull moving inside her pocket. She touches it; it's all warm. Its heart is beating normally. Its wings aren't broken. Hélène feeds it with some bread soaked in milk. She has never seen anything as beautiful as this white bird with its orange beak. Even the trees are less pretty. Even the wedding dresses. Even the countess who sometimes comes to the atelier in her fine car, with her lovely legs and doll-like face. Not a single landscape. Nothing is more beautiful than this bird. Hélène opens the window in her room to release it.

*"You who can reach heaven, could you ask God to heal my eyes and teach me to read, please?"*

*The bird takes off and flies around in circles. The full moon makes it shine like one more star.*

This morning, the ghost was waiting for me outside the door to room 19. I was almost unpleasant. Sometimes, too much beauty and too much blue is just annoying. And anyhow, I don't like being disturbed. And I sense he's going to cause me no end of trouble. He's the kind of guy who upends someone's routine with a click of his fingers.

"Hello, Justine. Could I have five minutes with you?"

I heard my colleague, Jo, chuckling behind me, and before I'd even replied, she said:

"Go on, Juju, I'll take over."

Juju. She actually said that. Juju. How dumb. In front of someone you fancy, you always end up hating those you love. Because of that familiarity they have, and you don't want them to have, especially when it's the not the time.

"Not for too long, because we're busy bees in the morning."

I actually said that. *Busy bees.* And blushed. Almost tripped over the cart and lost my balance. The shame. The total shame.

I suggested we go to the small staff room, next to the office, where there's a coffee-maker, microwave, fridge, table, and a few chairs. Normally, we don't bring residents or their family into our little den, but "he" isn't normal. With a face like his, he gets permission for life.

We walked along three corridors and, two floors later, I ushered him in.

In the morning, the corridors are really noisy. Doors stay open because all the care staff are coming and going. So you sometimes hear the "dependents" raving, insulting the walls, or calling for help. Through doors left ajar, you see some very old residents who resemble ghosts, their eyes gazing not out of the window but into the void.

The poet Baudelaire described a lunatic asylum that becomes harrowing as night falls because of the screams escaping from it. In retirement homes, it's when day breaks that emotions run high.

No one else was in the staff room. I put coffee in the filter and switched the water on. He sat down. I took two chipped mugs and filled them. Without shaking.

"Would you like sugar?"

"No thanks."

I put two sugars into my mug before sitting opposite him. He glanced at the posters on the walls and at the old 2007 calendar of firefighters who had stripped for charity.

"Would you be able to tell me what is on my grandmother's bedside table? From memory, would you be able to list all the objects on and inside it?"

I closed my eyes and said:

"A photo of Lucien, of Rose, of Janet Gaynor, a carafe of water, chocolates she doesn't eat, hydrangeas in a crystal vase."

"Who is Janet Gaynor?"

My eyes were still closed, but I could feel his eyes through my eyelids, just like when you close your eyes in bright sunlight.

"An actress. Who got an Oscar in 1929."

"And in her drawer . . . do you also know what's inside her drawer?"

"A load of papers rolled up in a hair elastic, a thimble, a photo of Louve, a white feather, paper hankies, and a single of Georges Brassens's 'Les Sabots d'Hélène.'"

"Would you be able to write them down, all these things you know about her? For me?"

I opened my eyes again. In his, there was only blue. An infinite blue. Red cheeks were all I had.

"Make a wish."

"Why?"

"You have an eyelash on your cheek."

I brushed my left cheek, an eyelash dropped onto the table.

At that moment, Madame Le Camus walked in, out of breath. She looked at us without seeing us, dived on the coffee pot, and then sipped her coffee while muttering:

"Here we go again. The family's downstairs. Wants an explanation, and I don't have one. Here we go again . . ."

I asked Madame Le Camus if there had been another phone call.

She stared at January 1, 2007 on the old stripper-firefighter charity calendar, took a deep breath and, as though to herself, replied:

"This time, someone rang yesterday evening. At 11 P.M.! To say that Monsieur Gérard had died of a pulmonary embolism."

The ghost gave me a questioning look as he finished his coffee. I explained that someone was phoning the families of those who were forgotten on Sunday and pretending they had died. His eyes again questioned me. And I let them.

Just before leaving, he looked at me as if I were a magician who'd just put his grandmother into a saw-in-half box. He left me alone with my boss, who was still staring at January 1 and the pecs of a rather strapping firefighter.

Since last Christmas, Madame Le Camus has seemed to be endlessly crossing a finishing line. She's in such a state, she's forever out of breath. She goes back and forth between the rooms and the office, gazing heavenwards, as if the wan ceilings could provide her with answers through their neon strips.

It began on December 25 last year, when three families were contacted by phone concerning the death of a resident. And when those three families turned up on the morning of December 26 to make funeral arrangements, their respective relatives smiled at them, happy to receive this unexpected visit.

Since then, management has been investigating to find out who's been making these "sinister" phone calls. That's what it says on the staff notice, pinned up in the treatment room, break room, office, and our cloakrooms. Because it's happened five more times since then.

These phone calls come from room 29. Monsieur Paul's room. He's been sleeping almost continuously for three years. The doctors are categorical: it's clinically impossible that the calls were made by Monsieur Paul himself. But no one has seen anything irregular. No one has seen anyone slipping into room 29 to call those families on the sly. Families that all have one thing in common: they never visit. It's as if someone were counting the number of visits per resident and then making these phone calls to fill the flowerless rooms.

Consequently, everyone suspects everyone else: it's like an Agatha Christie with no dead body. Just imagine a novel by her in which Miss Marple was investigating because *no one* had died . . .

If Miss Marple investigated me, what would she say? That my "libraries," with all their stories, cost me dear? That I'm too young to look after people who are so old?

1930

*I*n the garden outside the house, Lucien sniffs a large red rose. It's his favorite smell: it reminds him of his mother.
Every morning, Emma would clean his face with cotton soaked in rose water, which she made herself. She would collect the petals in autumn and leave them to macerate, in a white enamel basin, all year long. When her bottle was empty, she would dip it into the basin to refill it with the fragrant liquid.

Sometimes, Lucien would plunge his hands and forearms into the viscous rose water. A few scraps of torn petal would cling to his hairs, like wrinkled stars. His father would immediately notice the scent. You can't hide a thing from a blind person. Even lying has a smell. His father would say to him, "Girls wear perfume, not boys."

He misses his mother.

Lucien opens his eyes and gazes at the redness of the rose. It's the color of blood. Is it that color that gives it that wonderful scent? Does the blood flowing in his mother's veins smell of roses?

Does he really have her eyes? The eyes of someone who leaves? Lucien thinks his mother left them, him and his father, because it's no life, living with a blind man. Because, one day or another, you're bound to want to live with someone who looks at you.

At The Hydrangeas, there are three doctors, plus their stand-ins, two physical therapists, a maintenance man and two cooks, twelve nursing assistants, five nurses, and a manager. But the mystery caller could well be someone from outside: the priest, one of the ambulance drivers, the undertakers, the hairdresser, the one or two volunteers who come for a few hours. It could also be the offspring of one of the residents. Most have lived in Milly their entire lives, and here, everyone knows each other. It could even be one of those nurses who ring for us, like maids, to escort a resident to the bathroom, for example.

The nurses do have greater medical responsibility than the nursing assistants, but I prefer my job because we get to hold the residents' hands.

So that the families know whom they are dealing with, the medical staff wear different smocks. The nurses' ones are pink, those of the consultants white, and for the nursing assistants, they're green, garbage-can green.

I love my two colleagues, Jo and Maria. We're a team. Madame Le Camus calls us The Three Musketeers.

Mademoiselle Moreau, room 9, calls us The Three Ladybugs, because our hands are forever spotted with antiseptic and eosin. She likes to count the spots to discover our age. And Jo says to her: "We're lucky: ladybugs have no predators. Even birds spit them out because their wings taste bitter."

Given I lost my parents as a kid, I think to myself that I must have been damn bitter for life to spit me out so hard.

Ever since I began here, the staff have called me "Little

Flower," because I'm oversensitive and do lots of unpaid overtime. In the first few years, when Jo saw me crying every time a resident died, she'd repeat to me: "Keep your tears for your own loved ones, because no one will weep for them." And I'd think that I'd already wept for most of my loved ones long ago.

The heat wave that has hit us over the past three days has already wiped out Madame Andrée, the lady from room 11. Ironically, we called her "Miss Forecast" because whenever we passed her in a corridor she would say: "Anticyclone!" How absurd life is. I'd never have thought a hot spell would carry her off.

Her children arrived this morning. Too late. They didn't have time to say goodbye to her. But it's not their fault. I think that, at some stage, our old folk get too far ahead of us. They launch into sprints that no one can keep up with anymore.

Jo hadn't spotted this anticyclone on Madame Andrée's palm. Jo has a gift. She can read the future in the lines of the hand. Our residents regularly ask her for a consultation. Jo says it's impossible to read old lines on palms. That they're as scratched as an old LP. So she makes things up.

None of these frills—my massages, Jo's palm-reading, the priest's blessings (when he's not repeating to anyone who'll listen "Make the most of it! Make the most of life!")—lessen our old folks' desire to return home. They often run away. But we're not allowed to close the gates: it would be seen as mistreating our residents, locking them up.

The old folk run away, but they don't know where to go. They've forgotten the path that leads back to before. Their "homes" have been put up for sale to pay the monthly fees for their stay at The Hydrangeas. Their window boxes are empty and their cats adopted. Their homes only exist inside their heads now, their personal "libraries." Those libraries I love to spend hours in.

What saddens me is when I see them piling up at reception from ten in the morning, and staring at the two main entrance doors as they open and then close.

They wait.

When the weather's fine, we take them out into the garden to enjoy the sunshine from the shade of the lindens. Being visited by the wind in the trees, the bees, the butterflies, and the birds makes up for all their waiting. We give them bread to throw to the sparrows and pigeons, which some love and some are wary of doing, while some just kick at the birds. And then arguments break out. And as long as they're arguing, they're not waiting anymore. Whether at home or elsewhere, sunny days are all alike.

When I'm tired, I go up to the top floor. I sit down, leaning against the large window that looks out onto the roof. I close my eyes and doze for ten minutes. When the sun breaks through, it burns my nape, which I love.

Often, the seagull flies off and watches me from the sky.

When I return to my duties, I don't know whether I'm on a morning, afternoon, or evening shift. Rather than overtime, I just do extra hours when I don't feel like going home. Don't feel like seeing Gramps bored stiff because, to him, it's forever winter; don't feel like seeing Gran searching for my father's face in mine; don't feel like knocking on Jules's silent door, when he's shut himself away, either to play computer games or to download electronic music from Beatport.

I prefer to peel off Hélène's support stockings and massage her legs and feet. While she tells me about the tall blonde sitting beside her, who's in a one-piece swimsuit and has covered herself in monoï oil, hair included.

It's the same when I can't stand the daily routine anymore. When we have to work at a furious pace, when a nursing assistant is absent and we have to race through everything: nursing, washing, cleaning. If I sense that I might get annoyed with a resident who is insulting me, or just isn't interested, or has wet themselves on purpose while laughing in my face, I hand over to a colleague or rush to room 19 for five minutes. I ask Hélène to talk to me about Lucien or the customers at her bistro. She often remembers Baudelaire.

This man renamed Baudelaire was born in Paris. When his grandmother died, he had inherited her house in Milly and had moved into it, alone, at around forty years old. He had taught children for a few hours a week, at the mayor's request. This man had a disfiguring harelip, and the children had mocked him, or been scared of him, so the parents had asked for him to leave. He had wound up at old Louis's café, where, leaning on the bar, he would spend hours reciting his favorite poet's verses.

To me, Hélène recites the poem he would mutter from morning to night, between gulps of liquor:

*Often, when bored, the sailors of the crew*
*Trap albatross, the great birds of the seas,*
*Mild travelers escorting in the blue*
*Ships gliding on the ocean's mysteries.*

*And when the sailors have them on the planks,*
*Hurt and distraught, these kings of all outdoors*
*Piteously let trail along their flanks*
*Their great white wings, dragging like useless oars.*

*This voyager, how comical and weak!*
*Once handsome, how unseemly and inept!*
*One sailor pokes a pipe into his beak,*
*Another mocks the flier's hobbled step.*

*The Poet is a kinsman in the clouds*
*Who scoffs at archers, loves a stormy day;*
*But on the ground, among the hooting crowds,*
*He cannot walk, his wings are in the way.*[1]

---

[1] Charles Baudelaire, "The Albatross," in *The Flowers of Evil—Charles Baudelaire*, trans. James McGowan (Oxford: Oxford University Press, 1993).

16

*1933, before summer*

W*edding day at Clermain. Large tables covered in white cloths have been set up on the Place de l'Église. The whole village has come together to celebrate the union of Hugo, the mayor's son, and Angèle the redhead, daughter of the blacksmith.*

*Since Angèle is ashamed of being a redhead, thanks to the Jules Renard novel,* Poil de carotte, *she asked her dressmaker, Hélène Hel, to make her a veil out of very thick tulle to hide her locks. She's even used white tailor's chalk to cover up her freckles.*

*It should be the best day of her life, but Angèle feels ill at ease. And it's not because of her hair or her skin. Frédéric, Hugo's cousin, keeps staring at her. She can feel his insistent eyes on her. Much as she drinks wine to forget about him, whenever she looks in his direction, his obscene gaze meets hers. Even on her wedding day, he's still doing it.*

*It's been going on for months. Him waiting for her outside her house, or her turning around in the street to find him shadowing her. Each time, she remains cold, but he persists: "Hello, you're so pretty," "Good evening, I love your hair," "Hello, what a lovely surprise," "Good evening, you have amazing eyes . . ."*

*Angèle has never dared tell Hugo about it. During the ceremony, she was even afraid that Frédéric might oppose the marriage. There was nothing to justify him doing so, but she couldn't relax.*

*Frédéric takes advantage of Hugo leaving his seat to come over to her. Angèle didn't have time to grab her husband's hand to keep him beside her. Frédéric walks around the guests and approaches her, smiling. A smile like a bad smell. She closes her eyes, drinks a large gulp of wine, which burns her throat. When she reopens her eyes, he is there. She wants to slap him, scratch him, tear his hair out. She wishes she were a man with the strength to beat him up. She hears him whispering:*

*"I prefer the red veil of your hair."*

*To escape from him, Angèle stands up from the table, too abruptly. Her dress snags on something sharp and tears at the waist. There's a kind of silence that confuses her senses. She looks at her dress as if it were her own skin that has just been slashed. She's even surprised she's not bleeding. Just a few white beads fall to the ground. Her heart starts to pound. She looks up and says to Frédéric, almost formally:*

*"Disappear."*

*Angèle then asks her mother to go and fetch the dressmaker, who lives a stone's throw from the church.*

*In the meantime, she will wait in the presbytery. Luckily, no one has noticed a thing, not even Hugo. Angèle's mother knows Clermain's couture boutique well. It's closed: today's Sunday. She steps in through a half-open* porte cochère *and follows a corridor that leads to the entirely glazed atelier in the rear courtyard.*

*Hélène is in the atelier, sitting cross-legged, like a man, on a wooden table. She's deep in conversation with someone the mother can only see from behind.*

*She knocks on the door. A bird flies off. Through the glass door, she sees Hélène looking at her without seeing her. Like someone interrupted in the middle of a conversation they don't want to end. The young dressmaker beckons her in.*

*What Angèle's mother had thought was someone from behind is a dressmaker's fabric dummy. She realizes that the young girl is alone, and yet she could have sworn that she was talking to someone.*

*One hour later, Angèle's dress is as good as new. Hélène has restitched every seam. She's facing the young bride in the narrow corridor, near a mirrored coat rack, and has opened the presbytery* door to let in some light. Angèle admires Hélène's work as if it were a miracle.

"I'm so sorry, Hélène."

"Sorry? Sorry for what?"

Angèle gazes at the face of the dressmaker, who is three years her junior. She couldn't say whether Hélène looks older or younger than her. Her clear skin, messy bun, blue eyes, large mouth, high cheekbones. Hers is that Slav beauty that one either loves or hates, because every feature is exaggerated. Even her eyes seem to be reaching for her temples. In Clermain, people say that Hélène Hel is crazy, and children are wary of her.

Angèle takes Hélène's hands into her own.

"When the fittings began, I didn't like you. It's my mother who insisted that you be my dressmaker . . . I was scared of you."

Hélène replies:

"That's normal. I'm scared of me, too."

Angèle smiles at the young woman, who always seems to be somewhere other than the room she's in. It's true that she's attractive and disquieting all at once. There's a kind of turmoil in her eyes. And she never smiles. Even when saying yes. Angèle looks at Hélène's hands.

"You have such nimble fingers."

Hélène lowers her eyes. Angèle embraces her affectionately and returns to her guests in her new dress. She scans the crowd. Frédéric is no longer there. She smiles inside, relieved.

Hélène remains alone in the corridor. She gazes at her fingers, and then, finally, packs up her sewing things. She doesn't close the presbytery door behind her: she has a thing about letting in the sunlight wherever she can.

To get back to the atelier, Hélène decides to walk along the cemetery side of the church. She tries to read the names on the gravestones. She pushes open the church's small side door. The church is empty. Hélène kneels and speaks to God, tirelessly repeating: "Teach me to read."

"What you doing?"

I jump. Jules gave me a fright. I close the blue notebook.

"Writing."

"Think you're Marguerite Duras, do you?"

"Where d'you hear about Marguerite Duras?"

"In a French class. Found it boring as hell. Hope you don't write like her."

"No risk of that. Open the window."

"You in a bad mood?"

"Nah. You know I can't stand you smoking in my room."

"It's more me smoking that you can't stand . . . You're not my mother."

Jules opens the window and leans out. He's sulking a bit. So I say to him:

"Yesterday evening, there was another anonymous phone call at The Hydrangeas."

He turns around; I can't see his eyes.

"To which family?"

"You need a haircut. Gisèle Diondet's family. The tiny lady with purple hair who had a haberdashery store. I told you about her last week."

"Remind me."

"Before, she spent a lot of time in the card room and joined all the workshops. But since early summer, she just stays put at reception with the others. So she was there when her family arrived, all red eyes and dark clothes."

Jules flicks his cigarette butt out of the window. Tomorrow morning, Gramps will pick it up in the garden, grumbling. Then he'll pop it in a bowl of water with the others and use it to water his rosebushes to kill the greenfly.

He's back sitting on my bed.

"And what did they say, the family, when they saw her . . . alive?"

"Imagine their shock. But I think they were a little disappointed."

"What d'you mean, disappointed?"

"When old people kick the bucket, it means the guilt's over. It's complicated. It's grief mixed with relief."

"And the little old lady, what did she say when she saw them?"

"At first, she didn't recognize them, but she was still pleased. Especially when they took her to a restaurant for lunch. You know, it often happens with the elderly. At the time of the visits, they're not that friendly to their family, but afterwards, something changes. They're less anxious. At any rate, this afternoon, Gisèle returned to the card room. She hadn't set foot in it for three months."

"You see, it serves a purpose, this anonymous thing."

"Earlier, Madame Le Camus summoned us all to announce that the police were going to investigate internally"—I imitate her voice to make Jules smile—"*to solve the mystery of the anonymous calls.*"

But Jules doesn't smile.

"Will it be proper detectives, and all that?"

It's me who starts to laugh.

"Are you kidding? Starsky and Hutch are on the case!"

Jules starts to chuckle. Starsky and Hutch are Milly's two neighborhood policemen. "The cowboys," as everyone calls them. They're a few years from retirement and won't be replaced. Apparently, they've been called that for years. Since well before I was born. One's dark-haired and the other blond. Well, that was before. Now they're both white-haired. Gramps says they're the last people you should call for help if in trouble. They're not liked in Milly: stupidity is very hard to explain, and theirs shows on their faces. They're arrogant and never greet anyone. When they hold out a hand, it's to serve a parking ticket. The "causing obstruction" kind. But who can obstruct whom in Milly? The roads are empty. Personally, I only find them half-amusing, because they are armed, after all. Jules says their guns are toys. But I don't think so.

"Who do you think's phoning the families?" Jules asks.

I look at his perfect profile. I've never seen anything as beautiful as Jules's face. Even with hair that's too long.

"Don't know. Could be anyone. At any rate, it's doubtless someone who has access to the families' files. And who knows the names and habits of those forgotten on Sunday."

"The names of what?"

## 17

Sunday

The heat wave is over. It lasted six days. I'm exhausted. Wiped out. I don't count my hours as it is, but when there's a crisis like that, it's the hours that stop counting us. I started my shift at 8 A.M. Didn't sleep all night, went dancing at the Paradise until 5 A.M. I needed to be young, get drunk, go crazy, put make-up on, flirt, wear something low-cut, close my eyes and dance. Convince myself that I'm pretty.

Since last autumn, I often end the night in the same arms. Those of a guy who's older than me. Maybe twenty-seven, called What's-his-name. Between him and him, I have other one-night stands, but he often returns. Like some bimonthly apparition.

Sunday is visiting day. But not for everyone. I drank five coffees so I could look after the unvisited. Sunday is a day to "handle with care." It's steeped in sadness. You might think that every day here is like a Sunday, but there's no getting away from it. It's like a biological clock. Every Sunday, the residents know it's Sunday.

After ablutions it's Mass, broadcast on TV, and then a fancier meal. Avocado with prawns is renamed "seafood surprise with mayonnaise," and chocolate éclairs become "filled sweet treats."

It's a bit like the daily vegetable soup. It changes name every day even though it's just the same hot dishwater. On Monday, the concoction is called "soup of the season," on Wednesday "garden velouté," and on Friday, "vegetable-medley broth." The residents love getting their menus for the week. It's their treasure map. Apart from the obituaries column in the *Journal de Saône-et-Loire*, it's the only reading matter that still interests them.

At lunchtime on Sunday, glasses of kir, followed by wine, help with digesting the morning. But we have to watch out that no one nabs another person's glass, or else arguments can break out, even coming to blows. The dining room is a playground in which many residents sort out their problems by hitting others. Even I have received a few slaps.

At lunchtime on Sunday, my colleagues and I lay the tables with white cloths and stemmed glasses. Like in a restaurant.

After lunch, some residents return to their rooms, because of the afternoon visits, or the Michel Drucker TV show. The rest we entertain in the card room as best we can, with little shows, karaoke, lotto, belote, screenings . . . it varies. I like to put on Charlie Chaplin movies and make them laugh.

I also like getting them to sing "Le petit bal perdu" into a microphone connected to two speakers. It's their favorite song. They each take turns on the mike. Sometimes, we even dance. It's not quite *Dirty Dancing* with them, but their hearts are in it.

This afternoon, we got our magician to come along. It's always the same one. A volunteer from my neighborhood, a kid who carries around a clutch of turtledoves and white rabbits as if they were bunches of keys. His conjuring nearly always goes wrong because he's too clumsy, so his tricks are as obvious as the nose on my face. But for those forgotten on Sunday, simply seeing a turtledove or some rabbits in a hat is wonderful, and lightens the heaviness of their day.

At around 2 P.M., I sensed the blue eyes of the "ghost" on my back. I was just settling my residents down for the magic show. I heard his hello. One of the turtledoves escaped from the kid's sleeve.

He was standing behind me. He smiled at me. He smiled at me. He smiled at me. He smiled at me. He was holding a book. He was wearing jeans and a T-shirt that was slightly too big.

"Hello, I've come to read to my grandmother, but I wanted to say hi first."

Confirmation: when I see him, I completely fall apart.

He has the sweetest smile. His skin is pale and his hands are like a girl's, fine and graceful. Beside him, I, Justine, don't exist. I'm normal. An earthling. Blushing. And too lucid to imagine that a man like him could see me as anything but the girl who listens to his grandmother telling her about the sea.

"Hello," I replied. "That's nice, have a good read."

And I promptly turned my back on him. Pretended to search for a turtledove with the magician. Again, I sensed his eyes, behind me, insistent. What did he want? To burn my nape like the sun through the window on the top floor?

After the show, I went up to see Hélène. I knocked. He was still there, his book open in his hands. He was reading aloud:

> In the morning they met in the breakfast room: the one who got there first ate slowly, to give the other time to arrive. Every day grandmother was afraid that the Veteran might leave without telling her, or that he was tired of her company, or maybe would change tables and pass her by with a cold nod of greeting, like all those men of the Wednesdays so many years before . . . [2]

His voice, beautiful, light and strong all at once. Like fingers on piano keys, moving from deep notes to high. Well, I say that, but I don't know much about the piano. And even less about extraterrestrial specimens like him. Except for my brother. But he's my brother. I'm not afraid to ruffle his hair.

He saw me and immediately stopped reading.

"What is it you're reading to her?" I asked my feet.

"*From the Land of the Moon,*" he replied.

---

[2] Milena Agus, *From the Land of the Moon,* trans. Ann Goldstein (New York: Europa Editions, 2011).

I didn't dare tell him that she'd already read it. Or rather, that Rose had already read it to her. I looked up at Hélène. Saw her smiling from her beach. I replied to the walls:

"She seems to like it."

He nodded. Well, I think he did.

I left, silently. Because I don't exist when he's there. I didn't see him again that day. I took a quick look at the roof: the seagull was in its place and seemed to be sleeping. He left *From the Land of the Moon* on the bedside table, between Janet Gaynor and Lucien, with my name written on it in fountain pen. His handwriting is lovely. I'd never seen "Justine" written so beautifully.

"For Justine."

He'd signed, "Roman."

His name is Roman. The French word for "novel." You couldn't make it up.

It's 9 P.M. I'm aching all over. Monsieur Vaillant asked me to massage his hands. "This evening," I said. Then I'll go and do Hélène's. I like Monsieur Vaillant. He hasn't been with us for long. He's not happy here. He misses his house, much more than his wife. So he tells me every day. After Monsieur Vaillant and Hélène, I'll go and switch off the TVs of those who have fallen asleep.

Then I, too, will reread *From the Land of the Moon*, before writing in the blue notebook, which I haven't touched for weeks because of the heat wave.

## 18

*1933, before summer*

This morning, Étienne played Bach's "Air," and some preludes, at a wedding. It was his first time playing in the church at Clermain.

As usual, Lucien guided his father to the organ, holding his left arm.

Lucien closed his eyes and listened to Étienne playing. He has always associated musical notes with the colors of the roses in his garden. Even before his mother left. He didn't reopen his eyes to look at the bride and groom and their guests packed in the pews. He always avoids looking at what's going on around him. He prefers to feel.

At home, he still doesn't light the ceiling lamp. He lives in darkness and ensures that Étienne doesn't notice.

Although he's twenty-two and his sight is perfect, he can't reconcile himself to the idea that he won't go blind. He thinks his affliction has merely been delayed.

After the service, Étienne and Lucien take their seats at the large table that's been set up on the square, outside the church.

Lucien loves weddings for two reasons: he and his father are often included at the banquets that follow, and his father can be on his own with the other adults. He no longer needs his son.

Lucien listens to the din made by those around him. He hears them getting drunk and laughing. He hears Étienne doing likewise. He merrily wolfs down all that's served to him, checking, every now and then, that the Braille book he slipped into his pocket is there. He still purloins these books without his father knowing.

*A fat woman nearby is trying to make conversation with him, but Lucien isn't keen on talking. When he's alone with Étienne, he already speaks for two: Watch out for the step, on your right, no, a fraction to your left, the sky's darkening, there's a big water leak there, this door needs repainting, the weeds are taking over the stones, Madame Chaussin is just walking past the fence, your glass is filled, don't touch, it's very hot, your white shirts are on the left-hand shelves, the bread is sliced, this apple is maggoty, your pupil is coming into the garden, beware, it's going to be noisy. So Lucien smiles politely at his neighbor, nods without listening to her, and that's all.*

*He will never marry. Never will he slip a wedding ring onto a woman's finger. Never will he ask a woman to swear fidelity to him. Not after what happened to his parents. Never will anyone attend his own wedding banquet. His father often calls him an anarchist because he criticizes the army, politicians, the death sentence, priests, and marriage.*

*Among all the guests eating, drinking, and laughing, Lucien is the only one to hear the sound of fabric tearing. Even Étienne didn't notice. For the first time that day, Lucien looks up and focuses on something specific: the young bride. She's looking at her torn dress with horror; a man is leaning towards her; she's escaping from him.*

*Lucien sees the man move away from the bride, who whispers something into the ear of a woman in a mauve dress, who rushes off in the direction of the village. The bride swiftly slips away, behind the church, clutching at her dress. No one, except him, has noticed a thing.*

*A few minutes later, Lucien sees the woman in mauve returning from the village, accompanied by a young girl with eyes lowered, holding a sewing box. They both head behind the church.*

*For the first time since his mother left, Lucien suddenly feels immense sadness. Like a surge of melancholy on an autumn evening when the sky is low, closed up, with not a chink to let the light through. He realizes that when he's blind, he'll no longer see young girls lowering their eyes. How will he be able to recognize grace? Even the colors he sees while listening to Bach can't answer that question.*

*Just as he can feel tears welling up, something drops onto his head. He runs his hand over his hair and contemplates the white, viscous, warm liquid shining on his fingers. No question, it's bird shit. He looks up at the sky, sees nothing, then leaves the table to go to the fountain, in the middle of the square, to rinse it off.*

*He dunks his head in the freezing cold water and, when he raises it, sees the man who was standing in front of the bride when her dress tore. He's smoking a cigarette while watching him.*

*"Are you the brother of the bride?"*

*"No. I'm the son of the organist."*

*"The blind man?"*

*"Yes."*

*"Do you know Angèle?"*

*"Who?"*

*"Angèle, the bride."*

*"No."*

*"I'm in love with her. But I'm not her husband."*

*Lucien remains silent. He wonders whether his mother was already in love with another man when she married his father. He wonders how love is caught, and whether it can be caught by several people at once. He's already slept with prostitutes but— roses, books, and music aside—he's never fallen in love. He's read lots of books on the subject, and the last one, Simenon's* Les Fiançailles de M. Hire, *he devoured. He watches the man moving off, in the direction of the village.*

*On his way to the church, Lucien passes the bride. The sun is very hot. Lucien enters the coolness of the church. He settles down in the half-light of the confessional and opens his book. There's no risk he'll be disturbed by the priest because he, too, has joined in with the feasting and dancing. It's no day for confessing. Lucien starts reading with his fingertips:*

*"God conveys his visible will to men through events, an obscure text written in a mysterious language. Men immediately translate it, producing hasty, incorrect versions full of errors, gaps, and mistranslations. Very few minds comprehend the divine language."*

Lucien soon dozes off, lulled by some murmuring he can hear. He finds himself barefoot, beside the sea. The light is beautiful. The sun high in the sky. The blue of the water shimmers around the boats. A girl walks beside him, holding his hand. She smiles at him. He feels good. He no longer fears the dark. The girl lowers her eyes; he no longer fears not seeing her.

From time to time, her slender fingers stroke the palm of his hand. Around them, children are playing; further off, others bathe. They have almost reached the water, just a few more steps. The murmuring gets closer: it's the murmuring of the waves, a kind of music that Lucien's father has never played in churches.

Lucien wakes up. He wakes to the darkness of the confessional. The girl has vanished. His book has fallen to the floor. He closes his eyes again. He must return to that dream. But it doesn't work. You can't just dip back into a dream like into an anthology. And also, there's that whispering, in the church. At first he thinks it's an insect, the sound of wings colliding with stained-glass windows. But it's a murmuring. The murmuring of the waves, the murmuring in the dream. Someone is murmuring. Lucien opens the door of the confessional and sees a shadow, kneeling, a few meters away from him.

He moves closer. He moves closer to the shadow the way he moved closer to the sea in his dream. And the closer he gets, the more he can distinguish the words being murmured:

"READ. ME. READ. ME. TO READ. TEACH ME TO READ. TEACH ME TO READ."

Lucien is right behind the supplicant. She turns around, stares at him for a long time. It's the girl in the dream. The one who lowered her eyes beside the woman in mauve earlier on. Her face is partly illuminated by three candles, one of which is almost *spent. She looks a little like one of the girls at the Autun brothel. Lucien doesn't know why he's thinking of that girl, here, now. In a church, he's thinking of the Autun brothel, which is in a house that, from the outside, looks like any other. There are even flowers in the window boxes. Over there, he doesn't close his eyes; he contemplates the girls' bodies. Just as he contemplates the girl kneeling before him.*

*He doesn't dare look into her eyes. As if he feared getting burnt. He looks at her hands. The hands she presses together in prayer.*

*"Why are you asking candles to teach you to read?"*

## 19

How's it going today, Monsieur Girardot?"
"My wife has died."
"That was a long time ago, now."
"You know, when you've lost the person you loved most in the world, you lose her every day."

"How's it going today, Monsieur Duclos?"
"Shut it, stupid bitch."
"Well, I say, you're going strong this morning."
"How the hell d'you think it's going?"
"Like a late summer."
"Stupid bitch."
"I can be. Come on, time to get up."
"What the hell are you doing?"
"You need to have a wash, Monsieur Duclos."
"Go fuck yourself."
"Well, I wouldn't say no."
"Asshole."
"OK, I'll see if that's possible."

"How's it going today, Madame Bertrand?"
"Annie has just died."
"Ah. Who is Annie?"
"She was my friend. When she'd arrive at mine, she'd say, 'A small beer would do nicely.' D'you think there's a bar up at God's place?"
"If there's a heaven, there's bound to be a bar."

"How's it going today, Mademoiselle Adèle?"

"Fine. My granddaughter's bringing me donuts."

"You're lucky to have a granddaughter who comes to see you nearly every day."

"I know."

"How's it going today, Monsieur Mouron?"

"The pain in my legs . . . Didn't sleep a wink all night."

"I'll ask the doctor to come by this morning, OK?"

"If you like."

"Shall I switch the TV on?"

"No. It's just women's stuff in the morning."

"How's it going today, Madame Minger?"

"Someone's stolen my glasses."

"Really? Have you looked everywhere?"

"Everywhere. I'm sure it's old Houdenot who's at it again."

"Madame Houdenot? Why would she have stolen your glasses?"

"To annoy me, of course."

"How's it going today, Monsieur Teurquetil?"

"Where am I?"

"In your room."

"Oh no. This isn't my room."

"Yes, it is your room. We're going to freshen you up and, if you like, we'll take you for a stroll downstairs."

"You're sure this is my room?"

"Yes. Look at the photos on the walls, there. Those are your children and grandchildren."

"And Mommy, where's Mommy?"

"She's resting."

"Is my father with her?"

"Yes. He's resting with her."

"Are they coming to see me this afternoon?"

"Perhaps, but if they're too tired, they'll come tomorrow."

"Good morning, Madame Saban. I'm just removing the cheese and ham you hid in your cupboard. You could get food poisoning, and it stinks."
"It's because of the Germans: they requisition everything."
"Don't you worry, Madame Saban, the Germans went back home long ago."
"Are you sure? Because I actually saw them yesterday evening."
"Oh really, where was that?"
"In the bathroom."

"Morning, Madame Hesme, any good news?"
"Oh no, my poor dear, I so wish I could take the place of those children."
"Which children?"
"It's not right that old folk like us are still around when there are children dying every month in the *Journal de Saône-et-Loire*."
"That's life, that's how it is."
"The good Lord ought to be here, taking his pick of us old folk. We're no use anymore."

"How's it going, my beautiful Hélène?"
"When Lucien saw me praying in the church, on Angèle's wedding day, he asked me why I was begging candles to teach me to read. He looked like a kid. I took him for an altar boy. He was handsome. Much taller than me. I had to look up to see him. At first, he didn't look me in the eye; he talked to my hands. When he finally did look into my eyes, I saw the Prussian blue of one of my sewing threads. A blue I almost never used. He looked at me the way one looks at a liar, or a lunatic. So I picked up a missal left on a bench, opened it at random, and began to read a passage so he'd hear what I was seeing. I should have read: 'For this is the will of God.' But I read: *Thiforsisthwieoflldog.*

"He closed the missal and said to me: 'I'm not the good Lord, but I can teach you to read with your fingers.' He spoke to me as if we already knew each other. I thought of my 'nimble fingers,' as Angèle had just called them. In the space of an hour, two people were talking to me about my fingers. It had been ages since I'd spoken with someone of my age. I mean, someone talking to me about something other than lining fabric or trimmings. In losing school, I had also lost the other pupils' youth.

"The two of us sat on a bench facing the altar. He opened the book he was holding. There was no title on its cover, but he said it was Victor Hugo's *Les Misérables*. He handed it to me, and it wasn't like the books I'd been given at school. I could look at it without panicking: its pages were blank.

"Lucien took my hand and made me stroke the pages. They felt like baby's skin but covered in tiny, hard pimples. Next, he took my index finger and placed it on a specific bump. He said: 'Can you feel the "a"?' Then he placed it on an 'm.' I felt three bumps under the pad of my finger. He made me touch an 'o.' Then a 'u.' He turned several pages before making me touch the 'r.' And then he went over it again. And my fingers didn't jumble up the letters. For the first time in my life, I understood what I was reading. I'd finally got my miracle.

"Three days later, Lucien came to my parents' atelier. He was standing in front of the swing mirror. His eyes had turned sky-blue, and he'd put brilliantine on his dark hair. A stray lock fell across his forehead. Like a comma between his eyebrows. When he saw me, he smiled at me, and I smiled back at him. He had the charm of shy people who pretend not to be so.

"His thick lips ordered a flannel suit from me. Normally, I didn't make men's suits; my father took care of them. But I insisted. And my mother needed no persuading. She understood that this handsome young man was there because of me. Her illiterate, messy-haired daughter being courted was unhoped-for.

"My father asked him for a deposit, all the same, because

Lucien really did look like a kid. He pulled three crumpled banknotes out of his pocket.

"I showed him the various suit styles in a brochure of designs. As he felt the different fabrics, he whispered to me that, if I agreed to sleep with him, he'd never be afflicted with blindness: losing his sight would become impossible. He told me that, since Sunday, he'd thought only of me. And I replied that, since Sunday, I'd thought only of Hugo's *Les Misérables*. And had been to see my old schoolmaster, Monsieur Tribout, to ask him if such a book really existed.

"Lucien picked a navy-blue flannel.

"I asked him if he was going to marry me, and he replied that, no, in his family, getting married brought bad luck. I said, 'I agree to sleep with you if, in exchange, you teach me to read with my fingers.'

"Girls who slept with boys outside of marriage were called sluts, but being a slut didn't bother me if I knew how to read. The facts of life, in 1933, weren't spoken about. Our periods would arrive, and we thought they came from the hole we peed through; we saw women getting married, their bellies swelling, but we didn't know what went on in our parents' bedroom. At school, there was always an older girl to tell the younger ones how to kiss a boy with tongues, but I wasn't at school anymore. When I met Lucien, I was convinced I'd end up an 'old maid.' That's what ladies in Clermain who'd never married were called. I was convinced that the 'old maids' were like me, that they couldn't read.

"I made him take his shoes off and then put him against a wall so he'd stand up straight. I grabbed my tape to take his measurements. I started with his wrist circumference, then the length of his arms, the width of his shoulders, his back, his nape, his armhole depth, his waist-to-knee height, waist-to-ground height, from the base of the neck to the tips of the shoulders, hip measurement, length of legs, crotch, thigh and calf circumference. It took ages. I even invented measurements

I'd never need to make his suit, so scared was I that he'd change his mind and wouldn't teach me to read. I was perched on a small stool. He closed his eyes. He didn't want me to know what color they were right then. I could feel him trembling under my hands. I'd taken measurements all my life, and yet I felt, on that Wednesday, as if I were doing it for the first time. 181, 40, 80, 97, 81, 36, 13; I remember him like a poem.

"Years later, he confessed to me that, on that day, measurement day, he'd felt as if he'd lost his virginity to my measuring tape.

"I didn't dare ask him 'which side he dressed on.' That's the question all tailors ask men, to adjust the seam at the crotch. I imagined he 'dressed' to the left.

"The following Sunday, I joined him again in Clermain's church. He'd said to meet at four, when there'd be no one around. With an organist as father, Lucien knew all the region's churches and their different schedules. He was right: when I pushed open the door, there was no one there but him.

"He'd been waiting for me for hours on the same bench as the previous time. The one we'd sat on to read from the missal. His hands were frozen. He took my hands and gave me the alphabet in Braille on a piece of wood. I immediately recognized the 'a.' The most wonderful present I've ever been given. I kissed him. I'd never kissed a boy. He said to me, 'I want to touch you. I beg you, let me touch you.' I unfastened my dress. Yes, I unfastened it. It was a white dress that had belonged to my mother and that I'd taken in at the waist. He gazed at me for a long time. Gazed at me as if I were an amazing view. The chill, in the church, made me stiffen. But I know he still found me soft. I took his hand and placed it on me. Then guided it all over, gently, for a long time, right up to my mouth."

"How's it going today, Madame Lopez?"

## 20

When I look at myself in the bathroom mirror, I don't think I'm pretty. My eyebrows are straight. I ought to have two arches above my eyes, like Janet Gaynor. It's as if my face hasn't yet made a choice, hasn't finished taking shape. I tell myself that what I don't find pretty about me will one day be someone's beautiful. Someone who'll love me and become my artist. Who'll continue me. Who'll take me from rough sketch to masterpiece, if I have a serious love affair. We're all someone's Michelangelo; the trouble is, we have to meet them.

Jules tells me I'm too naively sentimental, that I think like a novel.

It's true that when I sleep with boys, I do think like a novel, but it's not a novel that's suitable for everyone.

I never sleep with the boy I'm actually sleeping with. The boy in my arms isn't the one in my head. I think about someone else; more precisely, I think about many others. The scenarios change, but it can be up to five others. Five guys in my fantasy bed: that's when I'm really on form. The kind of thing one would never do in real life; well, at any rate, not in mine.

I like the idea of love, but I get bored when I fuck. I need to let my mind wander off. One day I'll send my pretend men packing and sleep with the boy I'm actually sleeping with.

The first time Lucien kissed Hélène, he felt a fluttering of wings under his lips. I'm waiting for the boy who'll feel that fluttering of wings from my lips. They say that that doesn't happen all the time. That you can spend a lifetime waiting for that fluttering.

Yesterday evening, I made love with the twenty-seven-year-old again. The one called What's-his-name.

I have one rule I don't break: never sleep with a guy from Milly. It would be like sleeping with a work colleague. Impossible to avoid bumping into each other every day. So, like all the others, What's-his-name lives close to the Paradise, thirty kilometers from here. I had a second rule I didn't break before What's-his-name: never sleep twice with the same person. I've blown that one, as I've been sleeping with him for quite some time. I even gave him my phone number. This guy annoys me, but at the same time, I feel good with him when he's not annoying me. Since we began sleeping together, he's been asking me questions.

Usually, my "one-night stands" get dressed again in silence. But that said, usually, I do it in the car, seeing as I don't have an apartment. But this particular guy has a studio. And he doesn't budge after lovemaking. Doesn't light a cigarette, either. He just looks at me, for a long time, then asks me a load of questions:

"What do you do for a living? And what would you like to do if you had the choice? . . . Oh yeah? No! . . . You'll let me hear it? . . . You still live with your parents? Oh, I'm so sorry. How did it happen? So you live alone? I know your brother, by sight."

"He's not my brother, he's my cousin."

"And yet he looks like you."

"Oh, really . . . I thought I didn't look like anyone. Maybe it's because our fathers were twins. Or because we grew up together. His parents were with mine in the car."

"Wow, your life's crazy, like some dramatic movie. Do you think about your parents?"

"Every day."

"Do you remember them?"

"No. My memories have lost their memory."

"So how do you think about them, then?"

"I listen to my father's Bowie and Bashung records. For my

mother, it's Véronique Sanson and France Gall. I search for women's smells, too. Her face cream. For a long time, I hunted for a cream that matched my memory of her, the one I can't remember. I've sniffed every cream there is on earth. Even today, I still collect samples, just in case . . . I don't know. In case her smell returns."

It was the first time I was talking about something so personal with a quick fuck. I keep that kind of thing for Jules. Or for Jo, if I've really got the blues.

I'm not in love with What's-his-name. I know that because I never think about him. With him, there's just the present. I couldn't say how long I've known him. I have no bearings in the past. And no future plans. I never say to him, see you tomorrow, see you next week, see you later, talk soon.

## 21

*1933, after summer*

Lucien's father remarried because of Bach's The Art of Fugue, *Counterpoint III, which he played at the cathedral of Saint-Vincent-des-Prés. After the service, a woman wanted to meet the man who had played it so wonderfully. She went up the stairs leading to the organ. An hour later, she asked Étienne to marry her. He said yes. He followed her and moved to Lille.*

*Étienne left the house, furniture, linen, crockery, and Braille books to Lucien, who didn't want to leave the area. He asked his son why he wanted the Braille books, and he replied: "To keep your fingerprints." Lucien watched his father getting into the fine car of his new wife. He looked happy. Lucien kissed him and, for the last time, told him what he was seeing and Étienne would never see:*

*"You look happy."*

*Since his father's departure, Lucien has been working at a café, the one belonging to old Louis. It's Milly's sole café. He helps with serving, and loading and unloading the crates of bottles and beer barrels; he returns drunk men to their wives every evening, and is in charge of washing the floors, windows, and glasses. He's also meant to help old Louis behind the bar on busy days, which is to say, never.*

*Since measurement day, Lucien takes the train once a week, on Saturday, to be with Hélène in Clermain. Sometimes, he cycles there. Always dressed in his navy-blue flannel suit. He goes straight to the church, never stopping on the way, looks at the statue Hélène was praying at that first time, and then hides in the* confessional. At around 6 P.M., Hélène joins him. They then wait in silence to be locked inside the church.

Lucien slips his week's tips into the collection box and lights up Hélène's body by burning candles. He guides Hélène's fingers towards reading, and his own towards loving. Hélène likes stories set beside the sea best, even though she's never seen it.

Since they first met, Hélène has changed a lot. Reading has unlocked her. As if daylight were finally penetrating her and then seeping out through every pore of her skin. She moves like a woman who is, at last, wearing floaty dresses after a very, very long winter.

When they start to feel sleepy, she speaks to him of her childhood, and it's like a lullaby. She tells him about the girls' school. About those feverish days, about the words that refused to be seen by her, about her mouth that went crazy and spat out any old thing, about the despair of isolation. She tells him about the only thing she could do before him: make dresses and suits.

She tells him about the evening she licked the words on the blackboard, thinking they were poisonous. And the little seagull that threw itself against the window to save her life. She assures him that every human being is linked to a bird. And that certain people share the same one. You just have to look up at the sky to see that your bird is never far away. She says that birds don't die, they're eternally devoted. That as soon as you put a bird in a cage, a man goes mad.

In return, Lucien says he loves her. He has never heard anything as beautiful as Hélène's voice.

"Talk some more . . ."

While she's talking, he breathes her in. This girl smells like a bouquet of roses and hawthorn blossom. A fragrance at once domestic and wild. When she's silent, he lights fresh candles to see her taking pleasure from him.

On Sunday morning, they leave early because Mass starts at 8 A.M. If he takes the train, Hélène accompanies him to the station. If he sets off on his bike, Hélène watches him disappearing over the horizon.

Once she's alone again, she returns home without going to the *atelier—she doesn't work there much anymore. Since knowing Lucien, she lies to her parents. Like when she was a dunce. She pretends to have terrible headaches in order to shut herself away in her room and spend hours reading with her fingertips.*

*She's not in love with Lucien. She's grateful to him. He got her out of jail when she had a life sentence. Thanks to him, she can feel the wind in her hair, the sun pricking her skin, smiles chapping her lips. He's her best friend, the brother she never had, her salvation. Thanks to him, she's lucky. He brings her luck every Saturday.*

*Lucien's beauty, know-how, and gentleness make her climax automatically, not amorously. It's not love as she'd imagined it, the love that leaves you reeling. Lucien isn't a prince charming but an entire kingdom. He could ask her for anything he wants; she'd give it to him.*

*He's madly in love with her. He thinks only of her. He'd like to breathe her in all night and all day. Her thighs, her sex, her arms, her skin, her mouth, her eyes, her back, her ass, her hands, her fingers, her voice. She has replaced everything. Even his fear of losing his sight. He doesn't read anymore, listen to music anymore, swim anymore. He barely eats, and his flannel suit is becoming baggy on him.*

*At the café, he rewashes the clean tiles and glasses several times a day to keep his hands busy, to avoid going crazy. He thinks only of Saturday. That when she enters the church he'll recognize her step, that she'll dip her hand into the holy water, greet her Lord with a sign of the cross, pull open the confessional door, smile at him, lift her skirt and expect just one thing from him: the new Braille book he'll have brought along.*

*At the brothel, he paid the girls with cash; this girl he pays with books. He knows she doesn't love him and gives herself to him the way the Autun prostitutes give themselves. Love is the art of being selfish.*

*On the last Saturday of 1933, a December 30th, Lucien Perrin makes his non-proposal of marriage to Hélène Hel.*

## 22

A re you reading your horoscope, Armand?"
Gramps shrugs his shoulders. Jules moves behind him
and leans over.
"'Aries, you are going to have an important encounter.'"
Another shrug of the shoulders. Gramps grumbles:
"Neverr rread that nonsense myself."
Jules persists:
"But you're still going to have an important encounter."
Gran chides Jules:
"Eat your potatoes instead of bothering your grandfather."
Jules returns to his seat at the table and drowns his fried eggs
in ketchup. At home, we eat at 6.30 P.M. Just like the hens. An
expression I hate because, when I was little, my friends would
say it to mock me. In fact, they weren't friends but neighbors,
or rather, on vacation next door.

At the table, I've always sat in the same place, opposite
Gran, with Jules to my left, Gramps to my right. That's just how
it is. And you'd better not change it, or Gramps sounds off.
Later, when I have my own place, I'll only eat from pastel-hued
coffee tables; there'll be no plastic-coated tablecloths, and I'll
never sit in the same place. At home, there's nothing but oak.
Everything's dark brown. Gramps says it's beautiful because it's
a noble wood. Personally, I think it's hideous. And at home, everything's covered up, protected. On the sofas there are covers.
On the armchairs, covers. And on all the tables, cloths. It's as if
our house had something to hide.

Every evening, after supper, Jules goes up to his room to revise, and I to mine to write in my blue notebook, if I'm not on

night duty. Gramps stays in front of the TV. And Gran goes up to her room to open a Danielle Steel novel, which she'll take a year to read because she nods off after two pages. I always give her several for Christmas. The covers of Danielle Steel's books are often pastel-hued, like my future coffee tables, and bear titles like *Now and Forever*, *Season of Passion*, and *The Ring*. I don't know what fires Gran's imagination in those books; maybe it's the covers.

At around six years old, I discovered that Gran and Gramps had first names. Gran is called Eugénie and Gramps, Armand. Jules often calls them by their first names: Eugénie, we're out of gherkins! Armand, I've found your glasses.

Jules is much cheekier to them than I am.

It's strange to see them young on their wedding photo. And even stranger to see Gran wearing a cinched-in dress. Time has exchanged her hour-glass figure for that of a Labrador. Gran no longer has a body. It's as if she were hewn out of a tree trunk. There's no distinguishing where breasts, waist, hips, buttocks are. Gran isn't fat, she's inflated, all of a piece. Her legs and feet are compressed into support stockings—even in summer—and her hands are forever rough, as though no one had ever stroked them. I just can't imagine that Gramps ever flirted with Gran. Can't imagine Gramps toppling Gran onto a bed. Can't bring myself to think that Gran ever gave Gramps a blow job. Whereas when Hélène talks to me of Lucien, I can imagine all sorts.

Gramps and Gran almost never speak to each other. All they ever do together is the shopping. They never row. It's as if they've agreed to just leave each other in peace. I've never seen them kissing on the mouth. Just a casual little peck on the cheek at Christmas, to say thanks for a gift. And because we're there. Some people hide away to kiss, out of modesty. With them, it's the opposite.

It can't be said that they're nasty to us, merely absent. They're always inside the house but never in the rooms. They're always at the table, but never on the menu.

In the evening, Gramps joins Gran in their room at around

10.30 P.M. Except on Sundays. Every Sunday evening, Gramps watches *Cinéma de minuit* on France 3. When he joins Gran in their room, she's already asleep. She's leant her stick against her bedside table, popped her dentures into a glass of water with an effervescent tablet, put a hairnet on her head, and it's a scary sight, believe me. When I was little, the thought of going into their room in the middle of the night terrified me. Even when ill, with a raging fever, I'd wait until she'd returned to being the morning Gran, with teeth.

I can't imagine, either, that she ever lived a youthful life, without suicide attempts or a chamber pot at the foot of the bed.

Two years ago, I came home earlier than expected. Gramps had gone to Mâcon for the day, for a fully reimbursable health check-up, a birthday present for his seventy-five summers. I heard a noise coming from the bathroom upstairs. A hammering sound. Like someone hitting the pipes. I immediately thought of the plumber because that very morning, there'd been a major leak between the shower and the sink. The tiles were literally passing water.

As I entered the bathroom, I saw Gran, in blue overalls, flat on her back, head under the sink. All I could actually see were her legs molded by the blue cotton. She had leant her stick against the bath. She was also wearing shoes I'd never seen before. They looked like men's shoes, but in her size. There was a half-open toolbox, and Gran's hand darted from pipes to box with disconcerting dexterity. Without saying a word, I watched her grabbing various spanners and other screwdriver-like tools. Lying under the lowest part of the sink, she didn't see me. I found myself in the position of a little girl discovering that her grandmother leads a double life. One life in which she reads romantic novels, and another in which she's a plumber. What startled me most was seeing her in trousers, legs apart, and with a suppleness suggesting she wasn't as old as all that. As disturbed and embarrassed as if I'd just found her in bed with a lover, I backed away and left the house. I went to have a coffee at the betting bar and returned home an hour later, making as much noise as possible. She was in the kitchen, in the gray dress she ordered three years ago from the Blancheporte catalog. I looked down at her feet, and she wondered why I was scrutinizing her scruffy old slippers.

The bathroom was spick and span.

That evening, Jules asked if he could take a shower upstairs, and I heard my grandmother lying to him. Yes, the plumber had come during the day; the leak was repaired. Gramps asked Gran how much it had cost, and she replied: 30 euros, cash in hand. I searched for Gran's perfect-little-handyman gear in the garden shed, the junk closet, the cellar, but never found a trace of it. Now I wonder whether I wasn't hallucinating and the whole thing was just the fruit of my overactive imagination. Unless the plumber in Milly happens to be Gran's double.

Since I've been writing in the blue notebook, I no longer go down to the cellar to listen to music. As a result, Jules is revising. Or pretending to revise while playing online games and downloading techno music.

Over the years, I think I've mourned for music the way I mourned for my parents. I think I started mixing to make the sound of their voices resonate around me: all of our records belonged to our parents. They were record dealers.

After our fathers died, Gramps and Gran gave up the premises in Lyon they had leased. But not knowing what to do with all the records and CDs, they brought them back to the cellar. The music remained in cardboard boxes until Jules and I found them. First we bought a turntable to listen to the LPs, and then, a few years later, got a mixing desk. The latter was a gift from Jules's grandparents, Magnus and Ada. When Jules was still speaking to them.

Next year, Jules won't be at home anymore. I can't quite believe it. Just as I can't quite believe that Gramps is going to have an important encounter.

I enter room 19. Roman is seated beside Hélène.
"Hello."
He stands up.
"Hello, Justine."
He indicates *From the Land of the Moon* with his eyes. I'd put the book back on the bedside table for him to retrieve on his next visit.
"Did you like it?"
"I devoured it."
He smiles.
"I hope that didn't give you indigestion."
I blush.
"It made me want to go to Sardinia."
He looks at me.
"I have a little house over there, in the south of the island, towards Muravera. I'll lend you the keys any time you like."
I lower my eyes.
"Really?"
"Really."
Silence.
"Do you come across the characters in the book there?" I ask.
He looks at me.
"Every day."
I look at him.
"Even the Veteran?"
"Especially the Veteran."
He picks up the novel and then immediately puts it back down. Then he stands up again.

"I'm running late, I must go, if I'm not to miss the last train. Hélène hasn't said a word to me today."

I look at Hélène. I think of the house in Sardinia and say:

"Next time."

And he, with sadness, says to me:

"Yes. Perhaps. Goodbye."

"Goodbye."

Whenever he leaves a room, a slight shadow descends. He never asks me if I've started writing for him.

Hélène turns her head towards me and smiles.

"So, my beautiful Hélène, it's the world of silence today?"

"Lucien non-married me on January 19, 1934, in Milly, his village. There was lots of snow that day. He picked the coldest day of winter on purpose so no one would be able to come . . . Justine?"

"Yes."

I move closer to her and take her hand.

"Do you know why Lucien never wanted to marry me?"

"Because the wedding ring encircles the only finger with a vein running directly to the heart."

She starts to laugh like a little girl.

"The left ring finger."

I sit down beside her. She resumes her monologue:

"We disguised old Louis's house as a town hall. It was a large square house, with three floors, right opposite the railway station. With a ladder, Lucien hung a *tricolore* from the gutter, and a large '*MAIRIE*' sign above the front door. My parents, who had never set foot in Milly, were none the wiser. And anyhow, the snow covered everything up.

"There was no one in the streets. We were waiting for my parents in front of the fake town hall when they emerged from the station. I was wearing a very simple white dress, with no lace.

"We told my parents that we'd marry in church later, in the summer, and I'd add lace and a tulle veil then. My mother was disappointed that the only daughter of the Clermain tailors should have such a plain dress on her wedding day. As for Lucien, he was proudly wearing his first navy-blue flannel suit. He'd lost a lot of weight; I'd had to make some alterations.

"When he took my arm and we entered the fake town hall, he kissed me with his eyes. On that day, it wasn't just my hand I was giving him, it was both hands: I was starting to read Braille on my own, without his help. I owed everything to him . . . Justine?"

"Yes."

"Do you know what that means, owing everything to someone?"

"I know what it means, but I've never met anyone I could owe everything to."

Silence.

"On the ground floor of the house, old Louis had removed all his furniture and installed a large desk and a few chairs. Lucien had hung up some fake bylaw decrees on the walls, and on a locked door had written "Public Records Office." Old Louis loved playing the mayor. He took his role very seriously, without really grasping why Lucien was going to such lengths not to marry me. Much as Lucien explained to him that marriage prevented the blood from reaching the heart, and enslaved men and women to promises that were impossible to keep, he never really understood.

"Old Louis was a stout man with a deep voice. With his *tri-colore* sash across his chest, he read out the civil marriage code to us. Article 212, the husband and wife have a duty to be faithful to one another, and supportive. Article 213, the husband and wife together maintain the moral and material welfare of the family, provide for the education of the children, and prepare for their future.

"My parents left after the ceremony, so they wouldn't be caught out by nightfall, which was very early at that time of year."

She goes quiet.

"Hélène?"

"Yes."

"Why didn't you say a word to Roman today?"

She shrugs to indicate that she doesn't know. Then opens her mouth one last time before returning to her beach:

"After the exchange of kisses, Baudelaire, our fake witness, recited a poem:

*My sister, my child*
*Imagine how sweet*
*To live there as lovers do!*
*To kiss as we choose*
*To love and to die*
*In that land resembling you!*[3]

---

[3] Charles Baudelaire, "Invitation to the Voyage," in *The Flowers of Evil*, trans. James McGowan (Oxford: Oxford University Press, 1993).

I n 1935, Lucien and Hélène buy old Louis's café, who sells it to them for a song. They don't change the name. Figuring there's no point as that's what it's always been called. Changing the name of this café would be like renaming an old man who's a regular customer. They repaint the walls, and that's it.

The main room of the café is bright, accessed through a door with red, blue, and green frosted glass. Two large windows look out onto a street, and another onto the square with the Romanesque church. The floorboards are of dark wood. Four columns covered in mirrors reflect a kaleidoscope of customers leaning on the zinc bar.

Behind the bar, a small windowless room is used for storage. To the right, four steps lead to another room that serves as kitchen and washroom, because there's a sink, a stove, a table, and two chairs.

From this room, a wooden stepladder goes up to a floor where a basic bedroom has been set up.

Hélène memorizes the names of the liquors on offer. Since she can't read their names, she goes by the pictures on the labels, the colors of the liquids, and the shapes of the bottles.

At first, it's the customers who tell her in which glass to serve the Byrrh Violet, the St Raphaël, the Amer Cabotin, the Eau d'Arquebuse, the Dubonnet, the gentian, the vermouth, the cherry brandy, the Pastis Olive, and the Malvoisie Saint-André.

No customer cheats with the measures, the price to be paid, or the capacity of the glasses. There are even some new lemon- and orangeade drinkers among the regulars and the barflies, the color of Hélène's eyes luring the village's youngsters like absinthe.

# 25

Generally, our residents stink. They don't like washing themselves anymore. As if arriving in Heaven grubby doesn't bother them one bit.

In the morning, during wash time, we often get shouted at. And when we point out to the independent residents that they need to take a shower, ditto. We have to insist.

As for Hélène, she never stinks. She smells like a baby.

The first time I found myself alone with her, it was Christmas Eve. I'd been working at The Hydrangeas for a month. I was on night duty. The nurse had told me to keep an eye on Hélène because she had a slight fever. I went up to take her temperature. She took my hand. It made me want to cry because no one had ever touched me so tenderly. Such motherliness was unknown to me. As a child, whenever my grandmother touched me, it was always with a wash glove.

"How's the weather on your beach?" I asked.

"Beautiful. It's August now. Lots of people."

"Don't forget to protect yourself from the sun."

"I have my big hat."

"Is what you're seeing beautiful?"

"It's the Mediterranean. It's always beautiful, the Mediterranean. What's your name?"

"Justine."

"Do you come often?"

"Nearly every day."

"Would you like me to tell you about Lucien?"

"Yes."

"Come over here. Put your ear to my mouth."

I leant against her. I heard what one hears inside a seashell: what one wants to hear.

I n 1936, they close their bistro from August 20 to 31. On a large sign, Lucien writes:

## CLOSED FOR VACATION

Even the seagull disappears from the roof.

For eleven days, the men of Milly are obliged to drink alone. To repair a leak, rake the garden, chop wood, oil the well pulley, go to Mass with the wife.

It's the first time the village café has closed since they were born. Even for the oldest customers who no longer remember their own age.

When Lucien and Hélène reopen their café on the morning of September 1, Baudelaire is stamping impatiently outside the door, clutching a portrait of Janet Gaynor that he's cut out from a magazine. He enters the bistro with his new companion as if entering a cathedral to marry her.

On that September 1, all the customers are a bit grumpy, especially towards Hélène. It's her they blame for the closure. The men are silent, apart from when, one by one, they hold up the picture of Janet Gaynor, declaring to Hélène that this is the most beautiful woman in the world. That some women would do well to emulate her and style their hair a bit better. Hélène pays no attention and returns to her old routine, mending holes in pockets and on elbows, while ignoring her glossy rival.

That evening, when the café has been closed for more than an hour, Hélène finds Janet Gaynor's picture, abandoned on a corner of the bar. Does she know how to read . . .? That's the first thing

*Hélène wonders about while looking at the portrait. It's always the first thing she wonders about when she meets someone.*

*Hélène learned to read at sixteen. When she first touched the alphabet, she felt as if she were being born, learning to breathe. Then the words came, and then the sentences. She will always remember the first sentence she was able to read. It came from Guy de Maupassant's* Une vie, *a novel that Hélène has read twenty, maybe thirty times since then. "As a child, since she was neither pretty nor difficult, she was barely kissed, and would stay nice and quiet in a corner."*

*When Hélène reads sentences as grim as: "Then the damp, rugged landscape around her, with its mournfully falling leaves and gray clouds dragged by the wind, made her feel so desolate that she went indoors so as not to weep," she is exultant. Nothing she reads can sadden her. Each word is a warming gulp that thrillingly intoxicates her. Before reading, Hélène was like Jeanne, Maupassant's heroine, shut away in a convent.*

*Hélène had always felt that she remained on the surface of things, of people. When reading, she's biting into a fruit she's coveted for years, and is finally feeling its sweet juice flowing inside her mouth, her throat, over her lips, her fingers.*

*Before reading, her life amounted to daily, routine activities that, by the end of the day, plunged her into a deep sleep, like some worn-out draft horse. Now, her nights are crowded with dreams, characters, music, landscapes, sensations.*

*Hélène gazes at Janet Gaynor, the dreamy, provocative, and distant look in her lovely eyes. Her perfect eyebrows, her perfect mouth, her perfect hair, her bare neck. Hélène daren't throw her away. She sticks her between two bottles of Malvoisie Saint-André.*

*Later, the photo of Janet Gaynor was glued, pinned, taped between the bottles of lemonade and the stem glasses behind the counter. Almost always in the same place for years. It ended up stuck on the coffee machine that was delivered after the war, along with the bottles of Coca-Cola. Every time a hot drink was made, Baudelaire would say that the steam was messing up Janet's hair a little.*

## 27

Autumn is approaching. This morning, I stopped by at the cemetery before work. I like going there since I'm no longer obliged to do so.

Dead leaves were covering the dates on the tombstone. One day I'll be older than my parents. They'll always be thirty years old. I wonder what I'll do when I'm thirty. Will I be married? Will I have children? Will Jules have a good job? Will I have been to the island of Muravera? Will Hélène still be here? Will I have met my own Lucien? Will Gran still scour her sitting room twice a day while listening to the radio?

I wouldn't want to know. Sometimes, Jo offers me a clairvoyance session, just for a laugh, she says, but I always tell her that the future is no laughing matter. Particularly when you're twenty-one.

I never attend residents' funerals. I look after them while they're alive, but I stop at the threshold when they pass over to "the other side."

Earlier, Rose visited with Roman. The first time they've come together.

Ostensibly, Hélène didn't move, didn't open her eyes, didn't say a word.

Roman came to ask me for a second vase for Rose's hydrangeas, because the other one was full of the white roses he had brought.

In the office, I found one of our ugly vases, which must be around my age. He asked, quietly:

"Have you started writing?"

"Yes."

My "yes" made him smile. I saw only sweetness on his lips.

I handed him the vase, thinking to myself what a beautiful bouquet the blue of his eyes would make. Even in such an ugly vase. I know I'm rambling, but I swear I can't help it.

"Thank you."

I haven't seen him since.

This afternoon, What's-his-name phoned me twice. The first time, I didn't answer; the second time, still didn't. I slept at his last night.

With him, I'm still all over the place, blowing hot and cold. One moment I feel like kissing him, and then three seconds later, when he's too clingy or puts on some hideous polo-neck sweater, any excuse will do to chuck him out the window.

I've always been that way. I dream of love, but as soon as it's shown to me, it exasperates me. I become nasty and unbearable. What's-his-name is very tender, and maybe it's because life's not been easy for me, but I think I need a lover who scratches into the corners, like sandpaper.

This evening, I'm on duty.

I feel nostalgic, nostalgic for what I've not yet lived.

## 28

*O*ccasionally, Lucien asks Hélène if she'd like to change her life, leave, close the bistro, stop breathing in the men's cigarette smoke and listening to them rambling on, do something different. Occasionally, Lucien asks Hélène if she'd like to meet another man. One who'd marry her for real and whom she'd love for real. To which she replies, No, certainly not, you bring me luck.

In 1941, old Louis's café still has its regulars. Most of the men are too old for compulsory labor. And all that remains of the trenches is their scars, their tremors, their wooden legs, and the war memorial erected on the Place de l'Église.

When the Germans turn up in the village, they requisition certain foodstuffs, but don't settle there.

While they are around, doors and shutters are bolted. And then the men return to work on the land. And the very old men hit the bottle to drown their sorrows or wash down their meager meal, under the bright gaze of Hélène, who still patches up the holes in their trousers.

After three glasses of liquor, or five depending on the customer's build, she fills the glasses with lemonade. The customers, thinking she's taken the wrong bottle because she can't read the labels, daren't say a thing to her. They discreetly ask Lucien to re-serve them "properly."

\* \* \*

In 1939, Lucien had been called up to fight for his country in the "phony war." He returned to Milly in June 1940.

The crossing of the Maginot Line by German forces brought most men back to their homes.

Just before he'd left, Hélène had discovered that Lucien hadn't been baptized. She'd wanted to be his godmother, but Lucien didn't believe in God and ridiculed the holier-than-thou. Which was bound to anger Hélène. She would tell him that he was blaspheming, to which he would reply: My blasphemy is you. Hélène implored him. Lucien agreed to be baptized. Now they just needed to find a godfather. It was decided that he'd be pulled out of a hat full of the customers' names.

Lucien wrote all the men's first names on identically cut slips of paper. That day, all the men of the village were present. Even those who normally drank only the water from their well. Jules, Valentin, Auguste, Adrien, Émilien, Louis, Alphonse, Joseph, Léon, Alfred, Auguste, Ferdinand, Edgar, Étienne, Simon. Hearing them reveal their first names was just as if they'd stripped off in front of each other. They were usually known by their nicknames—Titi, Lulu, le Grand, Quinquin, Féfé, Caba, Mimile, Dédé, Nano—or not named at all. Just hello and then silence. Only Baudelaire got a special "dispensation." Lucien wrote "Charles Baudelaire" on the slip of paper.

It was Simon who won the title of godfather to Lucien. The others were a little disappointed: they'd lost in the good Lord's lottery. They all went to the church. All without exception, because it was the first time they were attending the baptism of an adult.

Although Simon was of the Jewish faith, the priest turned a blind eye. It was a time of war: everyone turned a blind eye, even the Holy Ghost.

The priest doused Lucien's head with holy water and said:

"Godfather and godmother, the child you are presenting, Lucien, will receive the sacrament of baptism: God, in his love, will give him a new life. He will be reborn through water and the Holy Ghost. Be sure to raise him in faith so this divine life isn't weakened by indifference or sin, but rather, develops within him, day by day."

*The priest gave Lucien's baptism certificate to Hélène on May 7, 1939.*

*Three days later, on the morning of his departure, Lucien woke to find no Hélène asleep beside him. That had never happened before. Lucien thought it might be an early sign of his father's affliction. He rubbed his eyes for a long time. He looked for her, called out to her, in vain.*

*He finally found a sheet of white paper on the kitchen table. It was dotted with tiny holes, which Hélène must have done with a sewing needle. By passing his fingertips over them, Lucien read: "Come back, my dear godson, my gentle brother, my fine friend, come back."*

\* \* \*

*On the day the lots were drawn, Lucien had cheated. Hélène had seen the two berets. A first one to put all the men's names into, a second one filled in advance with the name "Simon."*

*Just before the lot was drawn, Lucien had offered drinks all around, and, during the hubbub, had sneakily switched the berets under the bar.*

*Hélène had plunged her hand into the second beret, and Lucien had pretended to discover the name of his godfather.*

*That evening, while sweeping up the sawdust, Hélène had found 29 "Simon" slips hidden behind some empty bottles. She hadn't been able to read them, but had swept them up and made them disappear down the drain so no one would find them. What Hélène didn't know was that the Nazis were in the process of doing just the same thing as her.*

\* \* \*

*Simon had arrived one snowy day in 1938. He had entered through the wrong door, the back one, through the storeroom, the door for the apologetic. He had drunk some coffee and* explained to Lucien, with a strong accent, that he had escaped from Poland to seek refuge in the land of the Rights of Man, and, since then, had got into the habit of not entering through front doors anymore. His only luggage was a case containing a violin and a jacket.

Simon was fifty years old. He was a violin-maker; his workshop had been ransacked and set on fire, and he had been left for dead, with an inscription cut, with a knife, into his forehead: zydowski (Jewish).

The scar was still visible. The "y" would reappear on his forehead when his skin caught the sun. He always wore a little hat that covered his forehead. He was tall and thin, with strong hands that contrasted with the rest of his frail body. And with his curly gray hair, the tiniest drop of water stood no chance of wetting his scalp.

Before speaking, Simon would smile. As if not a word could leave his mouth without being accompanied by a smile.

Lucien and Hélène suggested he stay for a few days, sleeping in the room of the child that was sure to come but was taking its time.

They offered him free bed and board, and in return he would play his violin in the café to entertain the customers, who had become morose with the threat of imminent war. But Simon was scared. Scared that the sound of his violin might attract malevolent types.

He took off his hat for the first time, rubbed his head, and suggested playing the violin for the two of them, just the two of them. Within hours, he became "our friend Simon." A genuine friend, the sort whose kindly presence is a delight.

For Simon, Lucien was an intellectual whom love had turned into a barman. This tall young man could have been teaching rather than serving glasses of wine all day. But he had made the choice to have just one pupil, Hélène.

From the moment Hélène had leaned over Simon to darn his moth-eaten sweater, he had understood Lucien's self-denial.

## 29

S urname. First name."
"Neige. Justine."
He enters it into his computer. He types with two fingers.
I didn't know that people who type with two fingers still existed.
I thought the last of them had disappeared in the late 1980s.
"Date of birth?"
"October 22, 1992."
"How long have you worked at The Hydrangeas?"
"Three years."
"Position?"
"Nursing assistant."
He stops typing and looks at me, attentively.
"Neige . . . Your name rings a bell . . . What do your parents
do?"
"They died in a car accident."
"Around here?"
"On the national highway, exiting Milly in the direction of
Mâcon."
"In what year?"
"1996."
He stands up abruptly, making his chair on casters bang into
some metal shelving.
"Neige. But of course, Neige. The road accident. I went to
the scene of the accident that day . . . Officer Bonneton even
ordered an inquiry."
Too much information in one go. Starsky saw my parents.
Dead. And Officer Thingy even opened an inquiry. An inquiry
for what purpose?

"An inquiry?"

"Yes. Something wasn't quite right about the circumstances of the accident . . ."

"The circumstances? You must be mistaken. My parents skidded on a patch of black ice."

"Perhaps."

I persist:

"It said so in the newspaper."

He just looks at me, retrieves his chair, sits back down and presses "Enter" on his keyboard.

"Right. Let's get back to business. More recent, but still *old* business! Do you have any idea at all of the identity of the person making these phone calls to residents' families?"

"No."

"And yet, these last few weeks, the anonymous calls have increased. You've not noticed anything untoward in your workplace?"

"My grandparents . . . do they know? That you opened an inquiry after the accident?"

"What are your grandparents' names?"

He has the eyes of a grasshopper. The green ones that come into the house in summer and sting you really badly if you pick them up. I think they may even be the ones that kill the male after mating.

"Neige. Armand and Eugénie Neige.

"I don't think so. It remained internal."

"So . . .?"

"So what?"

"The inquiry? What did it reveal?"

"Nothing. The case was closed. But you, on the other hand: I'm told you do lots of overtime at The Hydrangeas."

He looks at me with disdain. As if I suddenly smell bad. I think he's more indulgent towards bank robbers than towards employees who do unpaid overtime.

"That's because I like being there . . . And this file . . . on my family, could you show it to me?"

He sniffs long and hard before replying, like in some bad Czech or German TV cop series:

"If you find me The Hydrangeas' anonymous caller."

Once out of the policeman's office, I head straight for The Hydrangeas, without returning home. I want to see Hélène. I need to hug her. Breathe her in. I always feel better afterwards. Like at the end of a long walk.

I dash into the cloakroom to get changed. I'm on duty at 5 P.M. because, once again, I've agreed to swap schedules with Maria.

Outside door 12, I hear Madame Dreyfus calling me. She's after news of the "fat cat," a giant wild tomcat she was feeding before coming here. Three times a week, I go to fill his bowl with dry food. I promise her that, tomorrow, I'll take a photo of him with my Polaroid camera.

Right then, What's-his-name phones me. It's as if he avoids saying his name on purpose. He always says: "It's me."

I'm on night duty, I can't "see" him this evening. "Don't worry," he says, "I'll come and pick you up tomorrow morning."—"But I finish at 6 A.M."—"Don't worry, I'll be waiting for you outside The Hydrangeas at 6:05 A.M."

I feel like saying OK, because it would be the first time someone under the age of eighty would be waiting for me somewhere. But I say no. When I come off night duty, I need to go home. Alone.

## 30

Annette was born in Stockholm in 1965. Jules kept her passport. In the photo, she looks like the blond singer in ABBA, Agnetha. That's surely why my mother, who was called Sandrine, picked her as a pen pal, at school in 1977. My mother had gone for the Swedish option because she was a fan of the group. Which might seem strange, since they sang in English. As for Annette, she wanted a French pen pal because France has the largest surface area of stained-glass windows (ninety thousand square meters), and she wanted to become a master glazier.

Jules kept all their letters. They had written to each other in English for seven years. At first, they told each other what their bedrooms were like, what they loved eating, doing, how many children they'd have later on, described their cat and their gold-fish. Whenever they traveled, they sent each other postcards.

Normally, they would have stopped writing to each other before too long because, at middle school, there are other things to do than write letters in English to a girl you don't know. But they didn't do what was normal. They began their correspondence in 1977 and met in 1980. After that, they saw each other every year. Until they died together.

As the years go by, the letters become increasingly personal. They talk about their family, their love affairs, their joys, their disappointments, their desires. They send each other photos, mainly Polaroids, which Jules and I have shared between us. Some we even cut in two to have the half we were each after.

Thanks to Annette, I learned things about my mother that no one could have told me. Like her childhood spent in the lodge of a building in Rue du Faubourg-St-Denis, where her mother was the *concierge*. She never knew her father. In her letters, she talks about life in the building, the tenants, the landlords, the tiny space where she would dance to ABBA's "Gimme! Gimme! Gimme!"; the Michael Zager Band's "Let's All Chant"; The Korgis' "Everybody's Got to Learn Sometime"; and Visage's "Fade to Grey."

My mother always loved music, all kinds of music. When she met my father, who was planning to become a record dealer, she was bound to fall in love with him.

She belonged to a theater group called Plume Paradis. I think she was funny and naturally cheerful because, on the photos, she's always laughing a bit more than the others. She had brown shoulder-length hair, was small, a bit chubby, and had the smile of an American movie star.

In 1983, the year they were eighteen, Annette and Sandrine went camping near Cassis. They pitched their tent in a camping site close to a rocky inlet, twenty minutes from the harbor. They swam all day and feasted on apple donuts.

Jules has a small diary that belonged to Annette in which she wrote lots of sentences in Swedish, which we translated with the help of the Internet. Sentences such as these:

"The light is white."

"It's like someone's scrubbed the houses with bleach—there are never any puddles."

"It smells lovely."

"You get dry without a towel."

"There's sugar on the donuts."

"The insects sing."

"I'd never been sunburnt, it's like a long-lasting slap."

Six days later, while buying an ice cream at the harbor, they meet Alain and Christian Neige.

In Annette's diary, it says:

"I could tell the two boys apart straight away: one is always looking at me, and the other isn't."

"They're leaving tomorrow."

"They're leaving the day after tomorrow."

"They're leaving next week."

"They're staying with us till the end of the vacation."

The following year, Sandrine and Annette met up with Christian and Alain in Lyon to spend the summer with them. At Lyon-Perrache station, the twins were waiting for them with a green convertible 2CV. Which cracked them up.

They had seen each other since Cassis, but not all together.

Alain had been to Stockholm twice, to stay with Annette's family. Christian to Rue du Faubourg-Saint-Denis, numerous times.

After Alain's second visit to Stockholm, he'd asked for Annette's hand in marriage, which she'd found very romantic but a little hasty. And she was only nineteen, after all.

In any case, Annette had opted to do her stained-glass window training in France. She'd found a master to whom she could be apprenticed in the Mâcon area. Which was only about a hundred kilometers from Lyon. So Sandrine had also decided to move to Lyon with Christian. They'd just need to find themselves an apartment for four.

The twins, both studying musicology at university in Lyon, were planning to become record dealers and composers. Christian would root out the rare LPs, and Alain would compose pieces of music, as well as running their business.

From Lyon, it took them three days to drive up to Milly in their 2CV, even though there are barely 170 kilometers between the city and the village. Every time she spotted a church, Annette would cry, "STOP!"

While Annette was studying each stained-glass window and taking photos of them, the other three had drinks on terraces.

Dozens of churches later, when the car finally pulled up outside the house, it was already July—July 14, to be precise. Kids were playing with firecrackers on the streets.

On the radio, the Bronski Beat hit "Smalltown Boy" played constantly.

The father of my magician neighbor told me that they were beautiful to look at. But most beautiful of all was Annette's blond hair. And her face, too. He'd never seen such a pretty girl in real life. For him, they'd only existed in his TV-listings magazines. When I was little, this same neighbor said to me, "She was *bien roulée*, your aunt." I didn't know what *bien roulée* meant—well put together. I thought of the *roulé à la fraise* that Gran makes. That he meant my aunt looked like a Swiss roll.

So the four of them got out of the 2CV singing: *Run away, turn away, run away, turn away, run away*, all imitating Jimmy Somerville's voice. And then they kissed Gran. Well, not quite. The twins kissed Gran, and Gran shook hands with Sandrine and Annette. And then the four of them sat down under the so-called arbor (four bits of wood with wicker fencing over the top).

Gran placed a bottle of port, ice cubes, and six glasses on the cast-iron table. She said Armand would be home shortly.

That day, Gran had made seafood couscous. Not a traditional July 14 dish, but the twins had insisted on it.

31

Wintertime

"Good morning, Madame Mignot, they changed the time last night. You need to put your alarm clock back an hour."

"You know, for me, here, it's always the same time."

## 32

The craziest Sunday I've ever known since working here. Jo and Maria had never seen anything like it, either. Even the broadcast of Mass was affected: at 11 A.M., there was no one left in front of the big screen in the TV room.

Yesterday, there were fifteen phone calls between 2 and 3:30 P.M., from Monsieur Paul's room. And those were just to families living more than three hundred kilometers away. Because the anonymous caller is super organized. And, according to Madame Le Camus, he or she uses a voice modifier.

"Hello, this is The Hydrangeas retirement home in Milly. We regret to inform you of the death of . . . Please come to reception tomorrow morning before 11 A.M., when the body will be transferred to the funeral parlor at 3, Rue de l'Église, Milly. All our condolences."

To the families that live near here, the phone calls were made last night, after 11 P.M. So that no one could turn up before this morning.

I was on duty last night. I checked in on Monsieur Paul at around 10 P.M.; he was alone. If Peter Falk was still of this world, I'm sure he'd solve this in a flash.

Madame Le Camus is keyed up, and Starsky and Hutch are carrying out searches of the "victims'" rooms. It's like being in an American TV series. Except the cops aren't as sexy.

All the families have decided to lodge a complaint against The Hydrangeas. And The Hydrangeas is lodging a complaint against a person or persons unknown. Do you have the right to lodge a complaint against a person or persons unknown if you're one of Sunday's forgotten?

But it was the loveliest Sunday of all the Sundays I can remember: the reception, corridors, card room, and video room were empty. Our magician went back home with his flock of birds, Chaplin remained inside his DVD, and "Le Petit Bal Perdu" inside its microphone.

Roman came to see Hélène. I didn't see him: I was too busy giving news of the living to the living.

When I went to kiss Hélène goodbye before leaving, his cologne lingered on her. So I stayed awhile. I sat down beside her and read her some extracts from my notebook:

*Since October 4, 1940, all "foreign citizens of the Jewish race" must be interned. Simon never leaves the café's cellar anymore. Hélène and Lucien convinced the customers that he had left overnight without leaving a forwarding address.*

*The village of Milly is in the occupied zone. The French police monitor, frisk, conduct searches. German officers come into the café, drink, and go. When they come in, it's always Lucien who serves them. As soon as they open the door, he alerts Simon by kicking a steel trap door concealed behind the bar. The slightest impact resonates down to the cellar.*

*Simon then hides—not without difficulty and the help of a ledge—inside a false ceiling built by old Louis's father. And he remains suspended there until Lucien comes to release him. He couldn't get out of his hiding place on his own. Once it's shut, it can only be opened from outside.*

*After alerting Simon, Hélène is next. To warn her to stay back, there are two codes: lowering the volume of the radio that's on a shelf behind the bar, or taking the photo of Janet Gaynor down from its shelf and sticking it on the door to the kitchen. As if the picture had to be moved to do the dusting. Lowering the volume of the radio means: Germans having a drink. Moving Janet: French police, Milice, Gestapo, suspect strangers.*

*In the evening, when the bistro is closed and the chairs are up on the tables, Lucien and Hélène join Simon in the cellar. They have a supper of Jerusalem-artichoke soup and brown bread while listening to the radio.*

*Simon no longer plays his violin. He looks at the instrument lying in its case as if it were part of himself that had been put into a coffin.*

*When it's getting late, Lucien and Hélène go up to their bedroom. Lucien wants to get her pregnant. He dreams of having a child with her. But Hélène doesn't fall pregnant, and he tells her it's because she doesn't really love him.*

Hélène has fallen asleep.

End of the day. End of Sunday.

Hélène has retired to her beach, and I'll be returning to my father's old bedroom.

In the changing room, I see I have three missed calls from What's-his-name on my mobile. I never phone him. If he's at the Paradise, great. If he's not there, he's not there.

But watching all those false orphans filing in the whole blessed day has shaken me up somehow. It's as if Assumption turned up on All Saints' Day, just for a surprise.

I ring his number for the first time. One ring and he says to me, straight off:

"You coming?"

"It's late, I'm bushed."

"You coming?"

"My legs won't carry me anymore."

"I'll carry you for them. You coming?"

## 33

How are you doing, Hélène?"

"In 1943, I said to Lucien: 'Don't worry, we have no enemies.' He replied to me: 'As long as I live with a woman as beautiful as you, I'll have plenty of enemies.' And the following day, he got arrested."

She closes her eyes.

"That was a long time ago. Now, we're on vacation."

While listening to her telling me her life story for the hundredth time, I give the floor of her room a mop and try to imagine her beach of the day.

Roman opens our door. He walks on tiptoe and avoids the damp areas. Panic stations, legs like jelly, idiot, twit, awkward, clumsy kick of bucket, a puddle, I bend over to wipe it up.

From behind my fringe, I watch him plant a tender kiss on Hélène's hair. I watch them both from this world, her in limbo, him in a state of grace.

"I'm leaving tomorrow. For two months."

He throws these words at me, aims straight for my heart.

I stammer:

"Two months?"

"I'll be taking photos in Peru."

"In Peru?"

"On the Ballestas Islands. I'll be snapping the gannets."

"Greedy people?"

He looks at me as if I were a complete dope.

"No . . . the birds."

If shame could kill, I'd already be dead and buried beside my parents.

"I photograph seabirds all over the world. Giant gulls, cormorants, seagulls, albatrosses, gannets, frigate birds."

I go back to cleaning the room. I feel like telling him that he doesn't need to travel across the world to photograph seabirds, that there's one here on the roof of The Hydrangeas, and that bird must have some amazing tales to tell, quite different from those I write down in the blue notebook. But I do no such thing. We all have two lives: one in which we say what we think, and another in which we shut up. A life in which words are passed over by silence.

"Will you be back for Christmas?"

He smiles. A shy smile. Almost a grimace. He lowers his eyes.

"Yes. Well, I hope so. And you? Will you be here?"

"I'm always here."

"Don't you ever get bored here?"

"Never."

"But don't you find your work hard?"

"Yes, it's really though. I'm only twenty-one. My colleagues are older than me. They all started later. This job is often a second job. At my age, it's not normal to see worn-out bodies. I mean, well, it's . . . shocking. And then there's the dying . . . On funeral days, I close the windows because you can hear the church bells even from here . . ."

"What's the hardest thing?"

"The hardest thing is hearing, 'He never remembers my visits so I'm not coming anymore.'"

Silence.

"Why don't you look for a different job?"

"Because there isn't a single job in which I could hear the stories these residents tell me."

"Might I take your picture?"

"I can't stand it . . ."

"That's normal. People who like having their picture taken don't interest me."

He pulls an enormous camera out of his bag and hides behind it.

"But . . . my hair's not tidy."

"Justine, if I may be so bold, your hair's never tidy."

He says that to me as if he's always known me. It's the kind of thing Jules might say. But Roman, really, I've known him for such a short time. But it's true that my hair defies combs, brushes, elastics, slides. I always look a mess. That's what Gran says. There are some girls who always look as if they've just stepped out of a hair salon. I'm the opposite.

"I didn't have a mother, so I don't know how to do those braid thingies, and all that."

"Why didn't you have a mother?"

"She passed away when I was four years old. She didn't get time to teach me how to be a girl."

"I think you're very good."

He could have said, I think you're very beautiful, or very pretty, or it doesn't matter, or I like you as you are, or it's fine. But he said very good. Very good. Like an assessment on a written test.

"Should I . . . should I take off my smock?"

"Absolutely not. Talk to me."

"Well, I also have a camera. A Polaroid. I take pictures of my brother and stick them above the beds of residents who have no family. Because he's handsome. And he makes a perfect son to have up on the wall. I take landscapes, too. And animals. Will you be done soon? But residents with no family left are rare. Are you done?"

"I'm stopping. Look, I'm putting my camera away."

He says that as if putting a gun back into his bag.

Hélène starts to shout:

"I'm coming with you! Take me with you!"

Roman gives me a questioning look. I lower my eyes.

"She's talking about Lucien's arrest."

"Do you know how that happened?"

"I'll write it down for you. I don't like Hélène hearing it."

## 34

You should wear your red top, it suits you better, your hair's a mess today, tidy your room, don't leave your things lying around, you're the one who took my lipstick, OK, it's alright sweetheart, help me clear the table, you're coming with me to the shop, I'll come and collect you at four, you're asking for my opinion, I'm giving you my opinion, I don't have time now, have you done your homework, but what's that, have you seen how beautiful that is, you won't go, I bought you this, shouldn't have started, go lay the table, no, no, no, well, OK, but just once, don't get home too late, no chocolate, no soda after 6 P.M., you're not leaving without breakfast, put your jacket on, it's cold outside, but what on earth's all this mess, have you brushed your teeth, it's about time you grew up, go have your shower, don't worry, it doesn't matter, I love you, goodnight, how beautiful you look this morning, I love that thing on you, your history teacher just rang, it's late, go to bed, but yes, math is important, it's alright my darling, who is this boy, I know you don't like reading but you're going to love this, what time do I pick you up, what do his parents do, switch the lights off, don't walk around with bare feet, we'll go see a doctor, don't argue, come and give me a hug, if you don't do as you're told, I'll call your father.

Oh, to have a mother, even an annoying one, even a crazy one, even a mother-hen one.

I never know whether something's good. Whether I'm any good. Whether I've hit the mark.

Yesterday evening, I had dinner with What's-his-name. Just

before going to the restaurant, in the bathroom, as I was getting ready, I'd have liked to pinch my mother's lipstick. Gran doesn't own any lipstick. On the bathroom shelf there's just an old can of Elnett hairspray, some wash gloves, and a pot of Nivea cream.

What's-his-name asked me to meet him at a Japanese restaurant. Once again, he asked me loads of questions, while I struggled to eat my sushi with chopsticks. My parents, my brother, my grandparents, The Hydrangeas, my colleagues, my childhood, middle school, high school, my exes.

With him, no lulls in the conversation, or fear of being like those couples who say nothing to each other at the table, who pretend to study the light fittings, or the flowers printed on their napkin.

And then he told me I was beautiful. When he said that, he seemed so sincere that I cut him short, particularly as I don't fancy him at all. Well, not really. I don't fancy anyone really. Except Roman.

"I have to go home. I promised my mother I'd help her with something tomorrow morning."

He stared at me.

"I thought your mother was . . ."

"Dead. But she's waiting for me at the cemetery. At 8 A.M."

"You live with the old and the dead. You're a with-it kinda girl . . ."

"You're neither old, nor dead."

"But you're not living with me yet."

" . . . "

" . . . "

"We should stop seeing each other."

"Shall we meet at the Paradise tomorrow evening?"

"No. Tomorrow evening I'm on duty."

"Shall I give you a lift home?"

"No. I came in my grandfather's Renault . . ."

In the car, I thought about What's-his-name for the first time.

I spend my time asking questions to the residents at The Hydrangeas, to my parents in their graves, to my grandparents in their kitchen. With him, it's the opposite. It's me who answers the questions.

And something in me still can't quite get rid of him.

What's-his-name is like those annoying tunes you hum all day because you can't get them out of your head. One day I'll tell myself, it's over, I won't see him this weekend, but when he turns up on the dance floor at the Paradise and kisses my neck, I can't bring myself to say get lost.

I didn't go straight home. They were showing *Amélie Poulain* at the cinema. I love that film, and have a soft spot for Monsieur Dufayel . . . Yet another little old man.

The cinema was empty. I settled down in the front row, middle seat, and, while licking a chocolate-and-strawberry ice-cream bar, slipped away into Amélie's world. Bliss.

# 35

G unshots. *Must be what woke her.*
*It's not quite five in the morning. Hélène flinches. She hears the sound of boots. Then hears her own heart making more noise than the boots downstairs. Lucien's not in the bed anymore. She thinks, the cellar. He's gone down to the cellar as usual. Nothing can happen to him since there's no light. Lucien has always been able to move in the dark.*

*She's naked. Yesterday evening, they read until late. She grabs a dress. Buttons it up all wrong. Goes down in her bare feet.*

*They are in the kitchen at the bottom of the stairs. There are six of them. Two are in uniform, two in civvies, and the last two are French policemen Hélène's never seen before. They smell of sweat and cigarette smoke. They undress her with their eyes, coldly. One of them is holding a gun. They say words she doesn't understand.*

*Just then, four other men, two civilians and two officers, come up from the cellar with Lucien. Blood is trickling from his mouth. He's very pale. He looks at her. She finds him thin. As if he'd already been gone a long time. As if he'd been deprived of every-thing for years, when in fact she's just spent the night by his side. Lucien shouts at her:*

*"Don't come down, go back up to the bedroom!"*

*But she doesn't listen to him, she rushes down the stairs and says to him: "I'm coming with you." Lucien says no. It's the first time Lucien has said no to her.*

*Then she addresses the four men who are gripping him tightly:*

*"I'm coming with you. Let me come with you."*

*One of the four leaves the group and slaps her, unbelievably hard, in the face. Hélène bangs her head on the banister and collapses, tasting blood in her mouth, hearing Lucien scream. She hears shots.*

*Hélène lies on the floor. She glimpses Lucien's feet moving away. Just his shoeless feet dragging on the ground, as if attached to the legs of a collapsed marionette. She doesn't have the strength to get up.*

*She can feel the howls in her chest. Those she's stifling so Lucien doesn't hear them. The two French policemen she's never seen before go back down to the cellar.*

*She tries gripping onto the walls of the corridor to lift herself up but is overcome with dizziness. Before her head hits the floor again, she sees Simon. One policeman is holding him by the arms, the other by the feet. His skull has been blown apart by the bullets. He's still wearing the gray sweater she knitted for him, in moss stitch. Knit one, purl one. She hears one of the policemen say, "Where do Jews get buried?" And the other one reply: "Don't know that they do."*

*At five-thirty, silence.*

*At six, Baudelaire finds her lying on the floor in the corridor and helps her up. Knit one, purl one is all she's able to say to him.*

*Hélène and Baudelaire go down to the cellar and find Simon's violin and hat on the floor. The few clothes she had made for him, burnt. His empty plate from that night's meal placed on a wooden crate. The three of them had supper together in the cellar yesterday evening. A clear broth of turnips and potatoes. Simon was always happy to eat. Even when it was disgusting, Simon would smile.*

*She looks at the imprint of his body in the old mattress. Caresses what remains of him with the back of her hand. She sees again the blood and flesh where his smile should have been. His smile, knit one, purl one. She lies down on the bed, in Simon's imprint, to offer to his memory what she never gave to him.*

*As the years passed, she had sensed Simon's love for her chang-
ing, growing, as a child grows. The child that Lucien and she
weren't able to produce. Simon's love had moved from childhood
to adolescence, and, in recent months, had reached maturity.
Like an adult. Lucien had noticed it, but had the good grace to
say nothing. There were plenty of guys who looked lovingly at
Hélène from the other side of the bar.*

*Where have they taken Simon's body? Why didn't they arrest
her, too?*

*For days on end, the villagers try to track Lucien down.*

*He'd left the village in a truck on the day of his arrest. Hélène
asks questions, implores, but gets no answer. She even cycles to the
German HQ closest to Milly. A manor house commandeered by
the Germans, set in open country at a place known as Le Breuil.
She pedals away for hours. She succeeds in meeting an officer who
speaks only broken French. He barks that Lucien was arrested for
high treason, that he hid a Jew. She doesn't understand the word
he repeats in a menacing tone: Royallieu, Royallieu.*

*Terrified, she senses that she must leave, she senses that Lucien
isn't dead, and that she now has only one thing to do: stay alive.
She gets back on her bike and pedals in the opposite direction,
towards her café. Night is falling. It takes her hours to get home:
every time she hears the sound of a motor, she dives into the ditch
so as not to be seen.*

*When she finally arrives, it must be three or four in the morn-
ing. The village is silent. And yet she can still hear someone talking, denouncing them, her, Lucien, and Simon. Which customer
was it?*

*She scratched her knees on the brambles. She's bleeding, but
isn't in pain. Her back tire is punctured. She enters her midnight-
blue bistro. She airs the entire place, and just sits at a table, waiting for the smell of the men, the sweat, and the cigarette smoke
to go away. She thinks again of what the officer had repeated,
"Royallieu." What could it mean? She thinks again of Simon; no
one knows where his body is.*

*In the silence of her café, as the wind blows through from all the half-opened windows and doors, she gradually becomes aware of it. Then, it's obvious: the seagull isn't there anymore. Hélène is so used to living with it that she hadn't even noticed. She hasn't heard it all day. Hasn't seen it. Hélène goes back outside. The church is plunged in darkness. The sky is black. The quarter moon is hidden behind a large cloud. Nothing. She calls it, stands back and looks up at the roof of the café. Nothing.*

*The seagull has gone. It's the first time since that day at school. It must have followed Lucien.*

*Hélène considers this; everything's going so fast. For as long as she doesn't see her seagull, Lucien will be alive.*

## 36

I walk into Jules's room. He's gaming online. He doesn't hear me: he's got his headphones on. I watch him mowing down German officers. Well, I think they're German. I end up tapping him on the shoulder. He jumps. Turns around. Takes off his headphones.

"I need you to look something up."

"Right now?"

"I need a date. Type in 'Kommando Dora.' Kommando with a 'K.' Dora like *Dora the Explorer*."

"What is it?"

"An underground factory set up by the Nazis. Their prisoners manufactured missiles."

Jules looks at me as if he doesn't understand.

"Why are you looking into that?"

"Because I know someone who was deported there in December 1943."

"Who?"

"You don't know him. He was part of the Compiègne convoy in December 1943."

Jules won't look anything up unless I tell him more.

"Lucien Perrin, Hélène Hel's lover, was interned in a transit camp called Royallieu. And then he was deported to Buchenwald."

Jules types in "Kommando Dora." And we see the list of the deported and the various deportations.

"December 14, 1943. The convoy arrived two days later at . . . [he struggles to pronounce it] . . . Buchenwald."

"Yes. And from Buchenwald he was immediately deported to the underground factory, Dora."

Jules reads the description of living conditions there. Daylight never seen.

Silence falls between us. The last time that happened, silence between us, was when our speakers were broken.

Suddenly, we hear explosions coming through his headphones. From his video game, *Faces of War*.

"Lucien was able to do everything in the dark. He must have withstood the darkness better than the other prisoners."

Jules appears not to believe me.

"But those prisoners . . . nearly all of them died. How did he manage to survive?"

37

If there had been no war, he would have had a quiet pee, would have shaved, would have woken her up with a kiss on the neck, would have put on any old shirt, would have opened his bistro with a slight lift of the damp-warped door, switched on the radio, silly songs would have got him whistling along, today's Sunday, so they would have been off for a swim in the Saône.

In the truck taking him to Royallieu, he thinks only of what would have happened had this war not tripped up their lives in such a monstrous way.

When the tarp lifts a few centimeters, he glimpses a bit of road, of sky, of seagull, or of tree. And like an artist, he redraws the days as they might have been by patching over the last few years.

There would have been no Simon turning up at the back door, no Simon the godfather and violinist, there would have been no living as a trio, without a child to fill Lucien's days with pride. In the cellar, there would only have been bottles stacked on top of each other, goat cheese, and cured ham, which he would have sliced thickly, with no fear of going without.

If there hadn't been this war, Simon would never have looked at Hélène, would never have lowered his eyes in her presence. He wouldn't have slept in the room of the child to come, or ended up on a mattress in the cellar. They wouldn't have eaten together every evening, for one year, two years, then three. If there hadn't been this war, Hélène wouldn't have spent hours down in the cellar when German planes were flying over Milly. If there hadn't been this war, she wouldn't have gradually opened her eyes to *watch Simon playing the violin during bombings. And without Simon, she would have remained seated on a bottle crate, ramrod straight, eyes closed, hands pressed over ears, praying to her tin-pot God. If there hadn't been this war, she wouldn't have spent hours closely watching the violinist's hands, his arms, his profile, his body moving. If there hadn't been this war, she wouldn't have knitted that sweater, gripping her needles. That sweater the musician never took off anymore, and was forever lightly stroking with his fingertips. If there hadn't been this war, she wouldn't have altered the trousers Lucien no longer wore, to fit Simon.*

*If there hadn't been this war, Lucien wouldn't have heard men banging on the door of the bistro at five in the morning, then storming down to the cellar and grabbing hold of him. He wouldn't have seen the despair in Simon's eyes when they opened the trapdoor and his body fell to the ground like an empty potato sack, he was so thin. Lucien wouldn't have seen them kicking him with the toes of their boots, and shooting him like a dog. In fact, he'd never seen anyone shoot a single dog. If there hadn't been this war, there wouldn't have been this morning that left Hélène on her own. He wouldn't have gone down to the cellar to talk with Simon.*

*He wouldn't have seen him praying by candlelight, eyes closed, mouthing silent words. He wouldn't have wondered what he was saying to God. Whether he was talking to Him about Hélène. And Simon, sensing his presence, wouldn't have opened his eyes, or smiled. And Lucien wouldn't have hated Simon's smile because it was both strength and beauty. And because he was increasingly drawing Hélène to the cellar. If there hadn't been this war, Lucien wouldn't have become that total idiot who allows his glass to be filled with adulterated liquor, his mind gnawed by unspoken jealousy, and who tells Dominique Latronche, the village Judas, that a person can be hidden in his cellar, inside a false ceiling built by the father of old Louis thirty years ago. And then repeats it, repeats it, repeats it straight into the eyes of Latronche, who pours him more liquor and makes him repeat it again. If there hadn't been this war, Lucien wouldn't be sitting in this truck, his body covered in bruises, weighed down with self-disgust and despair, thinking that if the seagull flies over his convoy of prisoners, it means Hélène is in love with him.*

## 38

When I was little, I lived in Lyon, in a building with a garbage chute. That's all I can remember. I'd open its black mouth and fling the bags into it. I'd hear them banging the sides as they fell. This gaping hole's breath stank like a latrine and terrified me, because I was convinced that, one day or another, the beast we fed with garbage would suck me up and take me away.

And it did. One morning when I woke up at my grandparents' house. In Gramps's garden, there was a bonfire. I went down in my pajamas to join him. Gramps's eyes were red and I thought it must be the smoke. I said: "But Gramps, why are you burning your garden?" He replied: "In Octoberr, we burrn the weeds. Beforre the clocks go back. It's winterr soon, have to help the earrth, this firre's like putting a coat on it, yesterrday your parrents had an accident, you and Jules will be staying with us."

He said it in a single breath. I looked at him and I remember so clearly, so clearly thinking, Good, like that I won't be going back to school.

Later, I learned that it wasn't weeds burning in front of me, but the two fruit trees he'd planted on the day his sons were born. Gramps had cut them down, doused them in gasoline, and burnt them in his garden.

Later, Thierry Jacquet, a boy in my class, asked me what it was like having dead parents, and I told him, *It's like seeing the October bonfire.*

"Gran?"

I wake her. She dozed off while I was putting in her curlers.

"Yes."

"If Jules gets his baccalauréat, we must start looking for an apartment in Paris for him, from July. If not before."

"Absolutely."

"After that, he can take care of his money himself. I'm going to make a transfer into your account, and you'll give him a check, telling him it's his inheritance from Uncle Alain."

"Fine."

"And he'll never know it comes from me."

"If that's what you want."

"You bet. I'd rather die than have my brother being eternally grateful to me. He's got better fucking things to do."

"Justine! Your language!"

"What about my language?! What kind of language do you use to lie to me?"

I shouted so loudly that she lifted her head full of curlers to check it really was me who'd just spoken, right there, behind her. Me who's never so much as raised my voice in this house. Even on the day I cracked open my head falling off my bike and got blood all over the kitchen.

"What's got into you?"

"What's got into me is . . . Did you know that the police had opened an inquiry after your sons' accident?"

She pauses a moment. She looks flabbergasted. Normally, Gran can't be crossed because of her suicide illness. I don't know if she's pulling that face because of my question, or because I'm daring to cross her. In a flat voice, she manages to say:

"What?"

"Absolutely! An inquiry!"

Gramps turns up, clutching his *Paris Match*.

"What's all this screaming?" he asks, already not caring a jot about the answer.

With a single hand gesture, Gran orders me to shut up. That's how it's always been: talking about the accident is strictly forbidden under this roof—it causes Gramps too much pain, and Gran to die on prescription.

And right then, I hear Gran lying:

"It's nothing. It's Justine pulling my hair, it hurts."

"That's not true, Gramps. I'm not pulling her hair, I was just asking her if she knew that the police had opened an inquiry after the death of your sons, because the circumstances of the accident weren't clear."

Gramps looks daggers at me: I've just desecrated the tomb of his memories. My legs are about to give way with the guilt. But I don't look down, I keep looking him straight in the eye.

"Who told you that?" Gramps asks me.

"Starsky."

He stares at me as if I've taken leave of my senses.

"He summoned me because of the anonymous calls at The Hydrangeas. And when I said the name 'Neige,' he remembered clearly that there was something not quite right about the accident."

Gran snatches her stick and stands up abruptly, though I've not yet finished setting her hair. I grab her shoulders and push her back into her chair. I think I've hurt her. It's the first time in my life I've dared to do any such thing. So she doesn't move anymore. Her head is sunk between her shoulders. I think she's scared of my violence. And as for me, I'm ashamed. I start thinking about all my forgotten ones, about how easily adults mistreat the elderly. About those stories you read in the papers, of care staff slapping and swearing at the old folk in geriatric facilities. I can feel myself welling up.

"Sorry. I would have liked . . . I would have liked you to answer one of my questions. For once."

I've lost the fight. They won't answer me. And I'll never raise my voice again. I spray lacquer onto Gran's head. The smell fills the kitchen. And then I stretch a net over her gray hair, which she'll take off only tomorrow morning.

Gramps has abandoned his *Paris Match* on the table to go

out and pick up the latest butts Jules has flicked out of the window.

As I slide on the helmet that blows hot air over Gran's fake curls, I tell myself that I must go back to see Starsky.

Even if it means sucking him off, I have to know the truth.

## 39

In 1944, fourteen months after Lucien's arrest, some Germans abandon one of their dogs at the side of the road. It's a bitch, a large, scrawny fawn-and-black creature.

The dog remains rooted to the spot, by the village's exit road, for a long time, like a statue staring out to the horizon.

One evening, the hound follows Hélène right up to old Louis's bistro. She lets it come inside, and it lies down in the sawdust. She gives it some soup to lap up. And then she names it Louve.

To celebrate the Liberation, Hélène offers free drinks to everyone in Milly. Even the women are there. Even those who give her dirty looks because she's possibly too beautiful for a bar owner. Louve, the sole surviving German for hundreds of kilometers around, watches them drink and clink glasses until late into the night.

Hélène also drinks that day. She drinks to waiting for Lucien. She drinks to being shocked every day by the silence of his absence. To the doors she hears slamming, but which don't slam anymore. To the pillowcase that remains immaculate, and that she punches every morning before making the bed. To the dark hairs she no longer finds on the white sheets. To the pages of books that she turns alone, to the meals she eats from a corner of the table, standing, turning her back on the empty chairs.

She drinks to the hope of seeing him return, wounded perhaps, but alive. She knows he's not dead, she senses that his heart's still beating, but doesn't know where and how. And anyhow, the seagull hasn't returned. She drinks, wondering if the person who denounced them is among this crowd toasting and merrily dancing on the wooden floor of her bistro. But she doesn't want to hate. She wants only to hope. Just as she'd hoped to learn to read.

Since that day celebrating the end of the war, she has seen men returning to her bistro. The village gets them back, gradually. Not all of them, but some of them. Those who fought in the 1914–18 war talk to those returning from the 1939–45 war. As for the farm workers who have done both wars, they don't seem to believe in their own survival anymore as they knock it back and gaze at the photo of Janet Gaynor.

Every day, the newspaper brings news of the war. As if the bullets shot years before were only reaching their targets now. The death toll is published. As are the photos of mass executions and concentration camps. And some personal accounts that Hélène can't read. No news reaches her in Braille. She asks Claude, a boy she hired to work at old Louis's café, to read them to her secretly in the evening, so no one knows she can't read. Though, in fact, everyone knows.

Claude was born with his left leg shorter than his right, and his limp prevented him from going off to do obligatory labor. And while men were becoming slaves, Claude had learned to read and write. That's why Hélène chose him, from among other far more experienced waiters.

Every evening, Hélène, with her fingers buried in Louve's coat, listens religiously as Claude reads various articles describing the war. Sometimes, when the words are too tough to hear, she says to Claude:

"Wait."

She breathes deeply. Then, with a nod of her head, asks him to continue from where he left off.

Sometimes—and she'll only find out about this much later—Claude avoids reading certain unbearable passages, describing prisoners' living conditions in the camps. He changes the words and makes up that some prisoners were better treated than others, eating their fill and sleeping in clean beds.

At night, when Claude has left for home, Hélène opens the bedroom wardrobe and looks at Lucien's clothes on their hangers. He left with nothing. Not even an "I love you" from her. Thank

*goodness the seagull followed him. She hopes he'll understand
this proof of love.*

*Since his departure, she's made other garments: trousers, jack-
ets, shirts. She hangs the new items beside the old. When he's
back, he'll choose what he wants to keep. Over the years, fashion
has changed. The Americans have brought over new fabrics. Will
this look appeal to Lucien?*

*In 1946, Hélène receives a letter in Braille. A letter from Étienne,
Lucien's father, mailed from Lille. The French government has informed him that his son, Lucien Perrin, born November 25, 1911,
was deported to Buchenwald and died in the concentration camp.
In the public records, Lucien Perrin is now included on the register
of prisoners of war "who died for France."*

*Buchenwald. She passes her finger over this word several times.*

*Claude shows her Buchenwald on a map of the world. With the
help of a ruler, he calculates that it's 905 kilometers from Milly.
Hélène looks at the tiny mark, close to Weimar. Barely bigger
than the eye of a needle. A tiny stitch on the heart of Germany.
Refusing to believe in his death, she stares hard at the map of the
world as if it has been drawn to show her where Lucien is, and
searches for a sign, a light, a bird.*

*As if hope were contagious, Claude embarks on some research.
He writes to all the hospitals that have taken in prisoners of war,
to the Red Cross, to all the associations and organizations in
charge of registering the deported.*

*Inside each letter that Claude sends, Hélène slips a portrait of
Lucien drawn in charcoal, because she doesn't have any photos of
him that aren't out of focus or taken from a distance.*

*Under each portrait, she asks Claude to write:*

Lucien PERRIN
Do you recognize this man? I am searching for any information that might help me to find him.

Write to Hélène Hel, old Louis's café, Place de l'Église,
Milly.

## 40

"Gran?"

"Yes."

"On the day of the accident, why didn't they take us with them to that baptism?"

"I don't know. I think it was Gramps who didn't want them to."

"Gramps?"

"Yes."

"Why?"

"I can't remember now. I think Jules had a slight temperature."

"Gran?"

"Yes."

"What did they say to you, Dad and Mom, before getting into the car?"

"*See you this evening.*"

I think back on my endless questions while waiting for Starsky outside the small police station. I've put on lip gloss and blusher. You'd think I'm ready to go dancing at the Paradise. As he comes up to me, walking like a cowboy, cap pulled down, he asks me, straight off, if I have information about that "dickhead anonymous caller who's starting to really piss me off." I give him my sweetest smile (three years of orthodontics to close the "lucky" gap between my two front teeth . . . ).

"No, I'd like to see the file you opened after my parents' accident. You know, they died in that car accident."

He looks at me with disdain and makes no effort to seem even remotely compassionate. I can't be his type.

"But I, young lady, have got the mayor on my back, so I need all the damn help I can get. Especially after what happened last Sunday."

He's referring to the phone calls that caused merry havoc at The Hydrangeas.

"But . . . last Sunday was good, everyone was happy."

"Happy? Are you putting me on?"

"There'd never been so many visitors. It was nice."

"And the guys thinking their mother had kicked the bucket, were they happy, too?"

"I'm more often on the residents' side than the families' side."

"Well, I'm more on the mayor-harassing-me's side, do you get me? He's harassing me . . . so, no anonymous caller, no Neige file."

"But I truly don't know who it is!"

"Try a little harder."

While this fat idiot talks to me on the sidewalk, I study the outside of the building. I stop listening to what he's saying to me. In my head, I'm working out a plan: returning one night to break the window at the back of the building, which is three meters up from the ground and the only one without bars. I'll bring Gramps's ladder.

"You're the youngest there, so the smartest. Sort it out."

"I'm not a grass."

"Oh really, so what kind of weed are you then, ha-ha!"

He's insufferable. I don't want to flash my teeth at him anymore, or attract him, and I'd never suck off a prick like him, even with a condom, even with my eyes closed, even while imagining that it's Roman.

"Goodbye."

I go off to feed Madame Dreyfus's "fat cat." He's waiting for me on the sidewalk. I pour five hundred grams of fish-flavor dried food into a bowl for him and change his water. I do this every three days. While he's eating, I take a photo of him to show to Madame Dreyfus. He's a total mess, a kind of grubby ginger, riddled with battle scars. I can't touch him, he's wary of me. I'd have loved to have a pet when I was little. Jules and I, especially me, we begged Gramps and Gran for years. Gran always explained that Gramps was allergic to animal hair. Pure fabrication, I'm sure. More likely, it was because animals are "dirty."

Right now, with Jo and Maria, we're getting all the residents to sign a petition to have a little dog at The Hydrangeas. Pets should be mandatory in retirement homes. And even funded by social security.

Once I've taken a photo of "fat cat," I head straight for Jules's room and look up "breaking and entering" on his computer.

What's good about Milly is that you can go from one place to another in five minutes. That's the advantage of living in a hole.

I read the instructions and then head straight for old Prost's store to order a wrecking bar and a crowbar. I say it's for my grandfather and, so it doesn't seem strange, I also order hair-setting products for Gran and batteries for my Polaroid. Old Prost tells me to allow three weeks for delivery.

I'm in no hurry. I'd even wait two months to get inside the police station: that's exactly when Roman gets back.

## 41

P aris. Gare de l'Est. A man shuffles around the platform. He measures 1.81 meters and weighs fifty kilos.

His head hurts. Hurts like hell. Something is hammering inside his skull, stopping him from thinking. Every new minute erases the one before.

There's noise around him, lots of it. Trains, loudspeakers, crowds.

In his right fist, he clutches some newspaper pages. He doesn't want to let them go. Mustn't let them go.

Someone tries to take his arm to lie him down on a stretcher. He doesn't want to. Pushes away, refuses, says "No." But not a sound comes out of his painful mouth.

Still that noise, those trains, those loudspeakers, those crowds.

A woman holds his hand. His left hand. The hand that's free. He lets her because she's gentle, reassuring. The woman leads him. He follows her slowly, unsteadily. She adapts to his pace. To him, it seems they're both walking for hours, but he may be wrong. It doesn't take that long. She helps him get into a truck. He lets himself be guided. He's scared and in pain. Pain. He lies down, at last. Closes his eyes.

The woman doesn't let go of his hand.

On both sides of him, other men. And although the truck's engine is noisy, there's silence. Everyone remains appallingly silent.

No one looks anyone else in the eye. But still that hand in his.

He dozes off. He doesn't dream. Everything is black.

When he wakes from his semi-coma, the truck is just entering *a park with ancient oak trees. It's spring, the sun is gentle. And the wind feels like a pardon.*

*Lying on his stretcher, he looks at the sky. And still that hand in his. And still the pain and that silence. He's carried into a large building. Inside, a smell of cabbage and paper, and long corridors bright with daylight.*

*He likes the smell of the woman holding his hand. When she lets go of it so he can be transferred onto an examining table, she says to him, My name is Edna, I'm a nurse, I'm going to look after you.*

*Edna carefully opens up his right hand, unclenching his fingers one by one. They are blackened with ink. In some places, Edna struggles to remove the paper that has stuck to his skin.*

*For how many days, weeks, months has this man been clutching these newspaper pages? He would like to scream, but doesn't scream. Would like to stop the nurse taking them from him, but doesn't stop her. He has no strength left.*

*A tear runs down his cheek. The cheek that's not gashed. And despite his emaciation, despite his wounds, despite his silence, Edna sees but one thing: the beauty of this man's eyes.*

*To reassure him, Edna immediately puts what remains of the pages into a cardboard box. She handles them as if they were diamond jewelry. She puts the lid back on and places the box close to him, clearly visible on a medical cart.*

*He is finding it harder and harder to breathe. The lacerating pain in his head is unbearable.*

*A doctor joins them and greets him. He places a stethoscope on his heart while Edna starts to unwind the bandage around his head. He tries to touch his dressings but Edna stops him.*

*A stench of carrion fills the room. Edna blanches. It's barely perceptible. But she blanches while smiling at him.*

*He wants to sleep. Closes his eyes. A fluttering of wings, and all goes dark.*

*He sinks into a coma.*

## 42

They talked about The Hydrangeas on TV because of the anonymous caller. On the France 3 regional news bulletin. The one Gramps never misses, watching it every evening with the volume as high as it can go.

A film crew turned up yesterday morning.

All the nurses had put make-up on, Jo and Maria had been to the hairdresser, and Madame Le Camus was wearing a fuchsia dress. But for our smocks, it could have been the Cannes film festival. Even the residents were looking their best. Madame Le Camus had asked us to "pay attention to their grooming."

The female journalist selected two residents to interview, a man and a woman, Monsieur Vaillant and Madame Diondet. Which prompted some jealousy among the others: *Why them and not us?* Unlike Madame Diondet, Monsieur Vaillant isn't a "victim."

Before selecting them, the journalist checked they hadn't lost too many of their marbles. Surname, first name, date and place of birth, number of children, and employment prior to retirement. Then she powdered their faces, necks and hands. Monsieur Vaillant couldn't get over it. And all the others made gentle fun of him.

Next, the sound engineer hid a mike inside their clothing. They didn't dare to move anymore; it was very funny.

The journalist began to ask them some questions. She asked them in a very loud voice and over-articulated.

I loathe people who speak to the elderly as if they were half-wits.

Then she "attempted to ascertain the psychological suffering inflicted on the residents by this anonymous caller."

Monsieur Vaillant replied that he couldn't care less, and that he wasn't deaf.

Next, the journalist "tried to understand the harmful impact of the trauma on the families implicated."

Madame Diondet, as a victim, replied that she felt pretty well, apart from a few pains in her legs.

Finally, all the residents were filmed side by side, and the film crew departed.

Monsieur Vaillant immediately asked me to get rid of his make-up. He let out horrified shrieks when I wiped cleanser over his face.

This evening, when it was time for the news bulletin, all the residents were in the TV room and had a good laugh when they saw themselves. Madame Diondet confided in me that she thought the TV had really aged her, that it was even crueler than the mirror in her bathroom.

## 43

I n 1947, a textile factory is established in Milly. Overnight, this new enterprise brings some fifty new male customers to old Louis's café.

Thanks to this extra income, Hélène hires Claude "officially," and buys tables, chairs, and a pinball machine. Claude serves while Hélène, having turned the old storeroom behind the bar into a small sewing workroom, returns to her original occupation. As if sewing was all she'd ever been able to do to wait for Lucien.

Many men tear their sleeve, trouser hem, shirt collar, or pull a button off their jacket so as to find themselves in Hélène's tiny workshop and feel her hands through their clothing. They watch her, bending, kneeling, crouching, concentrating on stitching a button back on, a hem, or adding a patch, with pins in her mouth and furrowed brows.

Her clients' biggest thrill is getting a bespoke suit made. The fittings take hours. She wraps her measuring tape around the whole body. She starts with the circumference of the neck, then it's the shoulders, the back, the waist, the pelvis, she goes right down the legs, measures you all over, lengthwise and widthwise. She traces your figure with chalk, and whenever they feel the pressure of her fingers on a muscle, they quiver like young grooms.

All the men of Milly, and the surrounding area, have fine suits. Even the farm laborers. You could swear that, from 1947 to the arrival of ready-to-wear, the men of Milly were more elegant than the men of Paris.

Sometimes, one of these men risks telling her that she's young and beautiful, that she could start her life again. But she doesn't want to start her life again. Just wants to carry on with her life. With Lucien.

*The portraits of Lucien she made Claude send to the associations registering prisoners of war produced nothing. No news whatsoever. Sitting behind her sewing machine, she makes a plan for the future all the same, to tell Lucien that she loves him.*

*From the windowless room, she hears men opening the door to the café, knowing that it isn't hers, her man. He has a very particular way of lifting the latch without making a sound. She knows, she keeps telling herself: he's not dead. He'll be back.*

*Hélène hears the men's voices ordering drinks. She hears Claude serving them. Rarely: What can I get you? Often: The usual? Sometimes he serves without asking a thing, long knowing what each barfly drinks to sink a little deeper into oblivion. Bottles knock against each other, glasses fill up, glasses empty into these men's bodies, not Lucien's body. They spit back out what they've drunk in unstitched sentences, while she keeps sewing straight lines in white cotton.*

*At first, it's the war that crops up most frequently in conversations. Tongues are loosened by the specter of those lost. And then, when life reasserts itself, there's talk of a wedding, a birth, a death in bed at a hundred, of the new factory where they're hiring a few more every day, of old mother Michèle who, like her almost-namesake in the song, has lost her cat.*

*After a few glasses, some venture to the workroom to give a timid wave. Hélène and Louve both lift their heads at the same time.*

*In 1950, the new coffee machine makes the same noise as the locomotive that will bring Lucien back to her. She knows it. He'll be back.*

\* \* \*

*Edna said to him: You have nowhere to go, would you like to stay at my place until you find work? He said yes.*

*He goes into Edna's house for the first time. She has made a bedroom for him under the eaves. She has hung a Gauguin print on the wall and a crucifix above the bed. She has bought him shaving soap and some* savon de Marseille. *She has put clean towels out and lavender inside the wardrobe so the linen smells good. She has been careful not to hang up a mirror, having noticed that he can't bear his reflection, that unknown, ravaged face that stares back at him when he comes across himself in a looking glass.*

*He has regained some weight. Can't circle his wrist anymore with thumb and index finger. His dark hair has grown back, apart from a few patches where his skull was crushed. The doctors reckon he was brutally and repeatedly hit with the butt of a rifle, and his face was slashed with a long-bladed knife, the sort used by hunters to finish off big game. A scar crosses his face from forehead to top lip, down the left side of his nose.*

*Edna said to him: You're an unknown soldier, without a military badge or identity papers. You don't appear on the register of people being looked for. We'll find you a surname and first name. What would you like to be called?*

*She gave him a list of men's names.*

*A beret, slips of paper inside it, a name. And that's it. A fleeting memory: names in a beret. Where? When? Why? Was it a dream? The dream? The one he has every night? The one he's never told anyone about, not even Edna?*

*He answered, Simon. I'd like to be called Simon.*

*Edna looked hard at him for a few moments. As though wary of him. No, it's not wariness. It's fear. He gets the feeling that Edna doesn't want him to remember. He, too, is afraid. He's terrified, haunted by a single question: Who am I?*

*He speaks and writes French. He knows what a shaving brush, razor, pen, scissors are for. And he smokes Gitanes. These are his only certainties. To other amnesiacs, they show photographs, pictures, faces, places. To him, nothing can be shown. He's lost all trace of himself. As if he's fallen from the sky. And there's no one looking for him.*

*He manages to read, to write, to walk, to run, to hold, to lift, to think, to remember a short while ago. His immediate memory is intact. The rest is darkness. His mind wears the black veil of widows. He's come across them occasionally. They scare him. Those great ghosts, those specters, he's wary of them, he's scared they'll take him to where he won't get better.*

*Thank goodness there's the dream, every night. A familiar presence, an answer, a defiance of amnesia. When he wakes up, he recloses his eyes to return to it, but the morning draws him towards the day, towards Edna, he must get up, have a coffee, retrain his body, get rid of that seawater taste in his mouth.*

*Since he came out of his coma, Edna sleeps close to him at the clinic. But he has never undressed her. Sometimes, she thinks she sees the flicker of a Lucien memory in Simon's eyes. Quick as a blink.*

\* \* \*

*Edna Fleming received the letter in 1946. On May 29, 1946. The white envelope was thick and large. That morning, it was she who had to take delivery of the mail and some medication. That had rarely happened. The director of the clinic was away for the week. As head nurse, the task had fallen to her.*

*She took it to be a sign. It was SHE who was meant to open that letter. SHE and no one else: the hand of God.*

*When she first saw the portrait of Lucien Perrin, she retched and her hands began to shake. The man whom the other nurses at the clinic called "Edna's patient" had a surname, a first name, an address:*

## Lucien PERRIN

Do you recognize this man? I am searching for any information that might help me to find him.

Write to Hélène Hel, old Louis's café, Place de l'Église, Milly.

*A woman was searching for him. She didn't have the same surname as him. Was she a mother, a sister, a daughter?*

*She gazed at the sketched portrait. No doubt about it. Despite the scars, the weight loss and the extra years, it was definitely him. His clear eyes. In the portrait, he was smiling. She'd never seen him smile. He just said thanks. As if that was the only word he could say. Thanks. The only word he could remember.*

*Milly, in Burgundy. That was four hundred kilometers from the clinic, which was in the Eure.*

*"Do you recognize this man?" Yes. She recognizes him. She recognizes him better than anyone. She recognized him on the platform at Gare de l'Est. Maybe because he had forgotten everything. A bit like a newborn baby. She fed him. Dressed his head wounds several times a day. Held his hand when he had a raging fever two weeks after his arrival, coming out of his coma. She helped him to piss and shit, and only ever left him to treat the other patients. She prayed for him like she'd never prayed for anyone when the surgeon told her he wouldn't pull through, that he was in too bad a state. She spoke to him. Read to him. Helped him take his first steps outside the clinic. Gave him back the desire to get up, walk, eat, sleep. Who could take care of him like she took care of him? Who could really love him like she really loves him?*

*The family searching for this man, this Lucien Perrin, knows only the smiling man sketched before the war. A lifetime separates before the war and after the war. As a nurse, she should know. How many survivors has she returned to distraught, shocked families, unable to recognize either a brother, or a son, or a husband? That Lucien is dead and buried. Simon was born from his ashes.*

*The man that remains is but a shadow of himself. It's not a shadow that this Hélène Hel is searching for, it's the past.*

## 44

He's just locked the main door on the ground floor. I'm stuck in a cupboard, between buckets and brooms. From time to time, I get rid of the pins and needles in my legs by gently jumping on the spot. I'm frozen stiff. And my heart's beating dangerously fast. If Starsky and Hutch return, I've had it.

If Jules knew . . . I couldn't tell him why I'm looking into the circumstances of our parents' accident. I'd have to lie and tell him that I want to know what the police have got on the anonymous caller. Just like I lied to Gramps when I gave him the wrecking bar and crowbar. He looked puzzled. He even said: "You want me to brreak into a bank?"

As soon as I collected the tools at old Prost's store, I realized that I'd never know how to use them. That it would be better to do as Hélène did when she let herself be locked inside her school on the day of the seagull.

Late afternoon, I just strolled into the Municipal and Public Space Department.

"Hello."

The Municipal and Public Space Department is situated in a small, square, two-story building made of concrete. Construction date: 1975. I remember that, when I was little, all the offices were occupied. That there were "real" policemen on the first floor, and that I came with Gran. But it's been several years now that no one's there except Starsky and Hutch.

Starsky asked me if I had anything new, any names of colleagues or residents to give him. I told him that since the report had been on TV, there had been no more anonymous calls. But that much he already knew. He looked at me strangely. I sensed that I annoyed him. Or that he suspected me.

The switchboard phone rang. Starsky seemed surprised. As if that never happened.

I pinched the palm of my hand so as not to laugh, because it was Jo who was phoning. I'd said to her: "You call the police station at four on the dot, about some neighborhood issue over parking restrictions, you mumble, you say any old thing, and you hang up. What matters is that the conversation lasts five minutes." She asked me: "Why?" I replied: "Please."

The moment Starsky picked up, saying "Municipal Department, hello," I pretended I was leaving.

"Bye."

I closed the door to his office behind me, switched my phone onto vibrate, and walked upstairs to the unoccupied part, where there'd been no "real" policemen for ages. If I got caught by Hutch, I could always say I was looking for the restroom. But I met no one on the stairs.

When I shut myself into the broom cupboard, it was 4:04 P.M. I've been waiting since then. In theory, there's no one left in the building by 6 P.M.

When waiting in a broom cupboard, there's time to think. About everything. I personally thought about Roman. The oh-so-handsome Roman busy photographing gannets in Peru. I thought about his big life and my really small life. His eyes, unique in the entire universe, and me, a messy-haired chick who shakes her ass at the Paradise on a Saturday night and pushes around carts of every sort of disinfectant. I must be far from unique.

We're not equal. We're not born equal. It's not possible. A specimen such as Roman is proof of that.

How could a girl like me share the daily life of a boy like him, except in her dreams? How could you imagine two individuals like us coming back home and saying to each other, "How are you, my love, did you have a good day?"

Everything must have gone right for him since the day he was born. And, also, he has a mother.

Our homes will never be alike. At mine, there'll be Swedish kit furniture, and at his, furniture he's garnered from around the globe. At mine, white tiles, and at his, parquet scattered with green and blue Persian rugs.

Even shopping at the supermarket with Roman must be something like a masterpiece. Life's a masterpiece when you wake up beside a Roman. At least, I imagine so.

I still regularly wake up beside What's-his-name. I don't know what work he does, but at the moment, he always arrives a little before the Paradise closes. My stinking of alcohol and sweat doesn't seem to bother him. He picks me up in the early hours every Sunday, but if I'm on duty later, lets me leave in Gramps's Renault.

In fact, he still asks me questions, and I never ask him any. Sometimes, I feel like I'm his investigation, a case he doesn't want to close. At his place, there's a whole load of books, and often, when I wake up, he's busy working at his desk. Maybe he's writing a report on me, the girl who only likes old folk. When he sees me opening my eyes, he squeezes me an orange juice and brings me coffee in bed—like in the ads. Then, smiling, he watches me tucking into my breakfast.

It's December 20. Roman told me he'd be back for Christmas. He's going to ask me where I'm at with Hélène's story. I'm making progress. The pages of the blue notebook are filling up like a bottle. I don't know what he knows about her. I don't know what his mother has, or hasn't, told him.

SLAM. Starsky's off. I hear the key turning in several locks. No more light in the corridor. It's dark. It's cold. I daren't move. I don't move. I blow on my hands and down the neck of my sweater to warm myself up.

Hutch could return here before going home.

Just as I'm making up my mind, the switchboard phone rings again. I jump, bang my head, drop my flashlight. I hear the batteries rolling on the floor. Lucky I've got the light of my phone to find them.

I go down the stairs using my flashlight. I turned it right down so I won't be spotted from outside. My legs are like jelly. I need to pee. I can't see a thing beyond thirty centimeters in front of me. I go into Starsky's office. A smell of stale smoke and alcohol. And yet there's neither ashtray nor bottle on the desk.

The archives room is behind Starsky and Hutch's offices. It's locked. I wonder if that's been so since the "real" cops quit, or if Starsky and Hutch still have the key.

I absolutely have to find it. It's pitch dark. My flashlight barely lights a thing anymore. The silence all around me is terrifying. Then I don't know what comes over me, but I start thinking about my father. I don't think about him the way one thinks about the twin of a twin, about someone in a frame on the dresser, about a brief news item, about a grave covered in flowers. No. I start thinking about him the way one thinks of a human being who was killed on the road at forty years old, abandoning a little girl at his parents' house one Sunday morning. A little girl who was afraid of a garbage chute. Do people who have a father realize how lucky they are?

Where are those damn keys?

My flashlight beams on a tall cupboard with a sliding door. I find a key inside an empty box for staples. It's not the right one.

Suddenly, a noise.

Someone's just opened a door. The main entrance. I hide under Starsky's desk. I hear whispering. No one's switched on the light. Two people enter Starsky's office. I can feel the cold from their clothes. They smell of winter, the night, and the clandestine, like me.

I curl up to disappear, become tiny again. It's over, I'm over, I'm going to get myself arrested. My face will appear in the paper. The name Neige will be dragged through the mud. Gramps and Gran will die of shame . . .

A woman says: "I'm cold."

The man with her tells her he's going to warm her up. The man is Hutch: I recognize his nasal voice. I hear them kissing and sighing. As for her, she squawks like a guinea fowl until the two of them groan in unison.

They're lying on the floor. They still haven't switched the light on. They're right beside me. If I reached out, I could touch them.

I feel like laughing and crying at the same time. If they discover me, not only will they lock me up, but they'll also kill me so I can't talk. I close my eyes and put my hands over my ears. I even try to stop breathing.

It doesn't last very long. Hutch is a premature ejaculator. I hear them hurriedly getting dressed.

She says:

"I'd better get home, or he'll lose it."

"When do we see each other again, my lovebug?"

"I'll call you."

"Next time, I'll handcuff you."

"Can't wait."

"So why not right now?"

Oh shit, they're going to go at it again. Thankfully, she says she really must head home. They leave almost immediately.

Ten minutes of silence in the dark. I've never smoked in my life, but right here, right now, I'd happily puff my way through a whole packet. I turn my flashlight back on. And that's when I spot them: keys hanging under Starsky's desk. A nice touch. Impossible to find them unless you're on all fours.

"Our Father who art in heaven, hallowed be thy name, thy kingdom come, thy will be done, on earth as it is in heaven, these are the right keys."

The North Pole. It's less cold in the freezer at The Hydrangeas than it is in this room. My flashlight picks out around fifty box files, a dusty uniform, two metal trunks, some empty bottles, and books and posters all piled on top of each other. There's a smell of damp. Underfoot, it feels like soil, a bit like in a cellar.

The box files aren't ordered alphabetically but by year. From 1953 to 2003. Everything is recorded: hunting accidents, fires, suicides, disappearances, drownings, attempted homicides, burglaries, bicycle thefts, hit-and-runs, floodings, sabotages, altercations, forcible entries, verbal aggressions. Everything. I never thought so many things could happen in a small village like ours.

As the years progress, the files change format: they get thinner. They contain almost nothing. Evidence of how the village gradually emptied. Especially after the textile factory closed in 2000.

I take the file for 1996, the year of the accident. I open it. It contains three reports of car theft. And this:

*On October 6, 1996, at 9:40 A.M., the station is alerted by Monsieur Pierre Léger, an inhabitant of Milly on Route de Clermain, that a car has just crashed into a tree on the Route Nationale 217.*

*We go immediately to the scene.*

*When we arrive, at around 10 A.M., we find Monsieur Léger and the fire brigade, which has already been there for twenty minutes.*

*We note that the vehicle involved, a black Renault Clio, license plate 2408 ZM 69, has been partly destroyed by the impact.*

*At 10:30 A.M., fire officers proceed to cut off the car's roof in order to extricate four lifeless bodies from the vehicle.*

*Monsieur Pierre Léger, the only eyewitness of the accident, was present when the vehicle came off the road. The facts are relayed to us succinctly, as follows: the vehicle came off the road at very high speed after zigzagging forward several times, and ended up crashing headlong into a tree.*

*Monsieur Pierre Léger immediately alerted the fire brigade using his mobile phone; they arrived around ten minutes later.*

*While the fire officers proceed to extricate the four bodies, a request message is sent to the central database to identify the owner of the vehicle.*

*At 12 noon, we are informed that the vehicle belongs to Messieurs Alain and Christian Neige, domiciled in Lyon (69).*

*At 12:30 P.M., specialists from the investigations squad join us on the scene. Police officer Claude Mougin takes photos of the exterior and interior of the vehicle.*

*At 12:45 P.M., the four bodies—two men and two women presenting with fatal injuries—are taken to the mortuary at Poinçon Hospital, Mâcon (71), once the medical examiner, Bernard Delattre, has certified their death.*

*Tire marks: with Monsieur Pierre Léger having told us that the vehicle left the road at speed, we note the tire tracks. The tracks aren't clear. The tires, due to extreme acceleration, seem to have spun around on the spot. The clearest stretches of track were photographed (photo no. 13).*

*We search in the vicinity for any other people who may have been woken by the impact of the accident, or may have witnessed anything at all.*

*At 2 P.M., back at the station, we give an oral account to our force commander and station commander of the progress of the investigation underway.*

*In short, the situation is reviewed, and arrangements are made for different officers to carry out the various urgent checks on the identities of the three other "conveyed passenger" victims.*

*At 3 P.M., I and our force commander visit the home of Monsieur Armand Neige, the father of the owner of the car, Christian Neige, on Rue Pasteur in Milly (71). He confirms to our commander that his two sons, Christian and Alain Neige, accompanied by their two wives, Sandrine Caroline Berri and Annette Strömblad, left the domicile of the said Armand Neige, where they were staying for the weekend, at around 8:10 A.M. on Sunday, October 6.*

*At 5 P.M., formal identification of the four bodies is carried out by Monsieur Armand Neige at Poinçon Hospital in Mâcon (71). He identifies his two sons, Alain and Christian Neige, and his two daughters-in-law, Sandrine and Annette, married name Neige.*

*It wasn't possible to ascertain whether the driver of the Renault was Christian or Alain Neige, both owners of the vehicle.*

*In addition, the post-mortem toxicological tests conducted on the four victims turned out to be negative.*

*The vehicle—the Renault—was transported to the Millet garage, in Milly. It was noted that the braking system might be faulty, but it couldn't be established whether this state was prior to, or due to, the violent impact of the accident.*

*Furthermore, it would seem that the driver braked before leaving the road, but the tire tracks aren't sufficiently clear to be sure, considering that the official weather forecaster reported, on that October 6, 1996, the presence of patches of black ice in the area. The driver could have blacked out, or been distracted for a few seconds within the vehicle.*

*Having read the above statement, I stand by it and have nothing to change in it, or add to it, or remove from it.*

*First copy (with hand-written report) to Monsieur le Procureur de la République in Mâcon.*

*Second copy for the records.*

*Signed and sealed in Milly, October 6, 1996*

*Warrant Officer Bonneton,*
*Officer Tribou,*
*Officer Rialin,*
*Officer Mougin.*

At midnight in Milly, one November 20, even the hearths have long been asleep. Not a single light on inside the houses. I pee behind a trash can. It's perishingly cold.

## 45

Every morning, the night staff pass on any information to us. Madame Le Camus tells us who is going to which floor.

We wake up the residents. We help them to wash themselves. We bring them down to the dining room. We settle them. We give them the medications prepared by the nurses. We serve them their breakfast. We bring them back up to their rooms. We make their beds. Then, if requested, we shampoo hair or apply polish to fingernails. At noon, we bring them back down for lunch.

That's if we're doing the floors with "independent" residents. Jo, Maria, and I often look after the floor with the "dependent" residents. We wake them up. We wash them. We help them to eat. And, if the weather's fine, we take them down with the others into the garden, or elsewhere if it's winter, as it is now.

If I didn't do overtime, I wouldn't be able to listen to the stories they tell. So my extra hours are like summer solstices. Each time I work, my days get longer. With the women, I massage hands, feet, or apply face cream while asking them questions. With the men (far fewer than women at The Hydrangeas, as at "retirement" homes everywhere), it depends. I wash hair, trim nose or ear hair while asking the same questions I ask the women.

I could fill hundreds of blue notebooks. Sometimes, I think of turning each resident into a short story. But I'd need to have a twin sister.

It's incredible how well daughters look after their parents. When I was little, I wanted to have a boy. Since working at The Hydrangeas, I've changed my mind. Aside from a few exceptions, the sons visit every now and then. Often accompanied by their wives. As for the daughters, they visit all the time. Most of those forgotten on Sunday have only sons.

I always do Hélène's room last, to have more time. This morning, when I arrive with my cart, Roman is there.

I fucked What's-his-name all of last night. When I'm out of sorts, I either hit the bottle, or fuck.

After I'd jumped from the first story of the Municipal and Public Space Department, I went straight to his place. He wasn't there. I waited for him in the hallway for an hour. I couldn't go back home. Not after what I'd just read. The photos of the accident were inside a gray envelope. I stole it. I didn't look at them, apart from the top one. While I was waiting for What's-his-name in the hallway, I lifted the flap. I saw just a heap of scrap metal. I imagined that the photos underneath were awful. That they showed my parents' bloodied bodies.

As soon as What's-his-name arrived, he took the envelope from my hand and burnt it in his shower, using rubbing alcohol. When the burning was over, nothing was left but a foul smell in the apartment.

We aired the place. And I admit that I cried.

After that, we looked up Pierre Léger in the local phone directory. He was the sole witness of the accident. I'd never heard of him. He wasn't named in the newspaper article.

What's-his-name found seven Pierre Légers. He phoned them, one by one. Until he found the right one. He said:

"Hold on, I'm passing you Mademoiselle Neige."

He held his phone out to me.

"Hello, good evening . . . I'm Justine Neige, the daughter of Christian and Sandrine Neige, who died in a car accident in Milly, in 1996. Is it you who called the police station?"

A long silence. Finally, Pierre Léger replied:

"At the time, I asked the journalists not to publish my name anywhere. How did you find me?"

First lie:

"My grandfather, Armand Neige, gave me your name."

"How does he know my name?"

Second lie:

"I don't know. Milly's a small village, things get around."

Silence. Breathing down the phone. The TV was on in the room he was in. It must have been the news bulletin, I could hear rocket fire.

"What do you want?"

"I'd like to know what you saw, that morning."

"I saw the car coming off the road and crashing into an oak tree. The impact was so violent, it wrecked the tree."

"Was the car going fast?"

"Like a rocket."

Silence. Lump in throat. I could barely speak.

"Was there black ice on the road?"

"The car overtook me—the driver was going so fast that I shouted out and sounded my horn at him. I didn't get time to see the people inside the car. It's only afterwards that I learned there were four of them. I didn't even get time to catch my breath. The car sped two hundred meters ahead of me, started to zigzag, then rammed into the tree."

Silence. He continued:

"At first, I didn't dare get out of my car. Thought how man-gled they must be inside. You won't believe me, mademoiselle, but I'd been given my first mobile phone the previous day, for my birthday. The first ever number I called on it was the fire brigade. I threw it away after that, and never wanted one ever again. Between me phoning and the fire brigade arriving, it was a good ten minutes . . . I got out of the car, my legs were shak-ing. I went up to the wreck: it was concertinaed metal. All the windows had exploded. Looked like a bomb had been in it. Not a sound from inside. I realized immediately that they were . . . "

"Did you see them?"

"No. And even if I had, I wouldn't tell you about it. Speaking of the dead doesn't bring them back."

"It does, Monsieur Léger. I swear to you, it does bring them back a little."

I'm fairly sure I'm looking rough. Roman is, too. He's very pale. I thought it was sunny in Peru. But in his eyes, still that infinite blue. I'd give my life to drown inside him. And I definitely wouldn't want my body to be fished out.

"How are you, Justine?"

"Well. Thanks."

"You look tired."

"I had a difficult night."

"You were working?"

"Yes. Was your trip good?"

"Like all trips. Lots of learning, like at school, except the teacher's fascinating and unforgettable."

I smile. He's holding Hélène's left hand in his hands.

"My grandmother's never worn jewelry."

"No. She always loathed it."

"You know so many things about her. Are you still writing for me?"

"Yes."

"I look forward to reading it . . . It reassures me, knowing that you're close to her, all the time. If I were old, I'd want a young lady like you to look after me . . . You're gentle. One can hear it and see it."

I feel like convincing him that he is a hundred years old. I even pray that, all of a sudden, he becomes a hundred years old. But . . .

"I'm going to ask you to leave the room for ten minutes: I need to freshen her up."

He lets go of Hélène's hand.

"I know I'm not allowed to visit in the morning, but there's nothing I can do, because of the train, and then the car afterwards. It's so far away, this place."

"I know. That's what everyone says."

"I'll go and have a coffee."

"There's a new coffee machine on the second floor. The coffee's almost as good as a good coffee."

He leaves the room. I take Hélène's left hand in mine. It's warm. I kiss it. I kiss Roman's fingerprints. That's at least something.

She opens her eyes and looks at me.

"Hélène, I understand why you waited for Lucien. I understand everything now."

Her eyes are still on me, but she says nothing. It's been three weeks now that she's not said a word. In the blue notebook, it's me talking for her.

I put my sign up on her door: "Care in progress, do not enter."

"Yesterday evening, I read the report of my parents' accident."

I take her nightdress off carefully, so as not to hurt her.

"I did something crazy. I broke into the cops' building. I mean, the *gendarmes'*. I know you don't like the French police."

I remove her pillows and raise the head of the bed. I fill the first washbowl. For Hélène, I always make the water a little warmer because she's sensitive to the cold.

"I did what you had done in the classroom on the evening of the seagull. I hid in a cupboard and waited until everyone had left. And I managed to find the file on my parents' accident. They were driving like lunatics. Parents shouldn't drive like lunatics. Instead of reading books like *How to Be a Good Mother*, they should respect the speed limits."

I place a protective sheet under her body. I always start by washing her buttocks. And then her back.

"And apparently, the brakes were screwed up . . . but that's not certain."

I soap her arms, her thorax, her abdomen. And while I'm at it, I massage her elbows with sweet almond oil.

"We're Thursday today. Your daughter will come to read to you. And your grandson is here, too."

I move her onto her back again and uncover the lower half of her body. I soap and rinse, carefully. I know her body by heart. This body that so loved Lucien. Us nursing assistants, we're the guardians of the temples of past loves. But that doesn't show on our pay slips.

Hélène says a few words:

"All those years of waiting for him. At the café, the men would say to me, 'Lucien is dead, you have to accept it.'"

It's good to hear her voice again, and, above all, it's a good sign. As soon as a resident stops speaking, the doctors ask for neurological tests to be done.

I massage her heels. And after drying every square centimeter of her body, I slip a clean nightdress on her. Hélène picks up her monologue:

"He couldn't be dead."

Finally, I wash her face with fresh water and a little baby lotion. I finish by brushing her teeth, and make her spit into the kidney tray.

I throw everything away: wash glove, protective sheet, diaper.

I write on her care form that she's spoken.

I remove the sign. Roman is waiting behind the door. He comes in and glances at my cart. Then at me. He says, "Thank you." I reply, "I'll leave you with her."

## 46

Where were you last night?"

"At a friend's."

"Which friend?"

"What's-his-name."

Jules throws himself onto my bed, laughing, and bangs his head. I think he's decided to keep on growing until he's three meters tall.

"Any new calls to The Hydrangeas?"

"None. Anyhow, there's no point now."

"Why's that?"

"No one falls for it anymore. We even have to phone some families several times when a resident really *has* died. But since this whole business, our residents have been getting lots more visits at weekends, even the long-abandoned ones. They should start an Anonymous Call Day in all the retirement homes around the world."

Jules smiles. He looks like Annette when he smiles, has the same dimples as her. Sometimes I think to myself that, had our parents not died, we wouldn't have grown up together. We'd have only seen each other every now and then. We went from cousins to brother and sister one Sunday morning. Because of a tree on the side of a road, and one of our fathers driving too fast. That's all it can take.

When our parents died, mine were living in Lyon, and Jules's were planning on moving to Sweden. Jules speaks a little Swedish. When he was little, he went over there several times to stay with his grandparents, Magnus and Ada. And then, after one particular summer, I don't know what happened, but he

never wanted to go back there. He'd fly into such a rage whenever Gran mentioned Sweden. Magnus and Ada even came
over here, to Milly, to Gran and Gramps's. But he refused to
see or speak to them. He double-locked himself into his room.
I remember them both in our kitchen, distraught. I can't remember their faces that well. And Jules tore up all the photos
they appeared in.

Every year, they send him a letter and a check for his birthday and at Christmas. Twice a year, in our little mailbox that
gets only bills and brochures, that pale-yellow envelope stands
out. Gran places it on Jules's desk, in his room. Jules tears it up
without ever opening it. He refuses to talk about it. Whenever
I try to broach the subject, he gets angry and slams the door.
But this evening, for some reason, the question just comes out.
Like a hiccup that I can't hold back, and that echoes around
the room:

"Why do you hate your Swedish grandparents?"

His face doesn't redden, and he doesn't leave my room slamming the door. He just replies, coldly:

"Why do you always jump from one subject to another?"

"Because I think at top speed."

"Well, slow down then."

He opens the window and lights a cigarette. I daren't move.
I watch him. And, after the longest silence, he says to me:

"They made insinuations."

"Insinuations?"

"They told me, well, they didn't exactly tell me, let's say they
tried to make me understand that my father might not be my
father."

As usual, he chucks his butt out into the garden to feed
Gramps's watering can, but not without first dragging so hard
on it, I'm amazed he doesn't burn his lips. He turns back to me
and adds:

"I was ten years old. I wanted to kill them. I swear to you. I remember that, at that precise moment, I knew what a murderous

impulse is. In fact, if I'd been twenty, I think I would have bumped them off. It was my young age that saved their skins."

Images rush through my mind. They say that, at the moment of dying, you see your entire life in a fraction of a second. That's exactly how I feel. The garbage chute, What's-his-name, the cemetery, the Q-tips, the October bonfire, the seagull, the Neige file, The Hydrangeas, Hélène, Lucien, Roman, Monsieur Paul, the anonymous caller, my brother at three, my brother at four, my brother at five, my brother at six, my brother at seven, my brother at eight, my brother at nine, my brother at ten, my brother at eleven, my brother at twelve, my brother at thirteen, my brother at fourteen, my brother at fifteen, my brother at sixteen, my brother at seventeen.

## 47

A nd yet, they look like they love each other."
Jo hands me back the photo of Alain and Annette taken a few months after Jules's birth. I put it away in my bag.

This evening, I'm having supper at hers. I like her husband. Patrick is a tall guy whose face is pockmarked from past acne. To conceal it, he has UV treatment every week. He has three tattoos on his body, including a huge mermaid right up his arm. Jo says that, sometimes, she hears her singing. And Patrick says to Jo that she should leave off the meds she's supposed to give to her old folk. Patrick's a real sweetheart who looks like a real bad guy. The kind who rides a Harley-Davidson and stops at pedestrian crosswalks.

I like eating at their place because they touch each other all the time without touching. Like people who love each other do. The exact opposite of my grandparents.

They have two daughters of around my age. I don't know them. Like everyone, they left Milly after the bac. Jo read a great future for them in the lines on their palms.

"Maybe Jules's mother was raped . . ." says Patrick, in his gravelly voice, while looking for something in the fridge.

Jo and I are dumbfounded by that.

"There are plenty of women who get raped and don't dare to say so. Maybe the Swedish girl had told her parents but not her husband."

Jules the product of a rape—that really is crazy.

"You know, Jules was little when his grandparents said those things; maybe he didn't quite grasp what they meant," Jo says to me, while putting taramosalata on bread.

Despite the pink Jo's spreading, I see everything as black. It's at such times that Jo says to me: "Come and eat with us tonight." And puts color into her dishes.

"Jules has always understood everything. It was as if he even spoke languages that don't exist."

"Where is he this evening?"

"At home, pretending to revise."

"What are you going to do?"

"Go to the cemetery and ask Annette, when she cheated on Uncle Alain, who it was with."

## 48

B irds don't die. Or at least, only by accident."
Lucien looks at the sky. Edna looks at him looking at the
sky. She asks:
"Who told you that, Simon?"
"Birds are passed down from generation to generation. Each
man is connected to a bird."
"Did you read that in a novel?"
"No, look."
He points up at the sky. Edna struggles to keep her eyes open,
blinded by the light of a Sunday in August.
"What do you want to show me?"
"You can't see it?"
"See what?"
"My bird. She follows me everywhere."
"She? Who follows you everywhere?"
"My bird. It's a girl . . . I lost my memory but not the bird."
Edna can see nothing in the sky. Not even a cloud.
"And where does this bird come from?"
"I don't know."
"If it's passed down from generation to generation, it must
come from your father or mother?"
"Maybe."
He contemplates Edna's rounded belly. Touches it with the
tips of his fingers.
It's Edna who made the first move. It's she who first entered
the room and lay down beside him. Everything went nicely, po-
litely, in silence, with no excessive passion but with great gentle-
ness. Lucien seemed happy to have a hard-on, to feel desire, to

*fuck a woman. And he smiled for the first time since Gare de l'Est
when Edna told him that she was pregnant.*

*"It's a girl."*

*"Like your bird?"*

*"Yes."*

*Edna kisses him.*

*"I hope she'll have your eyes."*

*"She'll have my bird's eyes."*

*"What color are they?"*

*"I don't know. She's too far away."*

*He returns to his thoughts. Edna watches him delving into his
memory. But it's as if he were searching inside a room plunged
in darkness.*

*It's two years now since he got off the train at Gare de l'Est
and entered her life. Two years that she's loved him. She knows
that, without the war, such a handsome man would never have
shared her bed. But does he really share it? He always seems to be
elsewhere. Over there, perhaps, at old Louis's café.*

*Last winter, Edna went to the address written on the letter
that came with the portrait of Lucien/Simon. Old Louis's café,
Place de l'Église, Milly. She didn't go there to speak about Lucien
to the sender of the letter. Certainly not. Indeed, she burnt both
portrait and letter a long time ago. She went there so the place
could tell her about Lucien/Simon.*

*She went into the café at ten in the morning. It was cold out-
side. Inside, a wood-burning stove. A clock with broken hands
showed five o'clock. She sat down in a corner. There were just
two men drinking in silence, leaning on the bar. The others were
doubtless at work at that time. One of the two men kept repeating the same sentence, about an albatross; it sounded like a poem.*

*From behind the bar, the waiter asked her what she would like
to drink. Edna didn't know what to say at first. But then she said:
Something hot, please. When she said that, the two men leaning
on the bar both turned to look at her at the same time.*

*A large dog appeared and came over to her, but not too close.*

*It seemed to be sniffing her from a distance. Edna feared it might recognize the smell of Lucien/Simon on her. In her panic, she asked: How old is the dog?*

*The waiter looked surprised by this question. Then replied that he didn't know exactly, that the* patronne *had found the dog towards the end of the war, by the side of the road.*

*The end of the war. The animal hadn't known Lucien/Simon. Edna felt relieved. Just at that moment, the dog disappeared behind the bar.*

*Limping, the young waiter brought her a piping-hot vegetable broth. A war injury, no doubt.*

*She sipped her broth, blowing on it from time to time. It tasted good.*

*The "patronne," the young waiter had said, and not the "patron." Hélène Hel must be the owner of the place.*

*At around half past ten, a woman came in, holding some trousers. She greeted the two men at the bar, and then went behind it, beside the waiter. He left her to it.*

*Edna's heart began to race, her hands to shake, thank goodness she was sitting down.*

*So she was Hélène Hel, a woman who talked loudly to the two men leaning on the bar. A small woman, stout and graceless. The kind you come across everywhere. The kind you don't notice, like Edna herself. Lucien had gone from one ordinary woman to another.*

*The waiter reappeared. Followed by* Someone. *And the dog.*

Someone *who opened a door behind the bar, a door covered in mirrors between two shelves holding glasses and bottles.*

*Upon seeing this* Someone, *Edna's hands started to shake again. She pinched her arms hard to get a grip on herself. But it didn't work. And yet Edna had seen worse. She had a strong stomach. She'd held the hands of plenty of men who'd had limbs amputated, who were gangrenous, who were dying. And she'd never had the shakes.*

*Until she met Lucien/Simon.*

*Since the Gare de l'Est, everything had deserted her: her self-confidence, pride, coldness, authority, calm, integrity, faith. Since "him," Edna had become cunning, a liar, a cheat, a thief, over-sensitive. She could go from laughter to tears in seconds, would steal morphine from the clinic to inject into herself, would forget, dream, blush, sweat, love, thought only of the bed she'd rejoin him in at night. And that morning, at old Louis's café, when she'd discovered* Someone's *appearance, she had learned jealousy. That octopus whose acidic tentacles could reach deep inside you and re-appear in the form of nightmares, in which Lucien/Simon would straddle all kinds of women until he found himself, once again, in the arms of* Someone.

*The waiter,* Someone, *and the dog went over to the woman be-hind the bar.* Someone *pushed back a stray lock of hair; Edna noticed only her hands, her fine hands. Then her long hair pulled back into a chignon, her nape, her skin, her large mouth, her perfect profile.*

Someone *looked at the trousers the other woman held out to her, then took them into her hands. Next, she looked up and her clear eyes met Edna's. Blue eyes. Like a caress that doesn't last. Her eyes merely skimmed things, without ever penetrating them. Like Lucien's eyes.*

*Just then, lots of men came into the café all at once. It was break time at the factory. The place instantly smelt of smoke. The woman who wasn't Hélène Hel left the café.*

*The woman who was Hélène Hel went into the room con-cealed behind the bar, followed by the big dog, to leave the trou-sers there. Then came straight back to help the lame young waiter serve the customers.*

*For fifteen minutes, Edna heard, How are you Hélène? And her answer: Well.*

*No one mentioned Lucien/Simon. And yet, behind each "Well" from Hélène, Edna heard Lucien's absence. And that way the men had of watching her filling the glasses. None of them had ever looked at their own wife that way. Edna would swear to that. Before Lucien/Simon, she never noticed such things.*

*An hour later, Edna caught a train. In the station at Vernon, she fell over. She didn't trip, she lost consciousness. Too emotional.*

*Passengers rushed over to her. Among them, a doctor. Edna told him not to worry: she was a nurse. The doctor told her that she was a pregnant nurse.*

*So God had forgiven her for becoming that woman.*

*A child.*

*She must forget. Must empty her mind. Must never have drunk that vegetable broth, or heard that man reciting poems, or been scared of a dog, or seen a woman with clear eyes that emptied while staring at the glasses filling up.*

## 49

T he drawer of the bedside table is half-open. There's no water left in the carafe. I fill it. Hélène drinks a lot. I don't know if it's the heat of her beach that makes her thirsty, or having been a bistro owner. Usually, we have to force the residents to drink so they don't become dehydrated. No risk of that with Hélène.

With his girlish hands, Roman removes the hair elastic holding together some torn and stained scraps of paper. They are old pages pulled from newspapers or books. Roman touches them lightly, with his fingertips, and says to me:

"It's extraordinary."

I reply to my feet that, throughout his internment at the Dora factory, Lucien hid a sharp little stone inside his mouth, and every time he wanted to write something to Hélène, he would spit it out.

Roman hands me a piece of yellowing newspaper, now almost transparent from being kept so long in a pocket.

"So, what's written on this one?"

"'*Hélène Hel not-married on November 19, 1934. Milly.*'"

"You can read Braille?"

"No, Hélène read them out to me."

"And on this one?"

"'*We should pray only for the present. To give thanks when it has your face.*'"

"That's beautiful. My grandfather wrote well. But I think people always write well when they're in love."

This time, I can't stop myself from looking at him. As he says it, he pushes his blue eyes into mine, like a child filling two holes with modeling clay.

Without him asking, I unfurl page 7 of a Polish newspaper. On it, there's the black-and-white photo of a silver-birch forest. Against the light, I show Roman how the page is riddled with tiny holes.

"It's a kind of letter. A disjointed letter. The last words he 'wrote' in Braille. I don't know what happened next. The train he arrived in, at Gare de l'Est, came from Germany."

"Could you read it to me?"

I start to recite the words that I know off by heart:

"*Why do they shoot at the dead? Why? So no one ever tells? So we all keep silent, even beyond this world? When it was my turn to get a bullet in the head, when I felt the cold of the barrel on my temple, there were some cries from outside. No more barrel on my temple. The men aimed upwards, into the sky. They forgot me, they forgot my life that was there for the taking. She comes from you. The child before our child.*"

"What's he talking about?"

"About Buchenwald, the execution, the seagull."

"What seagull?"

"Hélène always thought that a seagull was protecting her, since her childhood. And that it protected Lucien while he was deported."

"Carry on reading, please."

I continue:

"*What's left of the man who wore flannel suits? Will you recognize me?*

"*I'm scared.*

"*First move one finger. Very gently. Then the hand, like on a piano.*

"*It's to make noise inside my head.*

"*I write to remember a memory. The one of us hanging that 'Closed for vacation' sign on the café door. But we never left. Our pretend vacation in the room above, with the shutters closed. You'd seen to the provisions, I'd seen to the blue suitcase. I placed it on the floor of our room. The Mediterranean on the floorboards. A blue lagoon full of novels that I read to you. I particularly recall those by Irène Némirovsky. Sometimes, you would lean out of the window, as if out of the porthole of a boat, to tell me about the village and the people who were bored without us. And I told you about your belly, salty like a sea urchin's."*

I look up. For the first time, I hold his blue gaze for a few seconds. The more I recite Lucien's words, the less fearful I am of Roman's eyes:

*"You never said 'I love you' to me, but I love you for us.*

*"My love, the first time I kissed you, I felt a fluttering of wings against my mouth. At first I thought a bird was struggling behind your lips, that your kiss didn't want mine. But when your tongue came in search of mine, the bird started to play with our breaths, as if we were volleying it back and forth between us."*

I'm no longer able to utter a word. I roll the papers up again, into the hair elastic. He asks me if that's the end; I say yes, it is. I put the papers back into the drawer of the bedside table.

"Is it a fable, this seagull story?"

"Hélène's fable. She says that each human being is connected to a bird during his or her time on earth. That the bird protects us."

He leans over to his grandmother and kisses her.

"Why aren't you wearing your smock today?" he asks me in one breath, without looking at me.

"I'm on vacation."

"Yet you still come here?"

"I came to say goodbye to Hélène before I head off."

"Where are you going?"

"Sweden."

"It's almost never daylight at this time of year . . . Well, what I mean is, it's almost always dark."

He smiles because he's getting his words mixed up.

I look at him now. I can't tell him that only Sweden will be able to enlighten me, even in the middle of December.

\* \* \*

"Hello."

"Could you take me to the airport?"

"Of course. What day?"

"Now."

"Where are you going?"

"To Stockholm."

"You're visiting Jules's grandparents?"

"Yes. How d'you know?"

"How do I know what?"

"How d'you know that Jules's grandparents are Swedish?"

"You told me so."

"You remember everything I tell you?"

"Yes. Well, I think so."

"And do I tell you lots of things?"

"On the days I don't annoy you, yes."

Outside terminal 2 of Saint-Exupéry airport, What's-his-name kisses my hair before leaving.

You never kiss the hair of someone you're just fucking. He touches me and looks at me as if we're "together." In fact, I no longer really know what we are to each other.

I don't have a suitcase, just a small bag with what I need for two days. In the departure lounge, my flight for Stockholm is listed, boarding gate 2. Terminal 2, gate 2. Jules was born on the 22nd. To me, that's a positive sign.

Between Milly and the airport, What's-his-name didn't ask me any questions.

He switched on the radio, searching at random for songs, telling me this was his favorite kind of lottery. He was wearing a mustard sweater that didn't go at all with his trousers. In any case, the color mustard should be prohibited by law.

What's-his-name's clothes are never well matched, but he gets two lovely dimples deep in his cheeks whenever he smiles, as if to make up for his poor taste.

agnus and Ada live really close to my hotel in
Stockholm, at 27 Spergatten. I didn't tell them I was
coming. It's nine in the morning. It's still dark. The
sun will rise at 11 A.M. and set at 3 P.M. I'm very cold.

Wrapped up in Jules's padded jacket, I walk fast. By my
calculations, Annette's parents, Magnus and Ada, are around
seventy years old. I also know that they don't speak a word
of French. So I've arranged to meet an interpreter outside 1
Spergattan before going to knock on the door of number 27.
All I know about her is that she's called Cristelle, is French,
twenty-six years old, and has lived here a long time. I also know
that she costs 400 Swedish kronor an hour, which is about 50
euros. Speaking two languages pays better than looking after
old folk.

She's waiting for me.

I see her blowing into her gloves. Her blond hair is hidden
under a bottle-green woolly hat.

As I approach her, she says: "Hey, Justine!" She recognized
me thanks to my Facebook profile photo, which shows me just
as I am. Neither slimmer nor fatter, neither darker- nor lighter-
haired, neither younger nor older. We shake gloves.

As we walk from number 1 to number 27, I explain to her
again that I've come here to meet the grandparents of my cousin
Jules, who is eighteen and whom I consider as my brother, that
we both lost our parents in a car accident, which may not have
been an accident, and that I've just discovered that my Uncle
Alain, Jules's father, may not have been his father. As I'm telling her this story, which sounds straight out of one of Gran's

novels, I see her warm breath gushing out of her mouth, while she emits only onomatopoeic grunts.

Number 27 is a red wooden door, hung with a Christmas wreath. Are they alone? Are they here?

Annette had a slightly younger brother. Jules has two cousins. What if it's them who open the door?

I take off my right glove and give three quick knocks. Nothing. I knock again.

And what if, three days before Christmas, Magnus and Ada have gone off to a fjord, or something like that? But since I have no idea what a fjord is, I can't picture Magnus and Ada at one. And what if they're dead, and we knew nothing about it? But no, because I intercepted the Christmas card and check they sent Jules only last week. They couldn't have died in a week. Although . . . It takes just a morning to die.

A man opens the door: Magnus in his pajamas. Jules in fifty years' time. Same eyebrows, same eyes, same mouth, same emaciated face, same size. I notice his hands, his fingers longer than *cigarettes russes* wafers. Indeed, if he were smoking, I could faint right here on the sidewalk, he looks so much like my brother. Even his white hair resembles Jules's: the same unruly mop.

"Hello, I'm Justine, Jules's cousin."

Cristelle repeats after me, in Swedish: "Hello, I'm Justine, Jules's cousin."

51

July 14, 1984

The twins are waiting for him under the arbor, along with their new fiancées. Armand comes home from the factory on foot. It's five past twelve. He started at four in the morning. On summer afternoons, after his nap, he does some gardening. Then, at 9 P.M., he goes to bed.

Today is Bastille Day. It's worth working on public holidays, double the pay. Still ten more years to get through, and then retirement. He might take the opportunity to travel. He's never seen the sea.

When he's about fifty meters from the house, he hears Christian's and Adrien's voices ringing out in the garden. He hears the laughter of the new fiancées. He pushes open the gate, which no longer grates. And yet he could have sworn it still grated this morning. Who oiled the hinges?

Before going to embrace his sons, he has entered the cool of the house. He soaps his hands in the kitchen sink. Rubs his fingers against the block of *savon de Marseille*, digs his fingernails into it.

He passes his reflection in the mirror. His hair's going gray. Since he was a boy, he's been called "*l'Américain*," owing to his good looks. For a long time he loathed the nickname. As if it implied that his mother had slept with a GI at the Liberation. But then he got used to it. At work, when a colleague asks him, "How's it going, *l'Américain?*," he no longer pays any attention. That's what it's like around here: people can't just be called by their name. They're given a whole new status with a nickname.

He's hungry.

Eugénie has made a seafood couscous. It's Alain's favorite dish. The stock is gently simmering on the gas stove. He lifts the lid, inhales and closes his eyes. He prolongs the pleasure. The pleasure keeping him from his two boys. He'll hold them tight in just a few minutes.

Since they left to live in Lyon, he finds that time drags and the house seems far too big. To have two boys for eighteen years, two rascals who break crockery in tandem, and then a void. Rooms where the light never gets switched on, except for dusting. But what he misses most are those Sunday-morning bike rides. The pride of cycling up steep tracks, his sons' T-shirts drenched in sweat, their napes, their similar smiles. Two sons for the price of one. Even if Alain is more reckless than Christian, and more talkative, too.

He walks through the fringed curtain, out of the house. He hasn't seen them since Christmas. Seven months is a long time. Since they've been working "in music," they don't bother coming back to Milly. He moves towards them. Past his kitchen garden, noticing that the tomato leaves are yellowing too early for the season.

He doesn't see her straight away. Her back is turned to him. Only her golden hair has the effect of the mirrors he puts in the fruit trees to dazzle the birds.

Upon seeing Armand, Christian deploys his full 1.88 meters to hug him. Armand closes his eyes the better to breathe in the sweet smell of his son, his eldest by thirteen minutes. Then it's Alain's turn to pat him on the back and say the word Dad.

She, in turn, has stood up. Her bangs are too long. With a flick of the hand, she brushes her hair from her forehead. Her skin is pale, almost white. Her cherry lips reveal perfectly straight teeth, as white as her skin. As though they're competing. He shakes her hand and tells her, inanely, that her accent's thick enough to cut with a knife. She doesn't understand what that means, he just drops it. Turns his back on her, even. Now it's Sandrine's turn to introduce herself. Pleased to meet you, she says.

He pours himself a glass of port. Doesn't add ice. Can't stand it. He thinks again of the sea. Of retirement. Of Annette's face. What's come over him? Usually, he never thinks that way. Usually, he never thinks. Not like that, in any case.

So, what's new? Things are going well at the shop. The twins are moving into import-export. There's a trend for thirty-minute singles. British music is all the rage. It is the best, anyhow. Alain composes between customers, while Christian does the bookkeeping. Annette has left Sweden and will live in France to restore stained-glass windows. Restore what? You know, those colorful windows with Jesus on them, in churches. Oh, them. They need a pretty girl to sell their records, it attracts customers, and, as luck would have it, Sandrine has joined them. At weekends, Annette is with us, too. Oh yes, Dad, we have some big news. We're getting married. Since my brother proposed to Sandrine, I proposed to Annette, well, I actually asked Annette first—don't want anyone stealing her off me, you know? We'll marry on the same day, so you'll only need one wedding outfit, we'll marry in Milly, no way are we doing it in Lyon, Mom, you'll make us your seafood couscous, no really, there won't be too many people, no, just Annette's parents and Sandrine's mother, no fuss. Are you staying here a while? About two weeks. Your couscous is good, Mom. I miss your cooking. What's the specialty over there, where you're from, in Sweden? What does "specialty" mean? What you all eat, the dish of the day. In summer, crayfish. The rest of the year, herring, salmon. Is salmon a saltwater fish or a freshwater one? Both, he thinks. Salmon swims from one to the other.

Armand thinks that even if Annette spoke to him in Swedish, he'd understand her.

When it comes to girls, Armand hasn't met many. Before

Eugénie, he did go out with one. She wasn't that pretty, but had a lovely smile. It didn't last. And then there was Eugénie; he promptly asked her father for her hand in marriage. He courted her swiftly, as if it were a burden to be rid of. As if he needed a woman to say yes to him to feel at ease. To feel able to sit down on any bench and breathe. Not that he's ever sat on a bench. The bicycle saddle's his thing. As if getting married was obligatory to begin real life, the life of adults, a pathway out of childhood.

At his home, there was only a brother. At school, there were only boys. At work, there are only men. As for Eugénie, she's always been a woman. Never a girl.

He had a restless, sleepless night. Why do they call it a *nuit blanche*? His was black. Last night, he went to bed earlier than usual, to avoid being seated close to "her" again, at supper.

This morning, her perfume had already permeated the house. The walls had soaked her up. Lapped up her scent. And yet he'd swear this perfume doesn't come in a bottle, that she was born with it.

What's come over him? He thinks back to Alain's previous girlfriends. Alain went out with one for just over a year—she spent the night at the house a few times. A certain Isabelle. One day, he'd left her for another girl. A Catherine, he believes. And then there was a Juliette. No, he's wrong. That one was Christian's girlfriend. Girls who would spend a weekend or an evening at the house, who would come to pick up the twins. Girls wearing a touch too much perfume. He remembers one with a run in her black pantyhose. He'd found that tacky. Unlike Eugénie, he'd never had anything to do with his sons' girlfriends. In fact, he'd never had anything to do with girls in general. He'd been fond of Eugénie, but not loved her.

At the end of each year, at the meal organized by the workers' council, she would look out for any of his colleagues' wives eyeing him up. According to her, there were lots of them. His wife's jealousy made him smile inside, but he merely shrugged his shoulders and said nothing.

He's never been so happy to leave the house. No, not happy, relieved. He's almost running away. It's only 3 A.M. He's early. It doesn't matter. Nothing matters anymore, apart from "her." The future wife of his son. The girl who's come from Sweden. This morning, he feels as if a tumor has lodged itself inside of him. And, as he walks towards his factory, he knows that nothing will ever be the same again. Say, he's never noticed that brick wall there, just before the factory.

At work, at the weaving looms, he sees only her. It's no longer printed fabric emerging, but her face, her smile, her voice. Indeed, he wonders why his son Alain spends hours composing. When your fiancée has a voice like that, you just need to listen to it. Her every syllable is like an operatic aria. Even if he doesn't know much about opera. He's seen only one in his life, on TV, *Madama Butterfly*.

Yesterday evening, when he kissed his sons before going up to bed, he saw the nape of her neck. She was leaning forward. She'd placed a book on the table in the small sitting room and, while reading it, her left hand unconsciously stroked her right arm. He was floored. Gazing at her bare nape, her hair gathered into a quite stylish pink elastic. And her hand moving up and down, the length of her arm. And now, now that he's here, facing the weaving looms and doing almost the same movement as her, but faster, all he can see is her hand, her arm, her chalk-white skin.

He talks silently to himself. What the hell's come over me? What's come over me? I've lost the plot. An old machine thrown by youth. Sent spinning by the mind. You old fool, you're pathetic. Pull yourself together.

And yet, at midday, he doesn't go home. Because he no longer has a home. His house, his kitchen garden, his dresser, his picket fence, none of all that belongs to him anymore.

The foreman, says to him: "Everything OK, Armand? It's

one o'clock, time you went home, old boy." He's right, I am old. I'm a thousand years old. Fifty summers next month, but where did they all go? What did I do with them?

When he does finally get home, Eugénie tells him that the boys and their fiancées have gone away for the day. He could have taken her into his arms and swirled her around. As if at the dances they never went to, because, when they were barely married, Eugénie fell pregnant and he had to work twice as hard.

Their sons made the most of life for them. They went out, had a wild time. They knew plenty of girls. A new girl every week. And Armand always looked at those girls the way one looks at a pretty photo of a landscape in a magazine before turning the page.

"Why are you back so late from work?" Eugénie asks him. "Just a sec, I'll warm up what's left of the couscous. You haven't seemed quite yourself since yesterday."

After eating, he goes into Alain's room. Eugénie has clearly been in, there's nothing lying around. The bed's neatly made. The linoleum's gleaming. On the walls, the posters Alain never took down. Posters of Téléphone, ACDC, and Trust. A safe-like money box and a globe abandoned on his student's desk. A few photos of him and his twin.

Armand never got them mixed up, unlike the rest of the world. It was about the look in their eyes. The one defiant, the other reserved, since childhood. They might smile and blow their nose the same way, but it's all in the eyes.

Annette's little suitcase is placed in a corner. Between the wardrobe and the bedside table. It's pink. Armand had never seen a pink suitcase. Those Swedes certainly don't do anything like the rest of us. They produce stunningly beautiful girls, stylish hair elastics, and pink suitcases. He unzips it. Since yesterday, he's turned into a stranger, a new person, someone he doesn't know. Someone who secretly opens a suitcase. Someone who looks for a perfume.

Her pale clothes are all perfectly folded. In fact, they're not really clothes, but light, soft little things. Nothing like the dresses Eugénie has hanging in her wardrobe.

He shuts the suitcase abruptly, like a slap. In thirteen days' time, they'll be back off to Lyon. He won't see her again before Christmas. And, knowing Alain, between now and then, he'll have replaced her with another girl. One who'll have no effect on him at all, like before.

During those thirteen days left to kill, Armand does a lot of overtime. When he gets home mid-afternoon, he goes to bed, exhausted. Avoids evening meals, claiming to have a headache.

On the seventh day, Eugénie calls the doctor behind his back. Grudgingly, Armand agrees to be examined. The doctor detects mild depression, maybe from overworking. Armand turns down the sick leave he suggests to him. Staying at home is unthinkable. He comes across her often enough as it is. On the stairs, in the garden, in front of the house. The other day, she even borrowed his bike to go for a ride. She put her ass on his saddle. He intentionally left the bike out in the rain for two days, until Eugénie, grumbling, wheeled it into the garden shed.

She's always wearing a different outfit, and Armand could reel them off by heart. Even though he daren't scrutinize her too much. But a single glance is enough for him to take her in. For her to be imprinted on his mind. And then he might look elsewhere, try to force other images into his head, but she's filling all the space. With just a look, he can recall every pore of her skin. It's like a talent he didn't know he had. His memory now serves only to remember Annette.

Anyhow, it's ridiculous to think that, between now and Christmas, Alain will have replaced her. She's irreplaceable.

\* \* \*

Emptiness. Between the end of summer and this Christmas Day 1984, there was just emptiness. Absence.

This afternoon, to take his mind off things, Eugénie gets him to wrap the presents. Presents for the twins, for Sandrine, and for "her."

He started with those for the twins. Two sweaters knitted by Eugénie that they'll never wear, and two top hats, in case they need them for their weddings. Because, yes, that's it, they've fixed a date, it'll be this February.

And Alain hasn't replaced "her."

The paper he's wrapping the twins' presents in has sprigs of holly printed on it. The leaves' sharp prickles have been left out. And yet they prick his fingers. He has the feeling that nothing's gentle or smooth anymore. That even the air he breathes hurts him. He doesn't know why this is happening, to him.

Falling in love with his son's girlfriend is despicable. For the moment, he's not considering suicide. In his family, they don't do suicide. They take refuge in the past, or switch on the TV. He goes over his childhood, his adolescence, his youthful years with Eugénie, the hills cycled with the boys when they still couldn't care less about girls and spent their afternoons pumping up inner tubes, degreasing and rinsing chains, oiling pedals and brake pads, and polishing frames with cloths cut from an old sweater.

As soon as he gets to the present, he returns to the past, or switches on the TV. That's his way of doing himself in, of throwing himself over a precipice, again and again.

*The children arrive tomorrow.* Before, that was his favorite sentence. Today, it's the worst thing he could possibly hear.

Before, when the phone rang, he'd rush to answer, just to hear one of his sons say the word "Dad." Now, he shuts himself away somewhere until Eugénie has picked up.

Over the Christmas period, the factory closes. He won't be able to escape into the darkness at three in the morning and then drag out the day. He'll be forced to encounter her in the stairs, the kitchen, the sitting room, on the landing. In any case, with a bit of luck, they'll be off soon to look after the store. During the festive season, people give each other lots of music.

Now he's wrapping the fiancées' presents. Cameo pendants. He puts them into little boxes and wraps them in the paper with the prickle-free holly. He thinks that, for young women, a cameo seems a bit old-fashioned. But he'll say nothing to Eugénie: there's enough upheaval in the house as it is, even if it is silent.

On Christmas Eve, when, hiding behind his bedroom shutters, he sees her getting out of Alain's car, he finds her even more beautiful in her winter clothes. Eugénie opens the door to them in her nightdress. They're arriving from Lyon. It's almost midnight. They'll go to bed without eating anything. We'll celebrate Christmas over lunch tomorrow. He hears their steps and voices ringing out in the stairs. The bedroom doors closing. Then not a sound anymore. Apart from Eugénie, who rolls into the bed where he's pretending to be asleep, her feet frozen. She presses them against his striped pajamas.

It's 11 A.M. when Annette shows up in the kitchen the following morning. Alone. They're alone. Eugénie has gone to buy the Yule log and some sliced bread. The twins and Sandrine are still sleeping.

"Good morning, Armand."

He's just shucking the oysters: he does so mechanically, tipping the liquor into the sink and placing the open oyster onto a dish. Between now and lunchtime, they will have produced fresh liquor and will be delicious. It's the secret. Letting them produce their liquor again after opening them.

"Good morrning, Annette."

She stands on tiptoe to kiss him. He's holding his knife in his right hand. He inhales her forehead, then the crown of her head. He shuts his eyes so as not to lose his balance.

"How have you been since the summer?" she asks, pouring herself a mug of the hot milk Eugénie has left on the stove.

Her Swedish accent cracks like a whip. He's incapable of answering her. He watches as she removes the skin from the scalding milk in the pan. She bites her lip as she lifts it off with a wooden spoon. Then, without warning, she looks up and straight at him, giving him one of her adorable smiles.

"It's funny, Armand, how you roll your rrrs."

"Yes."

"Are you OK, Armand? You're very pale."

"It turrns my stomach, opening oysters. Apparrently, they'rre still alive when we swallow 'em."

"Oh. Shouldn't do it if it makes you feel like that."

She sips from her mug, blows on it, sips again.

"Shouldn't ever do something if you don't feel like it, Armand."

She puts her mug down and almost stares at him.

He stares back at her.

"Have you and Eugénie been married a long time?"

"I don't know anymorre."

She starts to laugh.

"What d'you mean, you don't know anymore? Your head's forever in the crowds, like Christian."

"In the clouds."

He leaves the kitchen, where the air has become unbreathable. As he goes, he meets Eugénie, back from shopping.

"Have you finished shucking the oysters?"

"Not quite."

They all gather in the sitting room.

This year, Eugénie has bought a string of flashing Christmas lights. So she's lowered the main lights to get the full effect.

They have aperitifs in the half-light: champagne in glasses that date back to their wedding. Armand crunches salted peanuts while Alain tells them about the store's turnover, which has rocketed. Putting Sandrine behind the till was a brilliant idea. So now he gets time to compose. He's sent his tapes to a record company in Paris.

All Armand sees is Annette's face, disappearing and reappearing. Not a great idea, those flashing lights.

They take their seats at the table.

Armand switches the ceiling light back on, gets told off by Eugénie. Annette races up the stairs and returns clutching some candles, which she sets on the table and lights with matches. She then switches off the ceiling light.

"That's wonderful, my love," Alain whispers to her.

And it's true that it's wonderful. Armand sees the dining room he's known for twenty years in a new light. Like his life.

Annette doesn't touch either the oysters or the *foie gras*, but the boys devour it all, and Armand is already on his third glass of wine. Eugénie looks at him strangely. He pours himself a fourth glass. The kids talk about their weddings. So, it will be in February.

It's gift time.

Sandrine hands a golden package to Eugénie.

"From Annette and me."

Eugénie struggles to untie the ribbon around it, and utters inaudible words when she finally discovers a Hermès silk scarf. She doesn't know what to do with it. She looks at it as if she'd just been handed a newborn baby. Instead of throwing it around her shoulders, she carefully puts it back into its box. Then Annette turns to Armand and whispers to him:

"This is from me."

"Thanks."

He can feel himself blushing like a girl. Annette has given him a boxed set of David Lean films. *Brief Encounter, Great Expectations, Summertime, Doctor Zhivago, Ryan's Daughter, Lawrence of Arabia, The Passionate Friends, This Happy Breed.*

When he kisses her in thanks, he shivers as if coming down with flu.

The boys prance around the house in their top hats. Alain imitates Jean-Paul Belmondo in *Le Magnifique.* Sandrine and

Annette, with their cameos around their necks, have a good laugh. Annette doesn't know who Belmondo is.

On the morning of the 26th, Annette has to leave. Alone. She's off to Sweden to celebrate New Year with her family. So that Alain can enjoy more time with his parents, she hasn't asked him to take her to the airport at Lyon. She's booked a taxi that's already waiting for her. Alain and Annette kiss in front of the house.

As Armand, hiding like the thief he's become, watches her disappear into the taxi, he tells himself that he'll never see her again. At this moment, he's sure of it. She won't come back to France. France doesn't have a monopoly on the Baby Jesus. She was just passing through. She'll never marry Alain. She'll do her stained-glass windows in another country. There are stained-glass window all over the place. She'll meet someone else over there. You can see it in her eyes. Not like Sandrine's when they turn to Christian. Annette will never come back.

On January 2, at four in the morning, he'll set off for the factory once again, and, with time, he will forget.

## 52

Patrick and Jo came to pick me up at Saint-Exupéry airport. Strangely, I was almost disappointed that it wasn't What's-his-name, buttoned up in some weird checked jacket.

I can't tell them a thing. What I learned direct from Magnus, I'll never tell a soul. As he poured out a flood of words to Cristelle, I felt as if I was hearing Annette's words. The ones she had confided, one evening in Sweden, to her father, who was sworn to secrecy.

There are two things I've learned from being close to the elderly. Two immutable things that they repeat to me year by year, room by room, shift by shift:

"Make the most of life, it goes fast."

"Never tell a secret. Even to your brother, your child, your father, your best friend, a stranger. Never."

I hand them a box of Daim bars while making up a deadly dull story: Jules's grandparents weren't there. I met their neighbors, who spoke French and told me that Magnus and Ada had left Sweden two years ago to live in Canada.

Jo tells me it's just as well: I'm too stressed by the whole affair anyway. My parents died in a road accident. It's sad, but that's how it is, and when you're twenty-one, you have to think about the future, nothing but the future.

While she's talking, Patrick nods his head like those dogs at the rear windows of cars. What I like most about those two is their love.

I'm ashamed of having lied to them, but what else could I do? I can't betray Annette. And since I'm not sure she's resting in peace, I don't want to make any more noise.

My eyelids are heavy, I feel like sleeping. I see the streets of Stockholm again, the frozen canals, Christmas in the store windows, the beer drinkers, the snow. The aroma of those cinnamon buns dunked in the tea served by Magnus and Ada. Their beautiful faces, their tears, too, begging me to persuade Jules to write to them, to see them, to forgive them. And Cristelle, her bottle-green woolly hat still firmly on her head, translating the words, repeating to me, *You're our only hope of reconciling with Jules.*

"Juju, Juju, wake up!"

I was in the middle of a dream. Jules was getting married, I was holding the train of the bride, whose face I couldn't see, and when she did finally turn around, it was Janet Gaynor.

We've arrived. Patrick has parked his car outside Gramps and Gran's. It's already dark. Must be around 5:30 P.M. The light's on in the kitchen, and in Jules's room. Tomorrow I have to do their presents. Just two days until Christmas.

I can't face going into that house on my own. Still half-asleep, I suggest to Jo and Patrick that they come in for a drink. They can't: Jo's on duty tonight, she starts her shift in an hour.

"Justine, I have to tell you something."

Suddenly, Jo looks serious. She never calls me Justine, always Juju. And so Patrick looks serious, too. Those two can't look serious separately.

"What is it?"

"Hélène Hel was taken to the ER last night."

## 53

E dna gives birth to a baby girl on March 30, 1947, at one in the morning. The baby is in the breech position, and labor lasts seventy-two hours. Simon/Lucien never stops holding her hand, lets her bite, curse, scream, sob, plead. As soon as the newborn emits her first cry, Edna loses consciousness. She gives up.

When she reopens her eyes, Edna sees Simon/Lucien beside her bed with their baby in his arms. He's studying the child as if searching for a trace, an impression, something familiar on her face. Lucien doesn't smile at his daughter, he looks questioningly at her.

"Simon, what would you like to call her?" Edna asks.

He replies without thinking:

"Rose."

"Why Rose?"

"It's my favorite smell. I can remember that. It's my favorite smell," he repeats.

A few months after Rose's birth, they move to Finistère, in Brittany. To the Route des Anges in the harbor village of L'Aber-Wrac'h. Where the sea is crazy as hell and washes over everything several times a day; between the sun and the rain, folk lose their minds, running to take cover.

That's what Edna wants. To take cover. Never to come across familiar faces. Or someone who might have received the same letter as her, along with the sketched portrait of Lucien Perrin.

Simon/Lucien has found work in a canning factory. Edna is a nurse at a school. She intentionally kept away from any medical establishment. Because of the portrait.

*When it comes to her daughter, Edna has the same intense feeling as towards her husband, that of having stolen her from another woman. At night, when she gets up to rock her, she feels guilty. She thinks Rose is crying because she's calling out to her real mother. And when her arms don't soothe her, when her gentle words and caresses don't succeed in quelling her distress, she feels like throwing her out of the window, putting her on a train, or in an envelope on which she'd write: Old Louis's Café, Place de l'Église, Milly.*

*Edna preferred it before. When she had just two men to love: Simon and the ghost of Lucien. Since Rose's birth, she has the feeling that Hélène is getting closer by the day.*

*Edna would like to move them even further away. Go abroad. As long as they remain in France, they'll be in danger. She thinks increasingly of America. The place where everything's possible, where there are illegals, foreigners, usurpers, like her. A new language to learn, to speak, to write maybe that's what the man she loves needs to recover. Because he's gradually sinking into a silent depression. He spends hours delving inside his head, empty as it is of a past, by reading and rereading novels he thinks he already read, before his injury. He asks questions to the sitting-room walls: where and when? But silence is all he gets back, and around him, nothing ever echoes anymore. So, with his head full of holes, he goes up to bed. Only Rose can make him really laugh. A true laugh, a noisy laugh that comes from the body, where he still has a tiny reserve of joy.*

*At times, Edna wonders whether it's possible that a man in love might reproduce the woman he loves, feature for feature, with another woman. It seems to her that, as Rose grows, she sometimes resembles Hélène. A crazy idea that Edna carries inside her like some new blood type. Since the birth of her daughter, she's paying in full for her lie. Whereas before, there were peaceful times. Times that were brief but serene. In her nightmares, she sees Hélène again behind her bar, sees again her gaze that lands but never lingers.*

*When she wakes up, Edna doesn't know. Edna doesn't want to know. Doesn't want to remember. She opens the windows and lets the sea breeze sweep away the bad thoughts clinging to the curtains of the room in which she and Simon no longer make love.*

## 54

Hélène is in a coma. Her mouth and nose are hidden behind a complex harness of tubes linked to a ventilator. Her left hand and arm are attached to a drip from which various solutions seep into her veins. Right now, I wish I'd studied medicine so I could save her life.

Rose is stroking her hand. A woman stands beside her. She isn't a member of the hospital staff: she's not in uniform. Roman is sitting at the opposite end of the room, with a lost look in his eyes. When I knocked on the door, he was the one who said, "Come in."

Rose says my name, *Justine*.

The woman looks at me and smiles. Roman stands up and comes over to kiss me. It's the first time he's kissed me. His cheeks are cold. As if it were him arriving from outdoors, and not me.

The woman I don't know approaches Roman. Rose kisses me in turn and says:

"It's so kind of you to come, I thought you were on vacation."

Roman doesn't give me a chance to answer:

"Justine, let me introduce my wife, Clotilde, to you. Clotilde, this is Justine. She's the young lady I've often spoken to you about, who looks after Hélène at her retirement home."

Clotilde smiles at me again. I greet her politely. And yet I long to scream: How on earth can you have such an awful name?! She's exactly as I imagined her: perfect all over. Like some Grace Kelly poster.

I move closer to Hélène. I don't recognize her. If Rose and Roman weren't there, I'd think I'd got the wrong room. That's it: Hélène is old. She looks like the others. Life has let go of her.

I lean my cheek close to her hair. I breathe her in. For the first time, it's dark on her beach. There's no one on it. Neither woman, nor child, nor man, nor towel. It's not cold. The air's even balmy. The sea is calm. Hélène isn't waiting for Lucien and the little girl, eyes fixed on the horizon, or on a romantic novel. She has dozed off. The moon is high. And full.

When I turn around, Rose, Roman, and Clotilde aren't there anymore. They've left the room. Like all those on Hélène's beach. We're both off-season.

For the first time in my life, I feel alone in the world. I would like to die in her place. I would like to leave. To be the first to see Lucien.

I take the blue notebook out of my pocket. I can begin to read the last chapters to Hélène. Or, perhaps, the first.

*"How old are you, Daddy?"*
*Rose asks him this while tweaking his nose. It makes her laugh. She's light as a feather. Lucien hugs her. It's just been raining. The path to the house is one big puddle.*
*"I don't know."*
*She rests her little head on his neck. He feels her breath against his skin. He looks up and watches the birds waltzing around. The gulls are watching out for the trawlers' return.*
*Lucien and Rose have the wind in their hair; Lucien has holes in his head. Clouds that can resemble monsters.*
*"Are you sad, Daddy?"*
*Lucien pulls on his eyes while forcing a smile.*
*"No, I just have droopy eyes."*
*He hoists her onto his shoulders, she holds her little arms out like the wings of a plane, he starts to run towards the door of their house.*
*Running, with his daughter on his shoulders, the wind in his nostrils, the smell of the earth mixed with spindrift, the rain pricking his skin like sewing needles, it feels good.*
*They weren't able to leave for America. The French authorities wouldn't provide them with papers. Amnesia doesn't fit*

*into any box, and Lucien/Simon doesn't exist enough to obtain a passport.*

*Rose's laughter uplifts him. He makes the sound of a plane's engine with his lips, and the two of them all but take flight.*

*When he opens the door, he recoils. Inside, mattresses from the bedrooms are overturned and slashed, cupboards emptied, saucepans and plates knocked over. The bags of flour and sugar have been strewn across the kitchen floor.*

*Rose is too little to understand what's happened, she just repeats what she's heard her mother say: It's a mess.*

*Edna is behaving increasingly strangely. Her crying fits can last hours, and now she frequently disappears for several days at a time. But from that to wrecking the whole house—it's just not possible. Even the skirting boards have been ripped off.*

*An hour later, two policemen find some footprints and explain to Lucien that many houses have had such visits recently. Lucien feels uncomfortable, he can't say why, but he doesn't like the presence of these men in uniform under his roof.*

*After they've gone, Rose has fun picking things up off the floor to help her father. Amid the laundry, the cans of food, and the bottles, she gathers old newspapers to put in the stove. She places them on top of the woodpile because she's not allowed to open the stove door on her own. Lucien cleans everywhere, wiping and sweeping. He likes doing this. Removing the dust. He so wishes he could dust inside his head.*

*Rose goes upstairs to play in her room.*

*Lucien opens the stove door and places a few bits of wood inside. He takes some newspaper, crumples it, and is about to strike a match when he spots the photograph. Of a silver-birch forest. He smoothes out the page. He recognizes this photograph. He was clutching it in his hand when he arrived at the station.*

*Everything suddenly comes back to him. The clinic, Edna's hand, pieces of paper in a cardboard box, his hand hurting from gripping them so tightly, the treatment room, the dressings, a nauseating smell, the coma.*

*He had forgotten about those papers. Where were they? Why is he finding them again in Brittany, in his house, on the day of a break-in?*

*There's a knock on the door.*

*He notices that all the pieces of paper he was clutching at Gare de l'Est have been placed on top of the woodpile. Together. Once more. He studies them, sniffs them. They're from foreign newspapers.*

*More insistent knocking.*

*Lucien goes to open. The two policemen are flanking a young man wearing a cap and a few days' stubble.*

*Lucien suddenly feels dizzy. He holds onto the door. Why does he feel so bad in front of these men in uniform?*

*One of the policemen says:*

*"We've got our thief."*

*But Lucien doesn't hear him. He no longer hears anything. He holds up a newspaper page in the direction of the young man.*

*"Where did you find this?"*

*One of the officers replies:*

*"He was close to the station, trying to make a getaway."*

*"I'm not talking to you," Lucien says, drily, "but to him."*

*Lucien stills holds the newspaper page out towards the young man, who appears increasingly sheepish. With his scarred face and piercing eyes, Lucien is pretty daunting.*

*"Where did you find these pages?" he persists.*

*"It's not me, mister. I'm innocent."*

*The second policeman pulls a gold chain from his pocket. Lucien instantly recognizes it. Edna's baptismal medallion. The pendant—of the Virgin Mary—swings like a pendulum from the officer's fingers.*

*"Do you recognize this item, sir? We found it on the person of this individual."*

*"I never stole it! My mother gave it me!"*

*Lucien stares at the thief. He, clearly uncomfortable, shifts from one foot to the other, sniffing noisily.*

*"That item doesn't belong to me."*

*Lucien's reply surprises the fellow in the cap more than the two sergeants. They press him, in turn, but Lucien sticks to his statement: he's never seen that item of jewelry. It doesn't belong to him. Neither to him, nor to his partner.*

"Justine, shall we go?"

Gramps is behind me. He brought me to the ER. He didn't want me to drive—I was in too much of a panic. I kept shouting: *Why did her heart give up right when I was away for two days? Only two days!* And yet I know very well that residents often fall ill when a loved one is away.

Is it my fault that Hélène has fallen into a coma? Am I being punished for going to Sweden to poke around in Annette's past? For having forced Magnus to talk?

Jules asked me whether my little weekend in Lyon was good. I said, *Yes, really good.* If he knew the truth, he'd probably kill me.

Gramps is standing behind me; he's taken his cap off. Seeing him here, in this hospital room, makes me realize that it's years since I've seen him anywhere other than in his house or garden. He seems embarrassed, awkward.

Between us, there's silence. Broken by sounds from all the equipment.

"How is Madame Hel doing?" he asks me.

"She's in a coma."

He says nothing more, just stares at Hélène.

"Gramps, do you know her?"

"Who?"

"Hélène, do you know her?"

"By sight, maybe. I was small when they rran the bistrro."

It's the first time he answers one of my questions with so many words: eleven.

I open my blue notebook and resume reading aloud as if Gramps weren't there anymore. In any case, has he ever really been there?

*Lucien finds the young thief a few hours later, at the bar of a bistro near the harbor. He seems lost in thought. When he looks up and sees Lucien walking towards him, he presumes he's come to give him a hiding. Instinctively, he covers his head with his hands to protect himself from Lucien's likely blows.*

"*I didn't do nothing, mister.*"

"*Where did you find those newspaper pages?*" *Lucien asks him.*

*The young man starts shifting from one foot to the other again. Why on earth is this guy so interested in those old papers when he's just ransacked the house?*

*Lucien stares hard at him. He won't let him go until he knows. He looks crazy, with his abnormally blue eyes. They're like two colored light bulbs, the sort you get on a fairground carousel.*

"*Behind a skirting board . . . in yer kitchen . . . thought they was banknotes, a real downer.*"

*Lucien pauses a moment.*

"*What's your name?*"

*This guy's definitely weird.*

"*Charles, mister.*"

*Lucien is still staring at him.*

*The young man then rummages in his pocket and pulls out Edna's chain. Reluctantly, he holds it out to him.*

"*Keep it, Charles,*" *Lucien says.* "*For your girlfriend.*"

"*I got nothing at all, mister. Let alone a girlfriend.*"

*Charles puts the chain back into his pocket all the same.*

"*Well, you never know.*"


*When Edna gets home from work, she stifles a cry. Simon isn't the same man anymore. It's as if he's got taller, he's straightened up so much. He's even more handsome this evening. More handsome than this morning when they said bye now, have a good day.*

"*I found some words,*" *Lucien says to her, looking her straight in the eye.*

"*Some words?*"

*Edna is surprised by the very sound of her own voice—flat.*

*"Some words I wrote on these newspapers. Why had you hidden them? Why?"*

*Edna goes to sit down and replies, as though to herself:*

*"I don't know. I don't remember."*

*He hands her the pages that she hadn't burnt. That she should have burnt.*

*"Braille, know what that is?"*

*"Yes," replies Edna. "It's the alphabet for the blind."*

*"I don't know why, but I can read it. And I think I wrote to someone."*

*"Someone?"*

*"A woman with a bird in her mouth. And then there's a place, too. A café with a sign, 'Closed for vacation.'"*

*"Would you mind . . ."*

*She stumbles on her words. Tries to speak naturally, but her heart is beating too hard.*

*"Would you mind reading those sentences to me?" she finally gets out, in one breath.*

*Lucien unfolds the pages with care. He touches the paper as he closes his eyes, and begins to read out loud:*

*"'My love, the first time I kissed you, I felt a fluttering of wings against my mouth. At first I thought a bird was struggling behind your lips, that your kiss didn't want mine. But when your tongue came in search of mine, the bird started to play with our breaths, as if we were volleying it back and forth between us.'"*

*Edna isn't listening to him anymore. He loved her. He was in love with her. Carry on? Take him back there? Stay here with the little one? Without him? Wait until tomorrow morning and tell him the truth: in 1946, I received a letter; "someone" is looking for you?*

*Separate him from his daughter? Return to Milly? Speak to Hélène? See what's become of her? Alive? Dead? Remarried? A mother and in love with another man? Kill her and run away in order to live once more?*

*Does one steal a man like a banknote? Does one go to prison for taking the life of a man from a woman?*

*Commit suicide. And in the letter she'd leave behind, she'd write: Hélène Hel, Old Louis's Café, Place de l'Église, Milly.*

*And my own life, at what address can it be found? Am I living? No. Let him grow old without ever saying a word. In any case, it's too late.*

*Lucien's voice rouses her from her torpor. It's the third time he asks the same question, crouching in front of her to be at her level:*

*"Do you know something about me that I don't know?"*

*"No."*

A nurse enters the room.

Gramps hasn't moved. I can see from the look on his face that he's disappointed that I've stopped reading. With a gesture that's meant to be affectionate, he squeezes my shoulder. His clumsiness hurts me. Both literally and figuratively.

The nurse replaces the empty IV pouch. She smiles at us and glances at the blue notebook that's wide open on my knees.

"You're right to read to her, she hears everything."

The nurse leaves the room. Gramps has sat down in a corner, arms crossed, seemingly lost in thought. As I look at him, I wonder why one falls in love. As someone who spends my days listening to stories, I should know that love can never be explained.

"Carry on reading," he says to me.

*June 1951. Between Milly's railway station and old Louis's café, Edna comes across no one. In the village, a blazing sun silences the scalding streets. All is silence: the trees, the sidewalks, the walls. The shutters on the facades are closed. The sun's reflection on the cobblestones is blinding. As Edna crosses the Place de l'Église, she observes her shadow, almost surprised that she's made of flesh and bones. No one at the terrace.*

*Inside, the café is empty. It's 3 P.M. Nothing has changed since the last time. The main door and the windows are wide open. Not a soul. As if everyone was having a siesta. Only the sound of a sewing machine, a cat's purr. "She" is there, tucked away in her closet, guiding a piece of material under the needle. Edna remains at the door of the café. She'd only have to take four steps forward to speak to "her," or four backwards to return to where she's come from, without saying a thing.*

*A fly brushes against her ear. Perspiration runs from her nostrils to her top lip, down the groove known as "the angel's mark." She wipes it away with the back of her hand while thinking about that legend, according to which we know everything about our life before we are born, but an angel places its finger on a baby's mouth to keep it quiet, leaving its mark above the top lip. Had she known everything, she'd never have let the angel place its finger there, she'd have just given up on this life.*

*The sewing machine has stopped. The dog she saw last time appears, like a mirage. It is panting, with head hanging and eyes half-closed, beaten by the heat. After vaguely sniffing Edna from a distance, it stretches out on the floor, keeping an eye on her all the while. Hélène appears. She's wearing a black dress. Behind the bar, she runs the tap and splashes her face. When she notices this customer standing beside the door, she ties an apron around her hips as she greets her. Have her eyes got bigger since last time? Her face seems engulfed by their blueness. Like Lucien's.*

*"What can I get you?"*

*Edna is still standing at the door.*

*"I know where Lucien is," Edna replies. "He's called Simon now."*

*Edna hadn't planned to say these two sentences. She would have liked to sit down, take her time; the lame young waiter was supposed to be there, she could have just observed, blended in with the other customers, waited for closing time, maybe even for nightfall. But no. Thanks to this heat hitting the region, they find themselves face to face, with no witness.*

*Hélène stares at Edna, whose words are still resonating*

*around the empty café, bouncing off bottles, glasses, cups, tables, chairs, bar, mirrors, the photo of Janet, the pinball machine: I-know-where-Lucien-is-he's-called- Simon-now.*

*Hélène silently studies Edna's fine, red lips.*

*"Here's his address."*

*She holds a piece of paper out to her. She hasn't moved. She's still rooted to the spot, at the café entrance, unable to cross an invisible barrier.*

*Hélène approaches Edna. She watches the nurse as if she might disappear from one moment to the next. She takes the piece of paper, unfolds it, and looks at it, pretending to read it, for a few seconds. Never, ever, would she admit to this stranger that she can't read. She looks up and asks:*

*"How do you know that it's him?"*

*"I received your 'missing person' letter, along with the portrait."*

*"But . . . that was a long time ago."*

*Edna lowers her eyes and her voice.*

*"He was seriously injured. But he's doing better now."*

*"Are you his wife?" Hélène asks.*

*"Yes."*

*Shocked, Hélène reaches for a chair to sit down.*

*"Where is he?"*

*"At our home. With our daughter."*

*"Why have you come here?"*

*Edna doesn't answer. She leaves the bistro and disappears as swiftly as she'd appeared. Swallowed up by the harsh light of the day.*

*At least an hour goes by between her departure and young Claude's arrival. Hélène, sitting on her chair, planted in the middle of the bistro, grips the piece of paper with both hands. The café is still empty. As if no one in the world is thirsty anymore, even though it's sweltering out there.*

*Claude struggles to understand what Hélène is telling him: a tall woman, very thin, Lucien's wife, dark hair, who's called Simon, seriously injured, a little girl, to tell me he's not dead. The heat stops Claude from thinking, understanding his boss-and-friend's garbled utterances. Hélène finally hands him a piece of paper, from which he reads, out loud: "Route des Anges, L'Aber-Wrac'h."*

\* \* \*

*Lucien opens the door. Hélène didn't remember him being that tall. He has changed a lot. He looks like a man now. They were both almost the same age, and now, she realizes, she looks much younger than him. His hair is darker. A deep scar crosses his face, from left temple to right earlobe, distorting his nose. His huge blue eyes stare at her. He steps back a little to let her in, as if he were expecting her.*

*Her legs struggle to carry her. Stupidly, she's dolled herself up, out of vanity. She shouldn't have. She should have known he'd changed, should have known not to wear make-up. That it's no party they're about to attend, but rather the burial of their youth. As she enters this unknown house, where portraits of Rose seem to multiply endlessly, she wonders if the two of them wouldn't have been better off dying on the day of the arrest. Departing with Simon under the bullets of the Boches so as never to live this moment. You could imagine all sorts in the cruelty of war. That your man might return dead, wounded, limbless, paralyzed, insane, nasty, violent, alcoholic, jealous, unbearable, traumatized, disfigured, but you could never imagine finding him in another house, in another life, with another wife.*

*"We know each other."*

*Lucien has just said these four words. She's not sure whether it's a question or a statement. His voice has become a bit husky. She can't quite believe that this scene is real, that she's in front of Lucien, that he never returned because he chose instead another house, another life, another wife.*

*Around her, there are only the objects he must brush against or use every day. She feels like a stranger who has waited too long for an unknown man.*

*"Yes, we know each other."*

*"The seagull, is that you?"*

*"It's mine."*

*He's looking at her hungrily. She feels as if he's caressing her. She's just reliving the summer of 1936, but without them touching each other. A summer going backwards, like in a nightmare.*

*"How did you find me?" he asks.*

*"I didn't want to come, a friend made me."*

*He looks her up and down. She forces herself to smile when every part of her body is actually sobbing, even down to the dress she's wearing, the new shoes pinching her ankles. He stares at her shaking hands, gripping a small blue suitcase that she finally holds out to him.*

*"Here are some belongings. Books, shoes, and the shirts you liked to wear. They may be out of fashion."*

*Lucien takes the suitcase without taking his eyes off her. He is incapable of apologizing to her, incapable of admitting to her that he can't remember her. How could he have forgotten this woman? He had the right to lose his memory, but not this woman.*

\* \* \*

*Usually, when Edna gets home, the radio is on, but not this evening. Rose is trying to open a blue suitcase on the kitchen floor, but her small hands can't quite lift the two clasps. As soon as Edna sees the suitcase, she knows that Hélène has come. She remembers the letter Simon/Lucien wrote: "You'd seen to the provisions, I'd seen to the blue suitcase. I placed it on the floor of our room. The Mediterranean on the floorboards. A blue lagoon full of novels that I read to you."*

*Edna had been waiting a long time for this visit, she thought it would happen sooner. It's already six months, now, since she went to the café to give their address to Hélène Hel, six long months, more than 180 days and nights of dreading. Would he leave with her? Would he recognize her? For six months she'd been preparing herself to find the house empty.*

*Rose seems disappointed by the contents of the suitcase: a few books, some old pairs of pre-war shoes, and three white shirts. Nothing to have fun with.*

*Simon appears at the top of the stairs.*

*"You're not listening to the radio?" Edna asks, stupidly, finding nothing else to say to him.*

*"No, I'm not in the mood."*

*He comes down the stairs to kiss his daughter. Edna is taking a look at the white shirts.*

*"What's this suitcase doing here?" she asks.*

*"I found it."*

*"Strange, the shirts seem to be your size."*

*Lucien picks up one of the old shoes still in the suitcase and puts it on.*

*"Yes, and look," he says, "this shoe fits me like Cinderella's glass slipper. Like in a fairy story, without a fairy."*

*"Why do you say that?"*

*"There's turbot for supper, I'll go and gut it," he replies.*

*He hates fish. Hates eating it, but also gutting it, cooking it, touching the scales, cutting off the head. The smell of dead fish makes him nauseous.*

*Rose copies her father, putting on the other shoe and bursting into laughter.*

\* \* \*

*Claude was waiting for Hélène in front of the Abbey of Notre-Dame-des-Landes. From a stone bench, he watched a bunch of kids playing soccer. When she appeared, the wind messed up her hair and the ribbon holding it flew off towards the sea. As he watched her approaching, he thought about how he'd never fallen in love with her. At the café, the customers had been teasing him for years: Come on, young Claude, admit you're stuck on your boss! No, he loved her the way one loves a great lady, a woman who makes no distinction between scouring the floorboards, sewing, and reading* Le Silence de la Mer.

*He had fallen in love just once, with a customer who had come to the café every Thursday morning for two years.*

*Thursday morning was market day in Milly, and once she had made her purchases, she would come for a beverage at old Louis's café. Her father always had a coffee and she, a grenadine. Claude would put his heart into pouring out her grenadine, and kept her glass hidden in a drawer under the bar. He would wash it separately from the rest, and wipe it with a soft cloth to let as much light into it as possible. While she was drinking, he would stop breathing for a few seconds, too engrossed in watching her swallow the red liquid. He blessed the market days when it was hot: he would keep topping her up for no extra charge until she had quenched her thirst. She would sit at the terrace and he would provide shade with a parasol just for her. She didn't smile at him the way she smiled at others, Claude was sure of it; she was in love with him, too. It showed in the way she looked out for him from the Place de l'Église, before reaching the bistro. She always appeared at around eleven, accompanied by her father. Their time was counted. They would arrive on the 9:45 bus, fill their baskets, have a drink, and then leave on the 11:40 one. Every Thursday, Claude lived twenty minutes of bliss, and that was worth years of marital happiness, he thought. Particularly in this post-war period, when one woke up amazed still to be alive. Once she had left the café, he would live only for the Thursday to come.*

*One Thursday morning, she didn't come, her father was alone. Claude thought she must be unwell. The following Thursday, she wasn't there either. On the third Thursday, Claude dared to ask the father if he should prepare the grenadine for the young lady, to which the father replied, No, Marthe has left for Paris to work for a notary. Claude almost fainted: he was losing her on the very day he discovered her name, which doubled his distress. Marthe never returned to the café, and Claude's Thursdays became just like all the other days of the week. Whether it was fine or raining didn't matter to him anymore. The glass remained in the drawer for a long time, and then, during a spring clean, it rejoined the other glasses up on the shelves.*

*When he noticed that Hélène was no longer carrying the blue suitcase, Claude understood that Lucien did indeed live in the house they had been directed to. Claude had insisted on their coming and her knowing, but seeing her approach, clutching her new shoes and looking so terribly unhappy that her features were distorted, he regretted having done so.*

*The two of them caught the bus back, and Claude didn't ask Hélène a single question. She would end up telling him everything once they were home.*

*During the journey, which took more than fourteen hours, Hélène kept looking up at the sky and saying to him: I don't understand why the seagull isn't returning with me. It has nothing more to do back there.*

\* \* \*

*On the day she returned from Brittany, it was the look in Louve's eyes that saddened Hélène the most. As if the dog had understood that it would never see its master. Hélène dreaded the moment she'd have to face her bed. Since the arrest, she'd always slept in it with the hope of Lucien, a hope that kept her warm. From now on, her nights would be cold, even if Louve did sleep at her feet.*

*Hélène didn't have the heart to empty out the left side of the wardrobe, where all Lucien's things were suspended in time— trousers, shorts, singlets, eau de Cologne. She'd see about it later. For now, she'd open only the right side, where her dresses hung.*

\* \* \*

*That same evening, Lucien put the blue suitcase away, behind the chest of drawers in their room. Edna was annoyed with him about that. In THEIR room rather than in a storage space such as the cellar, the attic, or the shed. He wanted to keep it close to him, that Mediterranean on the floorboards that had been a privileged witness of that other love. In the middle of the night, Edna would hear it raging. Like some creature crouching in a corner, a baleful and cruel creature that would end up drowning her.*

*To reassure herself, she swallowed morphine pills and told herself stories: he didn't leave with her, he decided to stay with me, that's his choice; he looked at me tenderly at 9:05 P.M. the day before yesterday; when he kissed me last week before going to work, his mouth almost touched mine; he smiled at me at supper; ten days ago, he asked me if I was cold and placed a shawl around my shoulders before I even answered. Edna logged all signs of this probable love in her emotional journal.*

*One Sunday morning, a few weeks after Hélène's visit, Lucien opened up the blue suitcase on the bed. For a long time, he just gazed at its contents without touching them. Edna was spying on him, hidden behind the door. And thinking that, when he was done, she'd change the sheets. He then took all the books out of the suitcase, closed it again and put it back behind the chest of drawers. He placed the books on the floor, beside an armchair, randomly opened a first one, then a second, and began to read them one by one, and then reread them every day. There must have been around twenty books. Of which about half were by Georges Simenon.*

*From that day on, barely would he be back from work before returning to his armchair and his books. He had the mindset of an explorer who discovers an unknown planet and searches, at all costs, for proof of former life.*

*From that Sunday on, Edna stopped telling herself stories.*

\* \* \*

Lucien could see Hélène again, standing in the doorway. He could smell her rose scent as she entered the house. A small, graceful woman, with her pale skin, big eyes, and ribbon in her hair. He could see her again, lips trembling, gripping her blue suitcase as if it were the rail of a ship, so as not to be swept away. He could see only her. For six years now, he'd been living alongside Edna knowing nothing about her—for her, letting oneself go seemed forbidden. Everything was held back with Edna, including her hair, which she scraped into a neat bun. Whereas, within minutes, he'd felt as if he knew everything about the Seagull. That's what he called her in his thoughts, since he didn't know her name.

Everything. He had known everything about her as soon as she had entered. That "délicatesse" was her favorite word, that she sang while washing up because she loathed doing it, that she never wiped the glasses, leaving them to dry beside the sink, that she liked to make love upon waking, that she felt the cold, that she ate red apples, that she wore woolen stockings, that she liked the wind, the sun when in the shade, funfairs, peeing on the grass, cycling through puddles, playing jacks, braiding her hair, drinking Suze as an aperitif, the color blue, the full moon, swimming, sewing, laughing, walking, dreaming, silence, creaking floorboards, hot water, face powder, white sheets, black dresses, the scent of roses, bunches of lavender in cupboards, beauty spots, touching things, that she had a sensitive throat, that she caught a cold at the slightest chill, that she got searing headaches and painful periods.

Everything. And yet he remembered nothing. Not even where she came from, or even where they were living. Because he had lived with that woman and, he was certain, Edna knew it. How, he had no idea, but she knew, she knew of the Seagull's existence. Her endless furtive glances betrayed her.

The seagull of the sky was still there, like an old friend, an extra shadow on sunny days. It often settled on the roof of the house and followed him when he set off for the canning factory.

*He didn't like his work, he stank too much of fish. He didn't like his life. He didn't like his ugly face crossed with a scar, which he shaved every morning in the bathroom mirror.*

*Only Rose enabled him to keep going. Rose, and cigarettes— he loved to inhale the smoke, in the evening, while gazing at a fixed point in the sky.*

*One Tuesday afternoon, when he had left work earlier than usual, knowing that Edna wouldn't be home before evening, he took the suitcase out again. He tried on the white shirts, one after the other, while looking at himself in the linen-cupboard mirror. In his reflection, he didn't recognize the man they had belonged to, but he envied him.*

* * *

*Hélène asked Claude to write "For Sale" in black on some white board. With thread, scissors, and ribbon, she made a loop. She hung the sign on the door of the café. Claude asked her if she was sure. What would become of her afterwards? She told him that she'd return, with Louve, to Clermain, to her parents' house. They weren't tailors anymore and had sold their store, but she could always find some sewing work. Claude felt even worse about having taken her to Aber-Wrac'h. He had ended up believing in Lucien's return even more than her. For years, he, too, had thought that, one day, Lucien would walk back into the café and stand behind the bar as if nothing had happened. He had ended up believing in Hélène's belief as if it were his own. That trip had dashed all hope of a return.*

*In Milly, news of the sale of old Louis's café was like a bombshell. Most of the men had gathered outside the door to be sure it wasn't a false rumor: Hélène Hel, THEIR Hélène Hel, was selling THEIR café! They were all there, the old, the young, the retired, the soaks, the employed, the farm laborers, the doughty, the lazy, the veterans, the artisans, the priest, the factory workers, the foremen. It couldn't be so. How could she leave, abandon them like used goods? What would become of them without her? Who would mend their trousers, and, on weekdays, serve them their drinks and food; who would listen to them rambling on, sell them their tobacco; who would take care of Baudelaire, tip their horses for the* tiercé; *who would smile at them the way she smiled at them? They all felt as if they were losing the lifeblood of their mornings, lunchtimes, and late afternoons. Because nothing was more of a tonic than this oasis of bottles in the midst of daily concerns, money worries, kids, women, pay to take home, than pushing open the café door and finding an old buddy to shoot the breeze with. Old Louis's café was the junction where their paths crossed, where they shook hands, chatted about the factory, the deliveries, the livestock, the bosses, the harvests, the latest news. In winter, it was always warm—Hélène herself kept an eye on the logs. And it smelled good in there, whether it was the aroma of the daily special, or the scent of roses. It's not because you get a bit tipsy that you don't appreciate the scent of roses. The radio punctuated the passing time, with the news, with love songs, and, with a cup or glass to sip from, life followed its course, felt lighter, as light as Hélène Hel, that idealized woman, whom you could have lifted on a fingertip, she was that slight.*

*Very soon, a terrible fear gripped the village: who would be the future owner? He'd never have bright eyes, never accompany them home on drunken nights, never darn a thing for them, never keep an eye on the fire, never. Whether victor or vanquished, one loses all wars, but they wouldn't lose Hélène. And what if this "owner" turned their café into a garage, or a haberdashery store? Very soon, the customers spread the rumor far and wide that anyone who set foot in old Louis's café, in Milly, to make a purchase offer to its owner would bitterly regret it (and their body would probably never be found.)*

*No one risked it. And Hélène never knew why no one bought her bistro. It was as if her sign was invisible. A sign she'd had to change three times owing to rough weather and some nasty types who'd torn it down.*

*At the start of 1953, Hélène finally asked Claude to write "For Sale" on the glass part of the door, but it made no difference, she received not a single offer.*

*At first, Claude had written "For Salad", knowing that Hélène would never notice. But then, feeling guilty, he'd wiped the "ad" off with turpentine and written "e" instead.*

\* \* \*

"Justine, it's midnight. We must go home."

Gramps's voice brings me back to the present.

I close the blue notebook after first kissing Hélène. I don't know if she can hear me reading her life.

In the corridor I find Roman, Clotilde, and Rose. I introduce Gramps to them. Roman says to me:

"Janet Gaynor got the Oscar for three films, *7th Heaven*, *Street Angel*, and *Sunrise*. At the time, an actress could be awarded for several roles."

I would have preferred him to say: Justine, I love you and Clotilde never existed, it was a bad joke, and it's not Hélène in this room, it's her double, Hélène's gone trekking in Nepal.

As for Janet Gaynor's Oscar, I already knew about it. I even know that Disney's animators were inspired by her face when creating their Snow White. I merely say to him:

"Goodbye."

It's one in the morning. And, as if the sky were paying tribute to Janet, it's snowing a little. The windshield wipers creak. Gramps drives at a snail's pace.

"Did you wrrite what you were rreading to Madame Hel?"

"Yes."

"It's good."

"Thanks."

I feel like telling Gramps that I wrote it for Madame Hel's

grandson, whom I'm totally crazy about, I feel like telling him that I went to Sweden and Magnus told me everything, I feel like telling him that on The Hydrangeas' roof there's a seagull, I feel like telling him that I sleep with What's-his-name, I feel like telling him that one day I got home early and found Gran dressed as a plumber, I feel like telling him that Patrick and Jo really love each other, but instead I pretend to sleep.

Behind my closed eyelids, the faces of Clotilde and Hélène merge together. From time to time, I open my eyes to look at Gramps's profile, which lights up when we drive through a village or past a streetlamp. I think only of Roman who's married and Hélène who's nearing the end. I think of the emptiness awaiting me around the very next bend. And him? What is my gramps thinking of? This gramps who never says a thing. Of her return?

Annette did return to marry Alain Neige on Saturday, February 13, 1985, at 3:00 P.M. at Milly's church. There were white flowers in her blond hair. That's all Armand saw: a crown of white flowers. He didn't see the beauty of Sandrine, hanging on Christian's arm, didn't see Magnus leading a trembling Annette towards the altar, didn't hear their mutual vows, didn't see Eugénie wiping away a tear, didn't hear Lennon's "Imagine" after the exchange of rings. He spent the day in a field of white flowers attached to some hair.

He couldn't say whether, upon leaving the church, they went home on foot or by car. Whether it was cold or very cold for February. Whether they made the cars sing out by sounding their horns. The grooms were wearing the same outfit. Armand always hated it when Eugénie dressed them the same when they were small. But on this February 13, 1985, he paid no attention to this detail.

They were fifteen around the dining-room table: Armand, Eugénie, Christian, Sandrine, her mother, Alain, Annette, her parents Magnus and Ada, Annette's brother, and a few of the grooms' friends.

Eugénie had asked Armand to push back the furniture. She'd used a white tablecloth for the occasion. Armand said yes, Armand said no, Armand smiled, Armand served glasses of champagne, or maybe it was something else.

They ate the famous seafood couscous. Eugénie had started preparing it the previous day. She had spent part of the night forking through the couscous, like her friend Fatiha had taught her to.

Magnus took a few photos with Christian's Instamatic. And then they danced. First the old ones, who weren't that old, then the young ones, who weren't that young anymore. Christian and Alain had made compilation cassettes for their wedding. Cassettes that Jules still has in one of the drawers of his desk.

When the old ones had sat back down, Alain played Prince's album, *Sign o' the Times.*

Next, they tucked into a *pièce montée* wedding cake, which Annette and Sandrine sliced together. On the top, four plastic figurines, for the four newly weds, stood arm in arm.

Annette removed one of the plastic couples and licked off the cream and caramel under their feet.

In the late afternoon, the slightly tipsy grooms went upstairs for a nap without their wives, who remained downstairs with the guests. Eugénie returned to the kitchen to make a large onion soup. Ada and Magnus helped her. In the meantime, Annette played The Rolling Stones's "Angie" and invited Armand to dance.

During "Angie," up close to her body, he thought, I'm disappearing. There are people who leave, who disappear overnight. I've seen that before in a TV program. During "Angie," he felt her little hand fluttering like a bird inside his fingers. He opened his hand, she escaped. The song was over.

The crown of flowers fell to the floor. Armand picked it up.

Annette started to cry and laugh simultaneously, snot was running onto her lips, she was sniffing and talking Swedish, and Armand had never seen anything as beautiful as that snot she kept wiping away with the back of her hand. Magnus came out of the kitchen, took his daughter into his arms and hugged her. Then she went to the bathroom and locked herself in for a long while. No one noticed, except Armand. Everyone thought she'd gone upstairs to rejoin her husband.

While they were having their onion soup and Alain was telling jokes that made everyone laugh, especially his brother, Armand, in turn, went to the bathroom. Annette had just come out of it. She'd fiddled with some mail-order catalogues and thrown tissues into the small Liberty wastebasket. They were still soaked with tears. Armand stuffed them all into his pocket to contain Annette's sorrow.

He stood in front of the can for a long time. He would have liked to stay there until he died. The two meters she'd just spent an hour in would be his dream tomb.

He lowered his trousers and sat on the still-warm seat. He'd not expected that warmth. The warmth she'd left behind her. He closed his eyes and began to weep.

# 55

1953

It's raining this morning. Hélène's eyes are swollen from grief. It's cold. She covers her shoulders with her shawl. Puts some wood in the stove.

She opens the café door at 6:30 A.M. Looks at the "For Sale" sign. The paint is fading and still no one is buying. She automatically glances up at the sky. She's no longer waiting for Lucien, but for her seagull.

Just like every morning, Baudelaire is the first customer. Over the years, he's become stooped. He looks at the ground as he moves forward, tirelessly reciting his poems as if reading them from the floor.

At seven, the textile factory workers come in for a coffee. They're silent. When they return for their break at 12 noon sharp, they're chatty.

By eight in the morning, they've all gone.

At around nine, the retirees turn up, those who play cards near the stove and then leave at around 11:30, just before the first team of men—who work the 4:00 A.M.-to-12 noon shift—show up.

Hélène switches on the large transistor beside the coffee machine from which Janet Gaynor smiles. She instinctively looks for Louve, then remembers that she died yesterday evening, just after closing time, as if she'd waited so as not to trouble anyone. Hélène knocks into Louve's water bowl, throws it away. She feels as if she has lost a silent little sister. She's hurting.

She hears the ten o'clock train pulling into the station. It's just a gentle five-minute walk away. Travelers are the only customers *who aren't regulars. They sometimes come into the café to warm up while waiting for a connecting train. This morning there are five of them.*

*They arrive at the same time as Claude. He goes up to Hélène and asks her if she's OK. She indicates to him that, yes, she's fine. It was he who buried Louve last night. Now that young Claude is here, she can return to her place behind the sewing machine, in the closet.*

*At midday she's back to help him. It's when most men are in the café. They come and go like on a station platform. There are those about to clock on, and those off home. The retirees leaving for lunch, the farmers, builders, and delivery men stopping for a break.*

*Once they've all gone, Hélène usually opens the doors wide to air the place. The smell of stale cigarette smoke reminds her of the day the Germans killed Simon and took Lucien away.*

*Simon, Lucien's gentle godfather. Behind whom Lucien is now hiding. Why is Lucien calling himself Simon?*

*Hélène has kept Simon's violin, sheet music, and hat, in case someone comes and asks for them. They are stored on a shelf in what serves as her workroom. Sometimes, she attempts to play a few notes, make the bow grind against the strings. The sounds she gets out of it are like the screeches of a trapped animal.*

*She often thinks of Simon's smile. And of what was "written" on his forehead, but less so. It's his smile she wants to keep. She never knew where Simon had been buried on the day he was executed. She was told all sorts of things, and any old thing: behind the church, in a meadow where numerous human bones were discovered in 1949, on the way to the then German HQ, the one she had cycled to, in a ditch on a road below Milly where, apparently, German officers would cover corpses with hydrated lime before burying them. She would have liked to take him back to Poland, among his own.*

*The 1:07 P.M. train pulls into the station. It's stopped raining and the café's facade is bathed in sunshine.*

*Just when she's about to retire to her workroom to finish making a tricky jacket, a female customer keeps her in the café—something about a trouser hem, a husband with one leg longer than the other. Thanks to Hélène's sewing, women increasingly come into the café. And not only on Sunday. And not just young women. In the early years, women would come to the café on Sunday morning, after Mass, to bring in their alterations. But now they come at all hours and take time to sit down and have a drink when their friends happen to be there.*

*Claude puts the chairs out on the terrace: it's mild for October.*

*Hélène crosses the square to escort Baudelaire home—he has a headache. She doesn't like him going home alone. She opens the shutters, airs the place, tidies his kitchen, makes his bed, puts some coffee on.*

*When she returns, she sees it. At first, a white blur. Her heart leaps: her seagull is perched on the roof.*

*Hélène stops moving.*

*On the Place de l'Église, a few meters from the café door, a little girl throws a stone and plays imaginary hopscotch. She hums "Bambino," a song by Dalida: "Je sais bien que tu l'adores, bambino, bambino, et qu'elle a de jolis yeux, bambino, bambino."*

*The child is too young to remember the words, but she knows the tune. She makes up her own words.*

*The sun reflecting from the café windows prevents Hélène from seeing the customers inside.*

*She trembles. Her eyes go from the child to the white blob perched on the roof.*

*"He" is there. He has returned.*

*Hélène places one foot in front of the other until she reaches the door. It's as if she's walking for the first time.*

*Is he just passing through? Has he done eight hundred kilometers to have a drink? Has he come to ask her for an explanation? Has he come for an hour, a week, for good?*

*How she regrets not doing herself up this morning and*

*throwing on this rather worn dress. How she regrets having cried all night over Louve's death and so having shadows under her eyes. How she regrets having such inane thoughts.*

*She takes off her apron.*

*She has imagined this moment a thousand ways: during the day, at night, in the evening, in winter, at lunchtime, on a Sunday, or in summer, but never did she imagine that she'd be outside the café and he inside. That it would be her pushing open the door, not him. She'd imagined that she'd run, that she'd throw herself into his arms, that he'd swirl her around in the air, that it would all burst out: the glory and the joy. Why do things always happen when we no longer expect them to? Why does it all come down to a moment?*

*She goes into the café. Looks around for him. He's seated close to the window, legs crossed, like a customer in his own bistro. He's wearing a black turtleneck sweater and black trousers. He's dressed like a widower when in fact she's there, very much alive. He tilts his head to watch the little girl playing hopscotch, and Hélène notices the blue suitcase at his feet. He's smoking. Lucien never smoked. The sunlight and wisps of smoke surround him like a halo, making the moment even more unreal. He turns his blue eyes onto her.*

* * *

*Since telling the truth to Hélène Hel, Edna no longer worries about that portrait of Lucien Perrin. She has left the school to work once more in a hospital. To return to those who really need her.*

*In room 1, a patient is dying, unlikely to last the night. He's called Adrien Moulin, he's young, twenty-five next month. Edna presses on a pump to release more morphine into his veins. She sees his features relax, almost imperceptibly, or perhaps it's just a figment of her imagination. She traces a sign of the cross on his forehead.*

*Edna watches death take hold of Adrien Moulin without feeling any shame, a bit like those tourists who invade Finistère's beaches in August. His white, waxen skin already shows not a flicker of life, and his clavicles are so prominent, you could cut yourself just brushing against them.*

*Edna has seen plenty of men dying. And even coming back to life, like her man.*

*Late into the night, when she gets home, Edna sits in an armchair beside the stove. She can't face going upstairs to sleep in her bedroom, close to that man and the blue suitcase stored behind the chest of drawers.*

*She waits until it's six in the morning before joining him. She watches him sleep, then lays her hand on his shoulder. He opens his eyes, doesn't immediately recognize her, being too occupied with Hélène in his sleep.*

*Edna says to him, Follow me. Follow me as you've followed me ever since the Gare de l'Est.*

\* \* \*

*On that day, as customers came into the café, they said, It's him, no it's not possible, I tell you it's him, no. And those who hadn't known him before the war asked the older folk, Who is he? And those who had heard of him said that his name was inscribed on the war memorial, that this man must be an imposter.*

*Baudelaire returned to the café, took one look at him, sat at his table and recited his namesake's "The Stranger" to him:*

*"Tell me, enigmatical man, whom do you love best, your father, your mother, your sister, or your brother?"*
*"I have neither father, nor mother, nor sister, nor brother."*
*"Your friends?"*
*"Now you use a word whose meaning I have never known."*
*"Your country?"*
*"I do not know in what latitude it lies."*

*"Beauty?"*
*"I could indeed love her, Goddess and Immortal."*
*"Gold?"*
*"I hate it as you hate God."*
*"Then what do you love, extraordinary stranger?"*
*"I love the clouds . . . the clouds that pass . . . up there . . . up there . . . the wonderful clouds!"*[4]

---

[4] Charles Baudelaire, "The Stranger," in *Paris Spleen*, trans. Louise Varèse (New York: New Directions, 1947).

## 56

G ramps?"
"Hm."
"Which was the best Christmas of your life?"

We're now just three kilometers from Milly. It's taken us three hours to get home from the hospital.

His profile is plunged in darkness. He focuses, rigidly, on the road. It's no longer snow falling on the windshield, but something more like ice.

I sense him stiffening at the question I've just asked him. Then he lets go. I don't know what he lets go of, but I see his shoulders relaxing.

I asked that question to hurt him. To take my revenge. To take my family's revenge. For the sound he never made by keeping his shitty silence. Keeping his love all to himself. I'm a granddaughter who'll forever ruin his life with her stupid questions. And he'll ruin mine because he'll never answer me.

"Could you take me back to the hospital tomorrow?"

"If you like."

Gramps drives into the garage. Jules appears in the headlights.

"Well?"

"Concussion."

Jules takes stock.

"Will she die?"

"I don't know . . . for sure."

I look at Gramps looking at Jules.

"Why arre you still up at this hourr?" Gramps asks Jules.

"I was waiting for you."

"You've got school tomorrrow."

"Armand, it's the middle of the school vacation, and I'd remind you that tomorrow's Christmas Day."

Gramps winces at the mention of Christmas. Then closes up again like an oyster.

Jules gives me a hug. He's at least three heads taller than me.

"Are you sad?"

"No. Lucien's waiting for her up there."

He instantly lets go of me.

"Come off it, no one's waiting for anyone anywhere. It's bullshit, all that. When you're dead, you're dead. Those stories, they're just to reassure people who mess up their lives. There's no second chance, Justine. It's now or never. That's why you need to get going! Need to get the hell out of this hole."

I don't feel like responding to Jules. Don't feel like responding to anyone anymore.

Lucien is waiting for Hélène somewhere, and Roman is married to a ghastly name. But it's only the name that's ghastly; the rest of her is sublime. I don't even feel like writing for Roman anymore because I'm sure he'll make his wife read what's in the blue notebook. And I write in that notebook for no one but him.

"Will you sleep in my room?" Jules asks.

"If you like . . . but I have to finish writing something, so you mustn't bother me."

"What d'you get me for Christmas?"

"I'm not telling you, even under torture."

"I give it less than an hour, and you'll have told me everything."

On December 24, 1989, at 6:00 P.M., Annette, in a wooly hat, told Eugénie that she was just popping out to the minimarket for something.

Eugénie, with her hands in the stuffing, insisted that Armand go with her—in fact, she'd prepared a list for him: *Hurry up, before the store closes!*

For once, Armand didn't look for an excuse to avoid Annette, maybe because the young woman's blond hair, which acted like a lightning conductor on him, was hidden under that hat.

And also it was dark, it was cold, it was the end of a year, a year of trying not to think about her, a year of dreading her visits, a year of avoiding her, of doing overtime at the factory, one more year. He was tired.

Annette wanted to walk there. Armand said no, they'd go in the car. Armand drove off, put the heating on "high." Annette turned the radio on. Changed stations. There was a song by Étienne Daho, "*Tombé pour la France.*"

Annette asked Armand what *tombé pour la France* meant. Armand replied that it was to do with civil action, something heroic, military. And yet, Annette said, the boy singing didn't sound like a soldier. This remark made Armand smile.

Within seconds he thought, I'll kidnap her, I certainly won't demand a ransom, and I'll never give her back to anyone. But he said: What do you need from the store?

She replied, Just girls' stuff.

He felt old. She's a girl, and me, I'm old. And she's my son's wife.

He parked the car.

He couldn't stop looking at the mist coming out of her beautiful mouth, once they were on the sidewalk. The trace of her breath on the cold air.

In the store window, they saw their silhouettes, side by side, reflected on top of the list of Christmas special offers. He thought his shadowy reflection looked younger than him. He thought about how he felt old, but wasn't.

They went into the mini-market, which has since shut down. It's now a garage. Not a garage where cars are sold, no, just a garage where they change the oil, replace parts, check tire pressure.

And so in they went, the last customers. After them, the store would close. Everyone had their Christmas Eve to prepare.

Armand read the list that Eugénie had written on a scrap of gift wrap: cooking salt, whole *champignons de Paris*, Q-tips. Why on earth did she need to buy Q-tips on Christmas Eve?

In one aisle, Armand bumped into Annette, who seemed baffled in front of all the boxes of tampons.

Armand blushed. His wife's sanitary napkins and other stuff were kept at the back of a drawer in the bathroom, and at the back of the cart when they did the shopping.

Eugénie had told Armand that Alain and Annette were desperately trying to have a baby. He had time to think that Annette must be sad. Embarrassed, he about-turned and headed for the condiments aisle. He finally found the cooking salt and paid for it.

As he left the store, Armand said, "Merry Christmas," to the cashier. He'd never said that kind of thing before. He'd never been a friendly guy.

Annette was already waiting for him in the car. She'd hurried to pay for her tampons so he wouldn't have to blush like a fool, once again, at the checkout. She'd taken her hat off. When she saw him approaching, she smiled at him. He didn't want to get into the car. He heard himself telling himself, quit now and run like hell. In front of him, the main street and the church were plunged in darkness.

Armand got into his car. Switched on the ignition, put the heating on "high," threw the bag of shopping onto the back seat. He released the handbrake, blew on his fingers, and kissed her instead of driving off. As he kissed her, he stroked her hair with both hands and slid his tongue into her mouth. Annette's palate, a field of strawberries. He closed his eyes the better to see her. She leaned towards him. Annette's kiss reminded him of those acid drops that explode between tongue and palate, leaving a fruity taste in the mouth. He used to steal them from the twins when they were small.

E dna feels nothing. She's neither hot nor cold. She has caught the 2:03 P.M. train back to Paris. She has just abandoned Rose, Lucien, and his suitcase at old Louis's café.

All is back in order.

From one moment to the next, Edna has become a widow and childless.

The widow of a man who never existed.

A child without a mother is an orphan. But what's a mother without a child called? The mother of a child who isn't hers.

Edna had loved a man she'd borrowed from life. For a few years, she'd flicked a duster over the fingerprints of another woman, but never managed to remove them. Now she's going to serve her punishment.

Strangely, Edna is neither sad nor happy. She's full of air. Like that balloon Rose held on a string at the fun fair not long ago. Empty of feelings.

As she thinks of her daughter's bright eyes, she feels a tear rolling down her cheek and settling on her top lip. Edna swallows it. A balloon now containing a tear.

When she arrives in Paris and steps down from the train, she'll cut the string that's keeping her down here, and fly off far, far away. But only once she's thanked heaven for giving her such a fine present, one day, at the Gare de l'Est.

On arrival at the hospital car park, I look around for it, as I did yesterday. This time, I spot it very quickly. It's perched on the roof to the right, between a window and a skylight. Close by, there are other birds. Birds of all kinds, scattered around the trees, the sky, the gutters, and the roofs.

Visits are allowed from two onwards. Rose is in the reception area. I hope that Roman and his wife aren't. Dear God, make sure I never cross paths with Clotilde again in my life.

Rose is waiting in front of a coffee machine that, judging by what's in her cup, is making tea instead. She smiles when she sees me and Gramps arriving. As usual, to avoid having to exchange greetings, Gramps says he's going to the restroom. Rose hands me an envelope.

"Here, this is for you."

"What is it?"

"A letter."

"What letter?"

"You'll see . . . Roman told me you were writing my parents' story. This letter will interest you."

I slip the envelope into my bag.

"How is she?"

"Still in a coma."

I allow myself to hope. Even though everything suggests it's over. Hélène will return to The Hydrangeas and enjoy the view from her armchair. Roman will return to take my photo, and, for once, my hair will be tidy. Rose watches me dreaming. Finally, she says:

"I'm off. Got to catch my train."

She throws her half-filled cup into a trash can. I daren't ask her if Roman and his wife are here.

I take the elevator. There's an elderly couple there. They're holding hands. I don't know why, but I start thinking about how people cry less when it's an old person who dies. They say, that's how it goes, that's life. So why am I crying?

Just like yesterday, I get out on the wrong floor. I look for a corridor I can't find. I go through swing doors hoping there'll be no Roman behind them, and along endless corridors. There are tinsel garlands everywhere. Under the hospital's neon lighting, they look strange. It reminds me of those department-store cashiers wearing Santa hats in December. In short, some combinations don't work.

I take another elevator and when, at last, the door opens onto the correct fifth floor, I find myself face to face with What's-his-name. He's wearing a white coat. It's the first time I see him smartly dressed.

The pens slotted into his top pocket prevent me from reading his name printed on the hospital badge. I'm so baffled that, initially, I'm speechless.

"Justine?"

"What are you doing here?"

"I'm an intern."

"Ah . . ."

"And you?"

"I've come to visit . . . a friend."

"Are you crying?"

"A bit."

"Are you OK?"

"Yes."

"Are you sure?"

". . ."

"I left you around . . ." he thinks for a moment, "forty messages."

"I'm sorry . . ."

"Was Stockholm good?"

"Very cold."

"If you need warming up . . ."

He kisses me on the mouth and disappears into the elevator. He's just kissed me on the mouth and I don't even know his name . . . First on the hair, then on the mouth. Next thing, I'll find out that we're married.

I didn't get his messages. I don't even know where my phone's hiding. The last time I saw it was, I think, in the drawer of the dresser on which the Neige brothers smile for the camera, flanked by their respective wives.

The woman in room 588 of the hospital in no way resembles the woman whose hand I've held for three years in room 19 at The Hydrangeas. Nothing's left of her, now. Can't even detect her body under the sheet. Since yesterday, she's shrunk some more.

I open the blue notebook. And resume reading her life to her:

*They lived like brother and sister. Hélène slept in what had been their bedroom, and Lucien in another room.*

*Hélène had found Lucien changed. The youthful spark in his eyes had gone. The war's effect on him had been a kind of overall subtraction. She didn't regret waiting for him, but he did disappoint her. She begrudged him for not being handsome anymore and for having forgotten everything. Even the scar he wore on his face like an apology note didn't excuse him. But that way he had of covering his top lip with his bottom lip when reading his paper, that old habit, she adored it. The war hadn't spoilt his gestures, or his attitude. And anyhow, Lucien would always be the one who had taught her to read.*

*And today, he was giving her a daughter. The child she'd so hoped for before the war. That child she no longer hoped for. Hélène hadn't needed to start loving Rose on the day she arrived because she already loved her. When she'd held her in her arms,* she'd recognized her smell, her skin, her breath, her hair, her voice, her fingernails. She'd felt as if she'd always known her. It was like a continuation, a sequel, a part of her, an organ or limb being reattached to her. Hélène had forced nothing, Rose had come naturally to her.

In the morning, they always opened the café at six-thirty.

At eight, Hélène would take Rose to school, making her promise to tell her if the slightest thing upset her. Rose promised.

Hélène would then return and sit behind her sewing machine, while Lucien served the customers. There was always one to tell him how things were before his arrest. And Lucien would listen to men with pitted noses recalling his youth, even though he was still young.

Some customers stopped going to the café after Lucien's return, since Hélène was no longer a widow. Having a drink there had just been an excuse to gaze at her and hope. Others started to view them with disdain. Avoided walking past this disreputable bistro, home to a couple with loose morals. Rose became "the poor kid," Hélène "the tart," young Claude "the lover," and Lucien "the deserter."

When Claude had suggested to Hélène that he should leave, now that Lucien was back, she had said, Stay, he isn't really back. Hélène couldn't have been without Claude: he was an integral part of the café. And thus of her life. In her eyes, he was as vital as the sunshine that came through the windows and lit up the bottles and glasses, the floorboards, the faces, from March to October.

Claude would arrive at ten o'clock every day to help Lucien prepare for the midday rush, when the morning-shift workers all turned up at the same time. Claude was Rose's adopted uncle. He was the one who knew where everything was kept, in the house, under the bar, in the drawers, in the bedrooms, on the shelves, in the cellar, on the work bench. He was the one who knew which floorboard creaked, where the meters were to be found, the cans of oil, the light bulbs, the water main, the keys, the trapdoor to *the attic, the coal, the fuel tank, the weed killer, the spanners, the reserves of beer, Rose's doll's blue dress, and how every appliance worked, where to give that magic little kick to restart a machine. The one who knew the strengths and weaknesses of every wall, floor, pipe, customer, player in the local football team.*

*In the late afternoon, Lucien would go to collect Rose from school. They'd walk back to the bistro hand in hand. Hélène would give Rose her snack. Later in the evening, Lucien would supervise her homework. It saddened Hélène not to be able to do likewise, Lucien could tell, but he pretended not to notice so as not to make her feel worse.*

*They all had supper together. Rose would talk about school, Hélène about her sewing, and Lucien about the customers. Sometimes, their stories would overlap.*

\* \* \*

*Hélène had begun by telling Lucien the basics. The way you might read out the headlines to someone from a newspaper. His blind father, his mother leaving them, Braille, Bach, the marriages, old Louis, the arrest, Simon, the baptism, the names in the hat, the villagers, after the war, the war memorial, the sewing, Louve, the years passing, the celebrations, the waiting, summer on the terrace, young Claude, the fashion changing, Royallieu, Buchenwald, the Dora mines, the Gare de l'Est, the letter, the portrait, Edna's visit to the café.*

*Lucien took her word for it but couldn't remember a thing. He would listen to her telling him about his life, and he liked the tone of her voice, her eyes, the way she was forever wiping her hands on her dress even when they weren't wet. He could see her beauty, but he no longer felt it. Nothing showed him the path to finding her again. Sometimes he felt like touching her hair, her face, just to know. But he'd never have dared. He wanted to re-discover the woman to whom he'd written in Braille on scraps of paper in Buchenwald.*

*Behind the bar, the old routine had come back to him. The routine remembered him, but without him.*

*When it came to intimacy, he had nothing left.*

*He could no longer feel the slightest joy. But he was filled with a profound inner peace. Indeed, that's how he realized that he didn't miss Edna.*

*Quite the opposite. He was relieved. Relieved not to be under surveillance anymore. To escape from her watchful eye. Edna's way of looking out for any traces of "before" had entrenched his fears. Living at old Louis's café had liberated him.*

*Hélène never spied on him, Hélène didn't hide behind doors, Hélène didn't poke around in his things, Hélène didn't search, in his every movement, for something that would betray him. Hélène wasn't scared of him, or his truth, or his past.*

*In time, Lucien had realized how unhappy and scared Edna must have been, knowing that his name wasn't Simon but Lucien. To the extent of abandoning their child.*

\* \* \*

*The thread that linked them hadn't broken, but Hélène didn't know how to reinforce it. So she compressed her stories, made them fit into an increasingly small bag. Until she got to telling him about their intimate relationship. The one they had nurtured in their bedroom, before Simon died.*

*She told him about their meeting in the church, the fitting of the blue flannel suit, the seagull, and their wedding.*

*One evening she didn't say good night to Lucien. She downed a large glass of Suze for Dutch courage, and then took him by the hand. She led him into the café, long closed.*

*Before lighting a candle and placing it on the bar, she told Lucien that she had slept with other men during his absence. Gypsies, fairground workers, traveling salesmen. So they left no trace of their passage. She told him that without shame or regret. It wasn't a confession. She wasn't waiting for any forgiveness from him.*

*He felt no jealousy, no hatred, no hurt pride. He told himself that he, too, had become Hélène's traveling salesman. A man passing through, among others. A stranger who had entered her house.*

*She untied her hair and took all her clothes off. The only light on her was from the candle. Her breasts and her downy tummy danced in the light of the flame. Her hips were wide and her thighs muscular. She had goose pimples and creamy skin. Lucien could see the blue of her veins through that skin.*

*He wasn't passing through, just one among other men. He had been her man. The first.*

*In the café, Lucien's breathing started to drown out the noise of the generator.*

*When he wanted to touch her, she gestured with her hand to stop him. And so he continued to look at her, for a long while.*

*As if relearning her.*

*Lucien did desire her. He felt like licking her, all over, to wash those other guys off her, wash the time that had passed off her, wash the silence, the absence, the abandonment, the forgetting off her.*

*The more he admired her beauty, the more Hélène's eyes shone.*

*She turned around and he saw the nape of her neck, her back, the small of her back, her bottom, and he began to hope. For the first time since the day of his arrest.*

*Hélène saw the sky returning to Lucien's eyes, a brief bright interval. While she kept turning, she told him how he used to caress her, hold her tight in his arms, what he liked to touch of her body, how she would arch her back, jerk him off, read aloud, and make love to him. Summer 1936. And then she put her clothes back on and said to him, see you tomorrow night. Same time.*

A nurse comes into the room, I close the blue notebook. After greeting me, she checks Hélène's blood pressure and temperature, changes her IV pouch, and smiles at me.

I'd like to ask her some questions about What's-his-name . . . but what would I say to her? How can you ask about someone whose name you don't know?

The nurse reminds me that tonight's Christmas Eve. That it's the 24th of December.

Gramps!

I lean towards Hélène to kiss her before I go. I don't want it to be the last time. Lucien can surely wait a little longer.

At the same moment, Roman arrives, alone. He looks wonderful. Sadness doesn't spoil him.

"I've come to read to her," he tells me, laying his coat on a chair.

"Thanks."

That's all I can find to say to him. Thanks. I still have the blue notebook, open again, in my hands. I close it.

"Is that my grandparents' story?"

"Yes."

I go up to him and kiss him on the mouth. He drops the novel he's holding and takes me in his arms. His hands are ice-cold on the nape of my neck. He strokes my hair. I close my eyes. I'm too scared I'll wake up if I open them. Never has anyone stroked my hair so gently; I can feel it growing beneath his fingers. I'm no longer Justine, I encounter a different form of myself. This kiss has the bitter taste of the ephemeral, of the end of a love story. I feel an immense sadness. Almost like a sense of death, of life ending.

I murmur Merry Christmas and leave the room, reeling, without looking at him. I don't want to know if this kiss really existed. I get lost in the corridors and my head goes on spinning for ages before I make it through the exit.

## 59

The jukebox had been delivered that very morning. Twelve 78s. Twenty-four red buttons with the song titles beside them.

There had been quite a crowd in that day. The customers were all fascinated by the way the contraption worked. Rows of flashing lights appeared on both sides when it was activated. So this was progress! You just had to press a number, from 1 to 24, to select a song. Even Claude and Lucien had abandoned the bar to join the customers and admire the choreography of the records.

It's Lucien who had ordered the jukebox. To surprise Hélène. She hadn't been able to read the song titles typed on the labels. But she'd made a discreet marker for herself near the button of song 8, "Petite Fleur" by Sydney Bechet.

Claude had squandered his entire month's tips on the jukebox in a single day. The machine had thrown the café into cheerful chaos because he'd stopped serving. As soon as silence fell, he would run over to put another coin in the slot, and stare, mesmerized, at the record turning inside the cabinet.

By late afternoon, Baudelaire and Claude had almost come to blows because Baudelaire only wanted to hear Tino Rossi's "Maman, la plus belle du monde," and Claude only Luis Mariano's "C'est magnifique." Hélène had resolved it by pressing button 8.

As for Lucien, he couldn't wait for everyone to leave, to be alone with Hélène and his jukebox. Since that first night when she'd got undressed, he was now impatient for just one thing from the moment he woke in the morning: being back in the closed café and seeing her undress by candlelight. Because she'd done so every evening since. And Lucien had watched her shedding her *clothes without once touching her. They never crossed the invisible line still separating them.*

*This evening, he would put on the B side of the Georges Brassens record, "Les Sabots d'Hélène," and invite her to dance. This was the first time he was planning ahead since the Gare de l'Est. At first he had just hoped, and now he was planning ahead.*

*It was strange, living under the same roof as a woman without ever touching her. Hearing the customers and storekeepers calling her "your wife" or "your lady" when mentioning her to him. It was strange having no memories to share with her, having nothing in common but the present, and yet still feeling what she was feeling, knowing what she liked, anticipating her reactions, reading her mind. It was as if some buried emotional layer of his brain had remembered her. Like on the day she'd come to Brittany to bring him the blue suitcase. He hadn't recognized her, but he could recite her off by heart. Yes. That's what Hélène was. A poem learned off by heart, of which he could recall only some rhymes.*

*The customers almost had to be thrown out that evening. And even Claude, who couldn't tear himself away from the jukebox, cleaning it as if it were a thoroughbred the night before the Prix de l'Arc de Triomphe.*

*Now that the café was closed, they'd had supper, and Rose was sleeping, Lucien pressed button 19, again and again. He was singing. It was the first time Hélène had heard him sing. He was out of tune, but he was singing. She lit the candle, started to undress, but Lucien stopped her. This evening, he would undress her. But first, they were going to dance.*

*He popped another coin in the jukebox:*

Hélène's clogs
Were all muddy,
Three captains, they say,
Called her ugly,
And poor Hélène

Was a soul in pain.
Look no more for a fountain,
If you need water, look no more:
With Hélène's tears
Just fill your pail.

*It was on the day of the jukebox that they picked up their thread.*

## 60

The hospital car park was deserted. It had long gotten dark and cold. Gramps had fallen asleep in the car. I watched him through the windshield. And found him very beautiful. His features were relaxed. Was he dreaming? I knocked gently on the window; he opened his eyes and smiled at me in his own way, lightly puckering both brow and mouth. But his mask of grief returned. He started the car without a word.

I looked in my bag for a tissue to wipe my eyes and mouth. I wanted to keep some trace of that kiss. I often look in my bag for things I never have. I came across the letter that Rose had given me at the coffee machine. I read it out loud:

*October 5, 1978*

*Edna,*

*I no longer remember the day you walked out of old Louis's café leaving your bag on the table. I was far too small. And in any case, losing one's memory runs in the family. In fact, it's pretty useful. That day, I must have thought you were leaving us on vacation, my father, your bag, and me.*

*My earliest memories go back to the Sunday afternoons when Hélène would close the café. It was the only day she'd wear make-up and her Sunday-best dress. We'd go for a swim in a river. We'd bring bread and hard-boiled eggs in a basket, and both tuck into them while watching Daddy come back to life in the water. I think I'd only ever seen my father's body stooped and clad in black. Little by little, I was discovering a very tall man with bronzed skin and the beginnings of a smile.*

*At the café, the customers were kind and gave me little gifts. Bubble blowers, marbles, crayons. They brought me sweets, too. Sometimes I would overhear murmured conversations about my father's "absence," and it was Hélène whom the customers called "the boss." But I barely paid any attention. I was the stepdaughter of a seamstress and I wore dresses as beautiful as those of the heroines in fairy tales. I would walk through the village in my princess dresses and invent a thousand-and-one lives for myself. Were you in one of those lives?*

*Until I was ten, no one mentioned you to me. You were silent. But I remember the day when Daddy started converting the attic into a bedroom for me. I said, But are we staying in this house, Daddy? He smiled and replied, Where else d'you think we'd go? He asked me to choose the wallpaper. I picked some with boats on it, sailboats. There's no sea in Milly. And yet I was sure I knew the sea, like an elder sister I'd lost touch with.*

*I have no photo of you. You're like a phantom whose image has never been captured. I did sometimes wonder if you'd ever existed.*

*I suppose that, at first, I loved Hélène the way one does a relation by marriage. But the only time I saw Daddy kissing her on the mouth, I hated her. I ran away from the house.*

*From that day on, they never kissed in front of me again. I only ever saw them loving each other without them knowing it. Although I always called her Hélène and never Mommy, she raised me like her own child. Indeed, I believe she always considered me as her daughter, and not as yours, just as you did. The one she should have had with Daddy if he hadn't been deported.*

*It's young Claude who first spoke of you to me. Young Claude is the waiter at the café. He was born with a limp, but he's the most upstanding boy I know. I've always considered him as a brother who would never lie to me. I understood that Daddy had had two lives, separated by the war. The second in which you hid him. Far away from the first.*

*I never waited for you. Or hoped for you. My parents did everything to make my childhood happy. A childhood full of light, leaving no dark corner for me to sit in and wait for you. I've become an illustrator, and in my drawings there's often a woman in the background. That woman is no doubt you.*

*Young Claude found you again, last Friday. He's been looking for you for years, without ever telling me. Apparently, you live in London, and you're still a nurse. How many children have you cared for while thinking of me? How many hearts have you heard beating while thinking of Lucien's heart? I'm writing this letter to you to tell you that it stopped beating last Friday. On the day young Claude found you again, Daddy moved into a third life that will be neither Hélène's, nor yours.*

*I was there when he bowed out. I'd come to spend a few days with them. I was helping them—a busload of tourists had descended on the café. Daddy was just serving a mint cordial. He fell down and didn't get up again. At first, I thought he'd tripped. Hélène immediately realized that, this time, the love of her life had gone, and you wouldn't be bringing him back to her. For the second time, she kissed Daddy in front of me.*

*The day I lose my father, someone finds you. Life takes away and gives back at the same time. But I don't know what it's giving me back. Apparently, in life, things often go this way.*

*Know that you will never read this letter. I'm putting it into your bag that's hanging on the door of my room. Daddy kept the bag and gave it to me when I turned eighteen. I've never dared open it; that would have been like rummaging in a stranger's bag. Daddy and Hélène brought me up too well. But I left it in my childhood bedroom because the sailboats are still on the walls and one day, perhaps, I'll set sail in one to visit you.*

*Finally, I wanted to tell you that you did well in bringing Daddy back to Hélène. He died happy.*

*Rose*

I read Rose's letter right to the end.

Gramps is still driving. There must be about fifty kilometers still to go. He says nothing. Makes no comment.

"D'you know what happens next, Gramps?"

". . ."

"Gramps, d'you know what happens next?"

"Next?"

"After Lucien's death, Hélène gave old Louis's café to Claude and left to live in Paris."

"And Rose?"

Never have I heard Gramps ask me a question about anyone. Not even whether I'd brushed my teeth when I was small.

"Rose and her son, Roman, found Edna again, in London. They stayed over there for a while."

At first, I don't see his tears. In the light from the dashboard, I see only his profile, and hear him sniffing, discreetly.

When I do finally realize that he's crying, I don't get a chance to say a word: he pulls over onto the shoulder and slumps onto the steering wheel. He is racked with sobs, and his wails break my heart.

Never in my life have I experienced such a tragic moment. I'm staggered. After a few minutes, or hours, I no longer know, I lay my shaking hand on his shoulder.

His cheap woolen coat prickles my fingers. Ever since Jules and I have lived with them, Gramps and Gran have only ever worn cheap clothes. In the old photos, they were far more stylish; I don't know whether it was the death of their children or the life of their grandchildren that impoverished them. It strikes me right then what a hard time they'd had of it.

"Gramps, are you OK?"

My voice seems to hit him like an electric shock. He instantly sits up and mutters:

"You wouldn't have a handkerrchief . . .?"

Once again, I search in my bag, just in case. But I'm not the kind of girl to carry handkerchiefs on her. I always search in earnest, but all I find is a cookie, some crumbs, a lip balm that's down to the plastic, my empty coin purse, and a little Pikachu that Jules gave me when he was small. It's a bag that serves no purpose. I search desperately in the glove compartment, and finally unearth a cloth that, apologetically, I hand to him. He blows his nose noisily, wipes his face.

We're still sitting in semi-darkness in the car. The engine is humming away, totally indifferent to my grandfather's feelings. It starts to rain. He puts on the windshield wipers, then his turn signal, and drives off.

And then not another word.

We've done around twenty kilometers when I dare to ask him a question that I've been dying to ask. I tell myself that now's the time. That never again in my life will the chance arise. Him and me in the car, on Christmas Eve, after a storm, a cataclysm that struck him upon the reading of Rose's letter.

"Gramps, what was Annette like?"

He tenses up, it's almost imperceptible, except to me, his granddaughter.

He moistens his lips. As if his reply were burning them.

"She was luminous . . . I could have used herr as a sourrce of light . . . She liked people who used shorrt sentences."

"She must have really loved you, then."

Silence.

"She loved me."

He said these words as if they were his last words. As if he'd been born to say them now, here in this car, and he'd done just that. If he'd died before my eyes, I wouldn't have been surprised.

He overtakes a truck. Takes ten minutes to do so. He's a real danger to the public. To dispel my fear, I say to him:

"Annette loved Uncle Alain. Jules is a love child. That's for sure. You can tell. You can see it. Breathe it."

He looks at me strangely. I'd even swear he's smiling. Suddenly, I feel as if I'm sitting beside a man I don't know. As if a magician had just switched my grandfather for another man. I

watch him, and everything about him has changed. Since utter-
ing his last three words, *she loved me*, he's looking younger. If it
continues, when we get home, we'll be celebrating his twentieth
birthday.

"Jules isn't a love child, he is love itself. In life, therre's gold-
plated jewelrry, and therre's solid-gold jewelrry. Jules is solid
gold."

At that, I'm the one who cracks and searches for tissues in
my bag. Just in case. But I find my faded Pikachu. And cry all
the more.

I have a vision. Gramps at the morgue, after the accident.
Gramps all alone. Gramps identifying the four bodies, one after the other. Who did he start with? One of his sons? One of
his daughters-in-law?

I see him coming out of the funeral parlor, getting back into
his car, and driving off. How he must have loved us, to return
home that evening. What did he say to Gran when he arrived at
the house? *It's definitely them. The four of them are dead?* And
why didn't Gran go with him to identify the bodies? I can see
him again, the following day, in his garden, burning the wood
of the two fruit trees. His eyes moist, and me a child. *Yourr parrents had an accident.*

"I love you, Gramps."

"I should hope so."

## 61

Hélène threw some gravel at the seagull so it would go, so it would return to Lucien, but it didn't move. The seagull was hers. It wouldn't be leaving anymore.

She finished sewing the clothes that Lucien would wear in the beyond. Summer clothes, in white linen. Front-pleated trousers and a short-sleeved shirt with a pocket to tuck a packet of Gitanes and his baptism certificate into. She picked his favorite shoes, his brown leather sandals.

Hélène turned the café's key in the lock and handed it to young Claude, saying to him: I'm selling you our café for a symbolic 1 franc. Get all the papers prepared at the notary's: I'll sign them on my return, and in any case, since I won't be able to read them, you can take care of them.

For the first time in thirty years, she took out the money she'd saved in a box. The money from her sewing, around twenty thousand francs.

And then she got herself ready. She certainly didn't want to wear a funeral dress. She wanted to celebrate Lucien. She put on her finest outfit, a white silk dress lined with organdy, with little pearl buttons down the back. It was always Lucien who did them up for her. On Sunday mornings, she would present her bare back to him, lifting up her hair and leaning slightly forward. As he did each button up—eighteen in all—he'd say to her, I love you, I love you, I love you, I love you, never stopping until the eighteenth was done. When he'd finished, he would plant a kiss on the nape of her neck.

On Sunday evenings, when he would unbutton her, he always started with the top button, at the neck, and then went down, very slowly, to the small of the back, all the while blowing warm air on the roots of her hair. And as he unbuttoned, he would murmur, Madly, madly, madly.

This morning, she didn't want to ask Rose to do them up. She dragged her standing mirror in front of the wardrobe mirror so she could see her back. She stretched her arms backwards, leaned forward, twisted her wrists, couldn't reach the buttons in the middle. She thought, Now, I am alone. Next, she put on a dab of lipstick, but not too red, to do justice to her sorrow.

Finally, she got up onto a stool, grabbed hold of the blue suitcase, and joined Rose, already waiting for her in the car. It was impressive, a woman having her driving license.

Lucien had never taken his driving test. And yet he'd still bought a Citroën Ami 6, in which the three of them would go on little jaunts on Sundays to amuse Rose. They would set off early in the morning and return at dusk, to avoid being spotted by the police. The car had packed up in the early Seventies, and Lucien hadn't replaced it. He'd said to Hélène, We'll take the train. But they never did.

They had always closed the café on Sundays.

During the journey from the café to the crematorium, Rose told her mother that her ailment was called dyslexia, and that specialist doctors could cure her. It wasn't her eyes that were ailing, but something in her brain that could be re-educated, just like someone with a broken leg who is helped to walk again.

Hélène thought her ailment had a pretty tricky name, and maybe she'd had to wait for Lucien's death to be cured.

Lucien wouldn't be buried in Milly, or anywhere else. A few years earlier, in front of Baudelaire's weed-covered grave in the cemetery, he had asked Hélène to have him cremated, to send him off on a journey for all eternity. Hélène had promised.

At the crematorium, classical music was the only option. Hélène would have liked some Brassens, Brel, or Ferré. She chose some Bach preludes for the period of reflection. She kissed the coffin several times. Not to kiss Lucien through the wood, but *to check that he really wasn't moving anymore. That he wasn't calling out to her. That this time, neither Edna, nor any other woman would bring him back to her.*

*Two men in dark suits took away the coffin. Inside it there was Lucien in summer clothes, and Simon's hat and violin, Simon who hadn't been entitled to a funeral. And since Lucien had been a kind of Simon in Edna's life, Hélène had thought it only right.*

*On that day, Rose didn't call her Hélène, she just whispered Mommy as she stroked her hair.*

*Hélène waited in the crematorium garden. It was a sad place, with poorly trimmed and, in places, jaundiced box trees. As if the earth were keeping to the bare minimum so as not to offend the bereaved with pretty flowers. And then there was Rose. She was much taller than Hélène, who sometimes wondered why, and then remembered that she hadn't brought her into the world.*

*"Being sterile doesn't surprise me," Hélène had said to Lucien on her return from the doctor's after the thousandth attempt to have a second child. "A woman whose eyes can't read can't have children. In humans, the stomach functions along with the head. If my stomach is like my eyes, it must do everything all wrong." Lucien hadn't responded because, when Hélène was certain, she was certain. He couldn't teach Braille to Hélène's stomach so she'd give him a son.*

*One of the dark-suited men handed her the urn containing Lucien's ashes. Hélène thanked him and put the urn into the blue suitcase. Rose said nothing. Asked no questions. She watched Hélène putting her father into the suitcase, and just wanted to get back on the road to take it back to Milly. Hélène refused. She told her that she was setting off on a journey with Lucien. That from now on, old Louis's café belonged to young Claude.*

I dozed off over the blue notebook. I still have my pen in my hand. Jules has just got back from the Paradise. He stinks of alcohol and smoke, and collapses down beside me. I'm almost ousted from my own bed.

"Fuck's sake, Jules, you're a pain in the butt!"

I was just dreaming. I was walking on Hélène's beach. She wasn't there. I'd come across Roman, in a white coat, and he was telling me that Lucien had come to collect her. Above our heads, a seagull was wheeling as Roman took me in his arms. He was going to kiss me . . .

Jules puts a wrapped gift on my tummy.

"A guy gave me this present for you. At the Paradise."

"Who?"

"Your guy."

"I don't have a guy."

"Well, yes . . . Your guy, you know, the doctor."

"How d'you know he's a doctor?"

"Well, he told me."

"You were dancing and he just told you that? *Hi, I'm a doctor.*"

"No. He was waiting for you in the car park."

"He was waiting for me?"

"He actually gave me a lift home, I was wasted. He's into you, for sure."

Jules lets out a kind of groan. Turns on his side and is instantly snoring. I try to rouse him with a shake, but nothing doing.

I feel the weight of the package. Carefully, I tear open the wrapping paper. It's very pretty, looks like velvet. It's covering a square box, much larger than a ring box, about thirty centimeters. I lift the lid and discover a little seagull of white gold, hanging on a chain.

No one has ever given me such a lovely present. After all his questions, What's-his-name knows a lot about me. I race down the stairs four at a time, barefooted. I must find my phone to call him, thank him, understand. It's about time that I, in turn, ask him some questions.

In the dining room, the clock tells me it's 7:00 A.M. Gramps and Gran are still sleeping. That's rare at this hour, but last night they went to bed at midnight, since it was Christmas Eve. No leftovers on the table. In the kitchen, everything's spick and span. Gran has never gone to bed thinking she'll clear up tomorrow. The first time I discovered that you could clear up the following morning was at Jo's place. And I was nineteen.

Last night, it was just the four of us celebrating, as usual. We've never had friends round. Gramps and Gran, because of their sadness, no doubt, their whiff of tragedy. Me, because no friend wants to hang out with an old-fashioned girl who never lets go of her little brother.

Jules and Gran were waiting for us in front of the small, artificial Christmas tree, which we fetch from the cellar every year. We no longer even bother to remove the decorations from one year to the next. We shroud the tree in a kind of fishing net, one that's never been near the sea, before putting it on a shelf. Then, on the morning of December 22, Gramps brings it up from the cellar and unfolds it. From time to time, we change some tired tinsel. Gran wipes the baubles with a sponge, brushes down the plastic branches, and then sprays the lot with air freshener. The magic of Christmas like in the movies? Not at ours.

When we'd got home from the hospital, Gran was watching a variety show with all the participants dressed as Santa, and Jules was playing solitaire on his phone. Gran immediately clocked that Gramps wasn't his normal self. That he was in a state. She must have put it down to me and Hélène, and the afternoon spent at the hospital, and all those bad memories.

The canapés she offered us had almost melted, the house was so warm. The thermostat was pushed to the max. As was the sparkling wine I forced myself to drink in large gulps. Jules told me I seemed strange. I said no. But I thought to myself that, now, I would always seem strange. I knew things that everyone else didn't. I felt as if I were ahead of the years, of time. Jules resembled Annette who resembled Magnus. That resemblance

244 · VALÉRIE PERRIN

had doubtless saved his life. Had prevented him from asking the wrong questions, or the right ones. Daddy and Uncle Alain had kept their resemblance for themselves, without passing it on. To the great displeasure of Gran, who had waited so long to see it on our faces. Especially on Jules's. And now I understood why.

Did Mom know this secret? Had Annette told her about it? What would have happened if Annette hadn't been killed? The answers of recent weeks have prompted new questions. It will never end.

Gran handed me my present as though she could read my thoughts—a gift voucher for the Fnac bookstore. The same thing for Jules, and a Carrefour gift voucher for Gramps. Since Gran discovered electronic gift cards, she's in seventh heaven. This twenty-first-century invention must have speeded up her recovery.

I drank another glass of sparkling wine and felt a little drunk. It did me good. I even started to chuckle at Jules's slightest dumb joke. Next, we had a hot meal. Even though what was on our plates was supposed to be cold . . .

I rummage in every drawer of the dresser. I finally find my phone, tidied away by Gran on top of a leaflet in Chinese or Japanese dating back to 1975. Why do my grandparents throw away absolutely NOTHING?

I close the drawer, which is just under the Neige brothers' wedding photo. How does Gramps feel when he passes it? Does he pass it, or does he do a detour, via the kitchen, to avoid it?

While my phone is recharging, I take a shower. This early, I can relax. At ours, there are two bathrooms—well, bathroom is a grand word. An old shower stall downstairs, in the laundry room, and a bathroom upstairs. If you're unlucky and turn on the hot tap downstairs while someone's having a wash upstairs, all you'll get is a trickle of water.

I come out of the shower, pull on some clothes, and listen to my messages. What's-his-name didn't lie to me. He left me forty messages. And he never says his first name—now I'm sure of it: he's doing it on purpose.

What's-his-name called me every day, several times a day. His messages are funny. Sometimes he sings, sometimes just tells me that he's having a coffee, that it's raining, that it's cold, that he's put on a red sweater that I'd hate, that he passed a florist and thought of me, that he, too, has a brother, that he'd like me to meet him, that he's on duty, that if I catch a cold he'll look after me.

He left the last message three hours ago:

"Justine, I was on duty tonight. I'm off to the Paradise. Shit . . . I'm hoping to end the night in your arms . . . If not . . . Merry Christmas."

## 62

It was the first time Hélène was in Paris.

Outside the Père Lachaise crematorium, before getting into the taxi, she kissed her daughter and gave her a letter for Edna, in case she went to see her in London. As she handed over the envelope, she explained that she'd dictated the letter to Claude that very morning.

Inside the envelope, there was a blank sheet of white paper, as Edna would discover a few weeks later. Rose took the envelope without a word.

Hélène felt it wasn't by chance that Claude had found Edna in London on the day Lucien died. It meant that Rose must go and visit her, over there. Hélène's letter would pave the way for Rose.

Hélène then said to the taxi driver:

"To the airport, please."

"Which one?" asked the driver.

"The one from which planes fly to hot countries with sea."

Between the crematorium and the airport, with her blue suitcase and savings box on her knees, Hélène sang Lucien's favorite song:

Hélène's clogs
Were all muddy,
Three captains, they say,
Called her ugly,
And poor Hélène
Was a soul in pain.
Look no more for a fountain,
If you need water, look no more:

With Hélène's tears
Just fill your pail.

*"You sing really well."*

*The sky was gray, overcast. It was autumn and Lucien had just died. The sun would now only rise for others, she thought to herself.*
*The driver asked her where she was from.*
*"From Milly," Hélène replied.*
*"Where's that then?"*
*"In the center of France."*
*"The food's good around there, isn't it?"*
*"Depends who's cooking."*
*On arrival at the airport, the taxi driver turned up the volume on the radio and swore:*
*"Fucking hell, Brel's dead!"*
*Lucien adored Brel. Hélène told herself that, since they'd died almost together, they stood a great chance of meeting up above, and must be waiting in the same line at the gates of heaven.*
*In recent years, Lucien would intoxicate their few remaining customers with music from his jukebox more than with alcohol from the bar. Brel, first and foremost: "Fernand," "Mathilde," "Frida," "Madeleine," "La Fanette." In the latest jukebox, there were a hundred singles, of which fifteen were by Brel.*
*Lucien would say to her, "My darling, what would all those names do without him? There's no one who can say names like Brel."*
*He called her my darling. And she called him Lulu.*
*One morning in 1954, when she was busy at her sewing machine, Lucien had come into her workroom to look at her, simply to look at her between serving two customers. She had looked up at him and said, I really love you. He had replied, I know. I lost my memory but not your love.*
*Planes were taking off and landing.*

Hélène asked the taxi driver to wait for her, she wouldn't be long.

"You're going to collect someone?"

"No, I'm accompanying my husband, will you wait for me?"

She took a hundred-franc note out of her box. The driver said that, at that price, he'd wait for her until the next elections.

"Oh, you know, I know nothing about politics, me, I just serve pastis and make dresses."

"Well, they must be really beautiful, your dresses," the man replied, still eyeing the banknote.

She got out of the taxi, her little blue suitcase in one hand and her box under her arm. She stared at the big departure boards, at the destinations, the names of distant capitals she would never visit, and, since she saw all the letters jumbled up, read the names of cities that would never exist.

Lucien had explained time differences to her. When they were going to bed, others, on the other side of the world, were getting up. He had also told her that there are more stars in the sky than grains of sand in the Sahara. She'd loved him for that, for all those things he'd taught her, that little girl from the dressmaker's, doomed never to know a thing if she hadn't met him.

She asked a traveler if he could see when the next flight was leaving for a hot country with sea, saying she'd forgotten her glasses.

Lucien had never succeeded in obtaining a passport. In the eyes of the French authorities, he was stateless. For them, Lucien Perrin had been deported to, and then killed at, Buchenwald. He had returned to Milly far too late to get his death certificate canceled at the public records office. What mattered now was that he should depart with his baptism certificate in his pocket. For Hélène, that was worth all the passports in the world.

Lucien had died twice. The second time, he'd decided to leave on his own. While serving a mint cordial to a young boy who could barely see over the bar. He hadn't even had time to pop the ice cubes into the glass. He'd barely poured in the cordial when his heart stopped.

*Hélène purchased a random plane ticket. She took out her own identity papers. Hélène Hel. She glanced at the photo before handing it to the attendant. It was strange how much Rose looked like her. Lucien must have loved her to have produced a child that looked like her with another woman.*

*"Would you like a round-trip ticket?"*

*"No, one way, thank you."*

*A little later, Hélène gently placed the blue suitcase on a conveyor belt.*

*"That's your only luggage, madam?"*

*"Yes."*

*"Have a good flight."*

*"Thanks."*

*Hélène watched the blue suitcase disappear into a dark tunnel.*

*When she got back in the taxi, the driver asked her where her husband was. She replied that he'd set off to see the world.*

*"Why aren't you going with him?"*

*"I'll be joining him later."*

## 63

Rose phoned The Hydrangeas yesterday evening. Hélène's condition is stable. That's what she said, "stable." I heard "seagull."

When I got home, the intro music of *Cinéma de minuit* was blaring from the sitting room, so I rushed in to watch. I've never seen anything as beautiful as that intro, with all those actors' faces in black-and-white appearing and then disappearing.

I curled up on the sofa opposite Gramps, who barely noticed me, and I cheered when I saw the title of the film that was starting, *Small Town Girl*, with Janet Gaynor. Gramps looked over at me.

"What's got into you?"

"Nothing. It's just that I know Janet Gaynor well."

He stared at me a moment, before returning to his black-and-white realm. Half an hour later, he was asleep. I thought to myself that he watched old films to have better dreams, to go to where he felt like going.

I couldn't take my eyes off the screen, and wondered whether Hélène and Lucien had ever seen a movie starring Janet Gaynor at the cinema.

I slept badly. I know that it won't be long before the phone rings. That I'll soon be told that Hélène is dead.

In France, we struggle with that word; at The Hydrangeas, we're not allowed to say it. The residents often refer to death with flippancy: kicking the bucket, croaking, snuffing it, pissing off, biting the big one, pushing up the daisies, being closer to Saint Peter than to Saint-Tropez. The nursing staff have to use dignified terms: disappearing, departing, passing away, leaving us, falling asleep peacefully.

As usual, Hélène does things gently. She has never liked drawing attention to herself. She couldn't have died dramatically. She's leaving quietly, on tiptoe.

Gran is waiting for me in the kitchen, with all her hair-setting products. Gramps has just gone out to get filters from old Prost's store. The coffee-filter box was almost empty. He can't stand almost-empty boxes. At ours, everything is doubled up: coffee, sugar, oil, vinegar, mustard, salt, soap, toothpaste, shampoo, matches, butter, flour. Everything goes two by two. We must never go without. It's an obsession.

I set Gran's hair. She notices my pendant. Tells me it's pretty. Asks who gave it to me.

"What's-his-name."

"You could make an effort," she retorts.

Her remark makes me smile. I part her fine hair with the comb, and roll it up on the multicolored curlers. I'm struggling to concentrate. I haven't phoned What's-his-name to thank him. After listening to all his messages, I pressed callback and, at the second ring, hung up. I'm terrified at the thought of being desired by someone. And if I did call him, it would be like making something official.

Gran intrudes, abruptly, on my thoughts. And "abruptly" is an understatement.

"Yesterday, while cleaning your room, I found your plane ticket to Stockholm."

I feel my face flushing, my hands go clammy. I struggle to roll her hair onto the curlers. I should have burnt that blasted ticket in the stove as soon as I got back. And yet I'd hidden it really well in my room. With her and her cleaning habits, any secret hiding places, any semblance of privacy, don't stand a chance.

"I threw it away. I presume you didn't want to keep it."

"No."

"Can you imagine if Jules had come across it?"

"Yes."

"Did you see them?"

"Yes."

"Both of them?"

"Yes."

Silence.

"You're pulling my hair now."

"Sorry."

Silence. A very long silence. I've finished putting in the curlers. I place the hairnet over her head. A curler drops onto the spotless tiled floor. I pick it up and roll a final strand on it. I fetch the dryer, under which she usually dozes off. But I sense that this morning, its warm air won't send her to sleep. I sense that she's watching me. She'd like to know what Magnus and Ada told me about Annette, about Jules. I can feel her eyes on me.

I can't say a thing. Because I don't know whether she knows, or what she knows.

Who, when passing our little house, with its vegetable garden, shed, and cement wall, could possibly imagine the secrets she holds in her poor head?

I set the thermostat and drying time. Twenty-five minutes under the dryer. Relief. I have twenty-five minutes to come up with a lie worthy of the name. But I can't think of one. I'm on my third cup of coffee when the alarm warns me that the drying time is up. It gives me a start. Just as I thought, she's not asleep. Usually, when I remove the dryer, she's gently snoring, head tilted forward and mouth half-open. But this time, she's looking, questioningly, at me. I remove the hairnet, and then the curlers, one by one. I fetch the boar-bristle hairbrush and use it as best I can, in silence. But she persists:

"Jules looks like Magnus, doesn't he?"

"Yes, like two peas in a pod . . . I went to see them on an

impulse. To reassure them. Tell them that Jules is happy with us. That he's doing his bac and going to Paris next year."

I know she knows I'm lying. So I come up with something else:

"Jules told me he'd like to do an architecture course that's really expensive. I went to see them to ask for money."

Gran's face changes color, verging on crimson.

"You went begging to the Swedes!"

"I wasn't begging, I'm protecting Jules, that's all."

Gramps comes into the room. Silence descends. I implore Gran to keep it shut, as she does me. This time she believed me. I can see from her expression that she believed me. All the coffee filters in the world couldn't hide the reproachful looks she's throwing at me. I hope she's not going to go off and commit suicide.

Gramps looks at us both, sniffs, puts away the coffee filters, and goes to the tap for a glass of water.

"I've told you a hundred times not to drink tap water, it's full of muck," Gran snaps at him.

Gramps looks at her and is about to say something, but then holds back. How many words has he swallowed? He turns his back on us and leaves the room.

I don't let Gran get a word in. I do a Gramps, saying I'm going to be late for work, and I beat it.

I'm almost an hour early. I stop off at the cemetery. I'm standing in front of the tomb of my childhood. I don't think I'll come here anymore. I think Jules is right. I have nothing more to do here.

My phone vibrates in my pocket. I presume it's What's-his-name. When I've not even had the courtesy to thank him for the pendant. I find potential emotions crippling. Only things that can never exist interest me.

I decide to answer him, because right now, at twenty-one years old, standing in front of my parents' tomb, I'm finally going to allow myself to be potentially "happy" with a real person who's under thirty years old. But it's not What's-his-name's number that's displayed, it's the landline at home.

"Hello?"

"It's me."

"Gran?"

## 64

Night of October 5–6, 1996

Eugénie woke up with a dry mouth. The previous day, she'd been a bit heavy-handed with the salt. Had salted the couscous twice. She'd been rattled that day because the washing machine had packed up. She'd had to force open the door—water had flooded onto the floor—and wring out the washing, item by item, in a basin. The repairman couldn't fix it. The machine was a write-off. So, with all this stress, she'd over-salted the couscous stock. In fifteen years, that had never happened to her.

She didn't usually wake up during the night. But since the twins and grandkids had come for the weekend, she'd heard Jules crying twice. He'd lost his pacifier. She wasn't that keen on pacifiers for babies. Had never given them to her sons. Christian had sucked his thumb and Alain the end of his cuddly rabbit's ear. She'd made the rabbit disappear on the day Alain was three. He'd hunted for it everywhere. She'd told him that Doudou must have gone back to the forest to find his mommy. It was just too smelly, despite frequent washing, and it was time Alain slept without it. She'd wrapped it in a plastic bag and then thrown it into the neighbor's trash can one night before going up to bed. She'd almost gone back down to retrieve it during the night, but Armand had fiddled with her left nipple, so she'd had to fulfill her conjugal duties. She'd fallen asleep, with Armand's breath on her nape, until she was woken by the garbage truck at 5:00 A.M. Too late, Doudou was gone.

The time had flown by. Dazed with exhaustion for the first

few years—barely would one twin drop off before the other one woke for his feed—she had let the shopping, washing, cooking, and cleaning get on top of her. Childhood illnesses had been multiplied by two, with a couple of days between them. When one had chickenpox, the other one would catch it two days later. There were a few summer Sundays when she'd felt truly happy. And the boys had grown like the two fruit trees Armand had planted in the garden on the day they were born.

She'd given them all the attention and care that two children need. All except for tenderness. She'd never learned that stuff, the kisses, the cuddles, the soothing words. She'd never known how to show affection. Never known how to love, to put love into her gestures the way one puts salt into one's cooking . . . Sometimes, too much.

And yet on evenings after school, when they came home ravenous, she would have liked to smother them with hugs, swallow them up whole, but she never did. She'd been reduced to just wrapping them up warm to compensate for her coldness as a mother. She, the farming girl, the eldest of seven children, "the only boy in the family," as her father would say. A beast of burden who could do everything: the cooking, the cleaning, looking after her little brothers and sisters, the machinery, the animals. Who could do everything but kiss.

She'd never managed really to love her sons. Her heart had always been cold. But at the birth of her grandchildren, something like love had happened, a kind of magic had taken place. She came close to caressing them.

She couldn't hear his breathing. She reached over Armand's pillow was cold. She opened her eyes in the dark. Switched on her bedside lamp. Squinted. The alarm clock showed 1:00 A.M.

She pulled on her socks. Had always hated walking barefoot. She went downstairs to the kitchen for a glass of water. Not tap water: she'd always hated the smell of chlorine. She poured some mineral water into a glass—she'd never drunk from the bottle, either. She was one of those women who wipe their glass with the back of their hand when eating out—which she did once a year, at the Christmas dinner at Armand's factory.

Before leaving the kitchen, she threw the washing machine a dirty look.

She'd met Armand at a dance. When he'd approached her to invite her to dance, she'd thought he must be mistaken. It couldn't be her that this man wanted to hold in his arms. She was wearing a dress her father had given her for her twentieth birthday. Her first dress, red with white polka dots. Femininity was a stranger in her life. One that would never cross the threshold. She had tried to put make-up on a few times, but her skin had rejected the colors, turning the powders into tacky streaks. She had always known that she was inferior to Armand. Inferior in every way: he was a very handsome man, she was plain; he was intelligent, she was uneducated; he was no handyman, she could repair anything; he wasn't friendly, she was easy-going. But she had finally understood that he had chosen her at the dance because she was one of those women who ask no questions. Who spin silently. One of those women who don't give men a hard time.

On the day of their wedding, she'd been proud to hang on his arm. She'd almost regretted not having any friends to make jealous. But the honeymoon night had been shocking: she wasn't prepared for it, she knew nothing. She'd seen animals mating, but she'd not seen the pain. Her mother had never told her a thing, except that, to be a good wife, she must do whatever her husband asked her to do. On that night, Armand had torn her insides. And he'd done it again and again, every evening, until her genitals, her thigh muscles, and her insides got used to it and no longer caused her pain.

She'd thought of that saying: *beauty can't be eaten as a side salad.*

The birth of the boys had been so painful, she'd promised herself never to go through it again. She'd produced no more children. The truth is, she hadn't liked being a mother.

Then, through television and women's magazines, she'd learned that one could orgasm when making love. She told herself that all that was for other women, pretty women. Until she discovered masturbation while flicking through the novel *Histoire d'O*, lent to her by her neighbor with some other books. Until she grew to like those nights up close to her husband, her big man.

She'd had just one friend, Fatiha Hasbellaoui. She'd met her when she'd worked at the village doctor's, when the twins were teenagers. Fatiha did the cooking and laundry there. She lived in, with her own room above the one for consultations. It was Fatiha who'd taught her to make seafood couscous. She, too, who had taught her to roar with laughter while savoring the crescent cookies and the stories she brought back from Algeria. As far back as Eugénie could remember, the three best years of her life had been those when she was doing the cleaning at this doctor's, particularly in the morning, when she'd sit at the kitchen table for a cup of tea, and Fatiha would tell her about the men, the women, the life "over there," with some belly dancing thrown in. With Fatiha, she'd had women's conversations such as she'd never had with the other girls at school because she behaved like a tomboy. Fatiha had spoken to her of love, sex, fear, contraception, feelings, freedom—nothing was taboo.

But the doctor, who loved the sun more than anything, had upped sticks to the south of France, taking Fatiha with him. Eugénie would have gladly followed them. The doc had suggested it to her and she'd spoken about it to Armand, who had laughed in her face: *And we'd live on your cleaner's pay, over there?* The departure of her boss and her only friend had plunged her into despair, and loneliness, for a long time. She'd found no more work after that. The textile factory had long stopped hiring. No wonder, given all the "Made in Taiwan" labels inside garments.

Fatiha would phone her every New Year. Eugénie would

respond cheerily to her *Happy New Year, Nini!* But until the birth of her grandchildren, every morning, every day, every week, every month, every year had resembled each other like peas in a pod. From one day to the next, only one thing changed: the clothes that she wore.

As she goes back upstairs, she almost slips. She puts too much polish on the wood. Armand says the house is a skating rink.

She hears some noise coming from Alain and Annette's room. Maybe Annette has got up to tend to Jules. Wretched pacifier.

When she opens her own bedroom door, she gets a start: Alain is sitting on the bed. He doesn't move. The last time she'd found him in her room, he must have been twelve or thirteen years old. He had mumps and was really suffering with it. He was crying and burning with fever. She hadn't been able to muster the tender gestures, the comforting he would have needed.

"What are you doing here, son? What's up?"

Alain doesn't reply. His eyes are vacant. He stares for ages at the wall opposite, the one on which all the family photos hang.

She switches on the ceiling light. Asks him if he'd like something to drink. He's white as a sheet. He's sitting on the edge of the bed as if on the edge of a precipice. She's never seen her son in that state. Of the two boys, Alain is the more cheerful, the more enthusiastic, the more talkative. Alain is her darling, her sunshine, the one who waltzes her around as soon as he steps through the door. As for Armand, he's always had a soft spot for Christian, who is more withdrawn, calmer, less outgoing. Alain is the elder of the two. Armand says he must have successfully negotiated the finishing line with his brother.

Eugénie moves closer to him, touches his forehead, then his hands. They're freezing cold. She covers his shoulders with a shawl. A strange sight. Her big son Alain in a T-shirt with "Nirvana" written under a photo of a blond youth, striped shorts, and a flowery shawl, draped around his shoulders. He seems traumatized. As if he's just seen a ghost. Then, robotically, he stands up. Before closing the door behind him, he turns back to his mother and mutters:

"So you never saw a thing, Mom?"

She doesn't understand. Saw what?

She follows him into the corridor. She sees him going into his room and closing the door behind him. She stands there, in front of the closed door. She daren't knock. Daren't go in. And anyhow, Jules and Annette are sleeping in there, they mustn't be woken.

Where is Armand? He must have had insomnia and gone off for a walk. That's happening to him more and more. He's changed. He suffers from insomnia and depression.

She gets back into bed, but doesn't go back to sleep. She sees her son again, sitting on the bed, wild-eyed. And yet he seemed OK last night. He made them laugh. Bounced Jules on his knees. Is he worried about his work? Does he regret giving up his half of the record store to his brother, to go and live in Sweden? Is he anxious about being apart from his brother for the first time?

*So you never saw a thing, Mom?*

No. She's not asking herself the right questions. She can't think straight. You don't look like that over concerns about work or moving. He's seen something he shouldn't have seen.

*So you never saw a thing, Mom?*

Armand returns to their room at 4:00 A.M. What's he been doing from one to four in the morning? She closes her eyes, doesn't move, holds her breath. He lies beside her. His body is burning hot. He hasn't just come in from outdoors.

"Where were you?"

Armand doesn't answer. Turns his back on her. She switches on the bedside lamp and looks at him. He's wearing a shirt, not his pajamas. One of the fine shirts he wears on Sunday. But what's he doing all dressed in the middle of the night? Armand still doesn't move. Doesn't say a word. She's used to his silences, which have always meant *I am superior.*

In fact, the only time he looked at her was on the day of the dance. The day he chose her. She's always been a housewife, not a woman one looks at. Armand has never had to complain of having a hole in his sock. He's always found his linen ironed and neatly folded in the cupboard. He's always come home from work to an impeccably kept house, and a full plate. He's never said thank you to her. Never really spoken, apart from the odd comment on this or that politician, sports reporter, singer, TV presenter. He's always behaved as if they didn't exist together. He has always lived on his side. Whereas she has so often wanted to cross over and join him.

She looks at his back, his strong back. She does something she's never done: she rips the sheet off him. He's wearing briefs. No pajama trousers. He turns towards her, his eyes full of both rage and shame. He has never hit her. And yet, insidiously, she has always been afraid of him.

His shirt is half-open. She looks at his chest, his muscular chest. They have always made love in the dark. She knows his body through touch and smell. Making love. He's just made love, he stinks of love. His face, hair, hands, eyes stink of another woman's genitals. And yet he hasn't been outdoors. He hasn't left the house. She looks at him, horrified.

*So you never saw a thing, Mom?*

## 65

I arrive at The Hydrangeas. Jo is there. She's about to leave. She was on night duty. Her face looks drawn. She immediately tells me about Hélène. Explains that her belongings have already been put away, and that another resident is coming at two, and will take her place in room 19. I ask to see her personal effects. They have been put into cardboard boxes and stored in Madame Le Camus's office. Her daughter is coming to collect them in the afternoon.

"And what about you, any news?" Jo asks me.

"I went to the hospital yesterday. She's still in a coma; I think her body has just given up."

"Justine, she's ninety-six years old: you can't expect a miracle."

"You all piss me off, going on about age! Hélène will forever be the age she was on the day she met Lucien in the church!"

Jo asks me if I'm OK. Tells me I look rough. I tell her that it's nothing, that I've just had my grandmother on the phone for an hour and she'd told me certain things, and since she's never told me a thing in her life, not even the story of Snow White before I fell asleep, it's shaken me up.

Jo suggests I have a coffee with her to get it off my chest. I feel like replying that, for once, the stories I've got on my chest are far crazier than those in the soaps the residents watch on TV. But instead, I give her a big hug and ask her what she's done to love Patrick all her life. She tells me that she's done nothing, that she's been lucky.

Before going to the changing room, I go up to the top floor, and the seagull has well and truly gone. For the first time, I feel like going, too. Leaving my work, my house, exiting this life to enter another one.

As I walk back down, I pass Monsieur Paul's room and the door is half-open. There have been no anonymous calls for months to the families of the forgotten ones.

I catch sight of someone from the back, leaning towards him, speaking into his ear. I see how gently the visitor holds Monsieur Paul's hand, I quietly close the door.

I go to get my smock in the changing room. I disinfect my hands. I come across Maria.

"How are you going to celebrate?" she asks me.

"Celebrate what?"

"Hey, wake up Justine, tomorrow night we change year."

I couldn't care less about changing year. And also, I don't like the look of next year one bit.

"Maria, there's a guy in Monsieur Paul's room, do you know him?"

"It's his grandson. He comes often."

"Really? Never seen him before. I thought Monsieur Paul never had visitors . . ."

"Well I see him all the time, he generally comes by early in the morning."

"Really. News to me."

I went into the storeroom. While preparing my cart, I thought of Roman, of unhappy love, lost love, nonexistent love. As I tackled the first corridor, the first door, the first room, the first hello, the first aches, the first memory lapses, the first insults, the first stories, the first protective sheets, I felt like dying in Hélène's place. But I knew very well that it was she who'd win. She had too much of a lead on me.

L ucien and Hélène made up their wedding anniversary. The first day of the year. The day of promises. On December 31, they would close the café at midday to set off on a honeymoon.

It's the only day of the year that Lucien would share Hélène's bedroom. Even after the jukebox and Rose's departure, they always slept in separate rooms.

Hélène's room never changed in forty years. A white, barred wrought-iron bed. A dressing table, a wardrobe, a standing mirror, pale-blue walls, curtains of voile and lace at both windows, one looking out onto the back of the café, the other onto the Place de l'Église.

As Rose grew up, there were new photos in new frames. Every ten years, Lucien repainted the walls the same color.

On December 31, at 1:00 P.M., Lucien would place the blue suitcase on the wooden floor of Hélène's room and they would go on the same cruise as in the summer of 1936. Every year, they would change destination, but every year Lucien would want to visit hot countries. Because of the sun. Countries where there was the sea. Because of the sea.

Every year, it was Lucien who was captain for the voyage. His favorite destination was Egypt. The Red Sea. He would dive into the sheets with his eyes closed and tell Hélène that he could see mermaids, one with eyes the blue of her room's walls.

At midnight, they would wish each other a happy non-wedding anniversary.

On the morning of January 2, they would reopen the café at 6:30 A.M., their skin glowing from the sun they had dreamt up and the love they had made. One must always insert some truth into one's dreams, or vice versa.

Sunday October 6, 1996

*o you never saw a thing, Mom?*
Well, yes. Once, she had seen. That way they had of avoiding each other. Eugénie just thought that Armand wasn't too keen on Annette, or rather, couldn't care less about her. He was more welcoming to Sandrine. And then, two years ago, shortly before Jules's birth, she'd caught Armand and Annette deep in conversation. Eugénie had been astonished by this sudden closeness. This complicity. The sort between those who know each other so well, they barely look at each other. A bit like her and Fatiha, when they'd drink tea at the doctor's. Except that Armand seemed to be lapping it up, savoring the moment. Eugénie had never seen her husband's face look like that. As if he had spotlights on him. Like on the stage where she'd seen Salvatore Adamo singing "*Laisse tes mains sur mes hanches*," under a canopy in Mâcon. Armand's usually hard, inscrutable features seemed to have been swept away by Annette's proximity. She had discovered the handsome, smiling face of a man under her own roof, a stranger. And it was her husband.

Eugénie hadn't dared disturb them. She'd gone back to see if the oven was the right temperature for her apple tart.

Eugénie, Alain, and Annette are sitting around the kitchen table. Sandrine and Christian aren't yet down for breakfast.

Eugénie doesn't look at Annette. Alain doesn't look at Annette. Eugénie and her son keep looking at each other.

Alain insists on taking Jules to the baptism. But Eugénie sticks to her guns, Jules will stay at the house, with her. The child is feverish, he must be kept in the warm. In any case, they'll be back late afternoon, won't they?

Alain is still in his pajamas. Annette is wearing a black silk dressing gown. Her fingers nervously stroke the tablecloth. Eugénie is already dressed. She has never undressed in front of her children, or appeared in her pajamas.

Christian turns up in the kitchen. Alain moves over to make room for his brother. Alain gazes at Annette's cup of milk, her spoon scraping off the skin and placing it on the plastic-coated tablecloth. This morning, thinks Eugénie, my sons don't look alike anymore. Alain is scarily pale. He keeps repeating that they're taking Jules with them. Annette is silent, and almost as pale as Alain.

"I will not let you take Jules."

It's final. Eugénie, who's never been domineering, never imposed a thing on her men, won't change her mind. Surprised, Christian stares at her. He's never heard his mother raise her voice, but this time, her statement was pronounced like a verdict. Alain leaves the table and goes back up to his room. Annette follows him.

Christian dunks his bread into his milky coffee and asks his mother if she's OK.

"Make sure Alain doesn't put Jules in the car."

Christian senses that's something's wrong. The tension is almost palpable. His father can be moody when annoyed, but his mother has always been even-tempered.

Armand is hiding in the garden shed. He wanted to leave, get away from the house, but his tire's flat. A gash at least two centimeters long. Did Alain want to take revenge by doing in his tire instead of doing him in? That's all he deserves. His son bumping him off.

This afternoon, Armand will hang himself. He'll kick the bucket. Eugénie will get a widow's pension—he gets good life assurance from the factory—and Alain will go live in Sweden with Annette and Jules. Nothing else will exist anymore. He feels nothing anymore, since Eugénie insulted him this morning. She'd done so in a whisper. He didn't know you could whisper the word *scum*. He thought it was inevitably shouted. She told him that she'd never forgive him, or let him leave. That he was her husband and would remain so. The way she'd said it, with that hatred that disfigured her, it was like a gob of spit full of love. Yes, it was as if she'd spat in his face while saying *I love you*.

When Armand passed Alain on the stairs earlier on, he received a virtual punch in the face. Alain had merely glanced at his father's shoes. Armand had seen the look in his eye.

When Alain was small, he had a habit of pinching his father's shoes. He'd get home from school and slip a pair on. There weren't many pairs. One for winter, one for summer. And the shoes often lasted several years. Alain would parade around for hours, impersonating his father. He even did his homework in his father's shoes. How often had Armand searched for them when leaving for work at four in the morning, and then found them beside the bed of his sleeping son?

The shoes had long been far too big for Alain. But at around fourteen, he'd started having to squeeze his feet into them. At fifteen, it was all over, no more messing around. His father's shoes had become too small. He'd gone up two sizes in a year, but from then on, Alain was more interested in his friends, and in girls. As for Armand, it came as quite a blow. That was all he could think of: My son can't get into my shoes anymore. It was the end of something, a sad end.

Armand hears someone pushing open the gate, walking through the garden, and ringing the doorbell.

It's Marcel, his colleague, who's just turned up in his van. Reluctantly, Armand leaves his lair.

"Hi, Marrcel."

Marcel's the guy he calls as soon as anything stops working in the house. To do odd jobs, to take stuff away. Yesterday evening, he came to mend the washing machine, and this morning he's going to take it to the waste collection site. But first, he just wants to check a part of the motor that always clogs up, which he hadn't thought of yesterday evening . . .

"If you knew how many machines get sent to the scrap yard because of that damn part."

Eugénie warms up some coffee while Marcel pokes around inside the belly of the machine. Armand hovers around and responds to his colleague with appropriate grunts as he goes on about drain pumps, solenoid valves, level sensors, heating resistors . . . And he must check the "object trap," too. Armand had no idea there were also traps in washing machines.

Christian has gone to his room to get ready. Annette returns to the kitchen with Jules in her arms. Marcel looks up; his eyes change when they fall on Annette. God, she's beautiful.

"This machine's really had it, nothing for it," Marcel declares.

Armand and Marcel want to disconnect the evacuation pipe and turn off the water supply, but someone's already done it. Armand automatically glances at Eugénie, not thinking for a second that it's her who's sorted everything. Together, the two men lift the machine. *God almighty, it weighs a ton.*

Right then, Annette hands Jules over to Eugénie. She takes the child into her arms, hugs him, but doesn't kiss him. The two women don't look at each other.

While he's dragging the washing machine with Marcel, Armand hears voices coming from the bedrooms, and one of the twins coming down the stairs. Alain or Christian? Armand can't bring himself to look up. No doubt they'll soon be setting off for that baptism. And this evening, when they return, he'll have hanged himself. Annette won't forgive him, but, in the end, that won't really matter. And life will go on, it always does. Life doesn't need him. What on earth can it do with a guy like him?

Armand and Marcel emerge from the house puffing and blowing like old steam engines—it sure is heavy. It's cold outside. Armand helps Marcel load the washing machine into the van and attach it with a bungee. He hears an engine starting, turns around and just catches sight of the Clio as it speeds off. The twins are in the front. Sandrine is resting her head on the back window. For a brief moment, Armand spots Annette's blond hair, his last sunset.

She would visit three times a year. Three days at Christmas, three at Easter, and the August long weekend. It had taken just one day in October for everything to stop. He didn't see much of her, and yet she took up all the space. He had nothing else left, not a crumb, not a minute to himself. He thought of nothing but her. Day and night.

The few times they had met up there, in the junk room, that toy graveyard, and snuggled in a corner where the ceiling light no longer worked, he had felt his life passing into hers.

Last night, neither he nor Annette heard Alain coming up the stairs. They saw the door opening. Then Alain called out to Annette. Several times. Annette gripped onto Armand. He felt her fingernails digging into his skin. They lay low, terrified and mortified at the thought of being discovered.

Alain moved closer, as if drawn by their breathing. The light from the corridor was enough to reveal them, like two creatures caught in a trap, two pathetic figures stuck to each other on the floor, between two boxes of crockery.

Paralyzed, Alain tried to say something, but not a sound came from his mouth. Then, after a seeming eternity, he backed away and closed the door behind him, soundlessly, to blank out what he had just seen.

Suddenly, Armand feels dizzy. Marcel asks him if he's OK, tells him he's looking a bit off-color.

"It's nothing, must be coming down with something."

Armand slips a few ten-franc coins into Marcel's pocket, for all his help.

"Forr yourr kids," he says.

Marcel bursts out laughing.

"I've never had any kids!"

Lucky you, thinks Armand.

With Jules in her arms, Eugénie watches them from the kitchen, hiding behind the window.

Armand thinks to himself that he must do the deed quickly. He can't put up with that accusing look a day longer.

"See you, Marrcel, until next time."

The morning passes smoothly; he acts like he's going to go on living. He plants some spring cabbages and winter lettuces in his vegetable garden. An old October habit. The earth is frosty. Winter's come early. All morning, he can feel Eugénie's eyes on his back.

At midday, he finds a plate, his plate, on the kitchen table. What's left of yesterday's over-salty couscous. He hesitates to sit down, then tells himself it's best to carry on as normal so as not to arouse suspicion. Since being married, it's the first time he's eating alone on a Sunday. He gazes at the empty space left by the washing machine and thinks that when he's no longer around, he'll leave no such void.

There's not a sound in the house. She must be upstairs with the children. While eating his couscous, he wonders why Eugénie had been so determined to keep Jules at home. He also wonders whether he should leave a farewell letter to Annette. No. To tell her what? I love you? She knows that. Nor to his wife. Nor to his sons.

Last night, before Alain discovered them, he'd felt the young woman's tears trickling down his neck while she told him about the face of a Virgin Mary she'd restored near Reims. As she described the cobalt blue to him, he could feel her mouth quivering against his ear.

She cries increasingly often, for an increasingly long time. It really *has* to stop.

While eating his couscous, he thinks of Annette's skin, and how the perishing cold of cathedrals and churches is harming it, of the scars she gets on her hands and forearms from handling the glass. He thinks of her wrists, fine as jewels. The image of his workman's hands on her white skin had always seemed like a mental one, but never a reality. Jules had brought him back down to earth.

The day he was born was the most beautiful and the worst of his life. The worst until last night, that is.

When he'd leant over the cot, in the maternity clinic, to take him into his arms, Eugénie had showed him the sign hanging overhead: "This baby is fragile, only his/her daddy's and mommy's caresses are permitted." Like on the evening he'd kissed Annette for the first time, Armand had felt like taking the infant and running away, kidnapping him and disappearing. But like on the evening he'd kissed Annette for the first time, he'd done nothing, had just gone home.

He washes up his plate, his cutlery, and his glass, places them on the edge of the sink. Eugénie will come after him anyhow, to rewash them. She doesn't like his way of cleaning things. Always says it's a botched job.

He's decided to hang himself in the room Alain caught them in last night. The ceiling's high, and it's the only door in the house that locks from inside. This time, he won't forget. Unlike last night. In addition to locking the door, he'll stick a terse note on it, so no one enters before calling the police.

There's a rope in the garden shed, wound around the big green ladder. He goes out to fetch it. He pretends to survey his planting first. Wanders around a bit. He's convinced that Eugénie is watching him from an upstairs room. In the shed, he daren't look at his bike, like when you pass someone you've loved too much. He unwinds the rope and slips it into a garbage bag that he conceals under his winter bomber jacket.

He opens the junk-room door. He switches on his flashlight and directs it at the roof beams. From his stepladder, he swings the rope several times until it wraps around the main beam, and then attaches it securely. He starts to tie his hangman's noose, has to try again, a few times. As he does so, he remembers that, when the twins were children, they used to perform magic tricks and tie false knots in scarves. They never revealed to him how they did it. He only knows how to tie real knots.

He goes back downstairs, he doesn't have much time left; Eugénie and the children have dozed off in front of the TV. Armand hears the sandman passing by. The children always want to watch the same video. He lifts up the gas cylinder that's under the sink and looks for the lock of Annette's hair that he hid at the back of the cupboard, inside a Treasury Department envelope. He opens the envelope and slips the lock of hair into his pocket.

He writes the warning note on the pad usually used for shopping lists: *Do not enter. Call the police.* He unrolls some sticky tape, tears it off with his teeth. He's about to go back upstairs when he sees a police car parking in front of the house. Armand can't believe his eyes. How can they already be here? Is he dreaming? He watches them pushing open the gate and entering his garden.

Shit, what the hell are they doing here? And they seem in a bad mood, too. Armand knows one of the two by sight. A guy from the village called Bonneton, a bit younger than him. The two officers are about to ring the doorbell. No. They mustn't. If they do, it'll wake up Eugénie and the children.

He screws up the note and puts it in his pocket, before going to open the door. He finds himself face to face with them. Officer Bonneton gives Armand a military salute and says:

"Good day. Monsieur Neige?"

Armand is surprised by the question. Bonneton knows perfectly well who he is.

"Yes."

"Are your sons, Christian and Alain Neige, the owners of a vehicle made by Renault with the license plate 2408 ZM 69?"

## 68

Hélène never went back to old Louis's café after Lucien's death. She would have been incapable of doing so. Thirty years later, when she returned to Milly to end her days there, as was her wish, she didn't want to go past her old café. She urged Rose to take her straight to The Hydrangeas, with no detour.

That café, so dated by the end of the Seventies, with its old jukebox, Fifties furniture, dark floorboards, and tinted windows, Lucien and Hélène could have sold it a hundred times. But they always found some excuse not to part with it, including young Claude.

From the Seventies onwards, more modern places had opened. Brasseries with big plate-glass windows, white tiling, plastic chairs, and video games with joysticks that drew in the youngsters. Smoky brasseries, where you heard anglophone groups playing electric guitars, and not Brel and Brassens soliloquizing all day long while Lucien, "the revenant," chain-smoked Gitanes behind the bar.

Claude ran old Louis's café until 1986. By the end, only a few old folk would come in for their glass of wine before ten in the morning.

After that, the café was turned into a medical practice, with a family doctor moving in for a few years. He saw his patients on the ground floor, and had the living quarters upstairs renovated, living in one apartment on his own, and his housekeeper living in the other.

It pleased Hélène that her café was replaced by a doctor's consulting office—in her eyes, there wasn't much difference.

*"Whether you go to a café or to the doctor's, what you're seeking is healing from lonesomeness," she would say.*

After the doctor left, no colleague took over. Young Claude, having fallen in love with the housekeeper, had followed her when she'd left Milly.

The whole place was razed to the ground in the early Nineties to build social housing which never got built.

\* \* \*

In October 1986, after selling the café to the doctor, Claude visited Hélène to bring her a box of personal effects. She was living in Paris and was sixty-nine at the time. She had worked for ten years at Franck & Fils, on Rue de Passy, as a seamstress, a "petite main."

There were thirteen seamstresses working on the seventh floor of the department store, in a light-filled workshop with a grand view of the Rue de Passy, and of the seagull. There they would do alterations on both prêt-à-porter and haute couture garments, and then iron them before wrapping them in tissue paper. They all sat around a large table sewing, either by hand or machine, depending on the alterations required.

Hélène was happy there, and had refused to leave for a long time. The personnel officer let her stay on until she was sixty-eight. She lived in the 16th arrondissement, a stone's throw from the store, where she still often dropped by to say hello to her former colleagues.

Her apartment had been lent to her by a countess, who lived on Rue de la Pompe. In lieu of rent, Hélène would supply the countess and her three daughters with a few handmade dresses. They would choose the fabrics and designs, cutting pictures out of magazines, and Hélène would make them.

She lived on the third floor. Claude didn't take the elevator. He knocked on the door, with box under arm and heart pounding, in part thanks to climbing three floors, but mainly because of Hélène, whom he was going to see again.

*When she opened the door to him, there was a good smell of polish and paper. Nothing had changed in her appearance, apart from the fact that she was wearing glasses and slacks. It was the first time he was seeing her not in a dress. Her hair had whitened. They hugged each other for a long time.*

*Claude told her about Fatiha, the housekeeper of the doctor who'd bought old Louis's café. A beautiful Algerian woman whose main quality was laughing a lot. Hélène said that Fatiha sounded like the title of a lovely song.*

*For the rest of the afternoon, while drinking tea she topped up every ten minutes, Hélène read passages from books to Claude. Books that weren't in Braille. She would pluck them randomly from her modest bookcase, open them at any page, and say to him, Listen, this time it's your turn to listen.*

*Many sessions with a speech therapist had corrected her dyslexia.*

*She spoke unduly loudly, and articulated so clearly, you couldn't possibly not understand what she was reading. Seeing her as proud as the schoolgirl she'd not been able to be brought tears to Claude's eyes.*

*Hélène told him that she was looking forward to seeing her parents and Lucien again up there, to surprise them all with her reading.*

## 69

Every October 6th, Gran places a wreath of flowers at the foot of the tree that killed her children. On the evening of the 5th, she has the white lilies and red roses delivered to her. The closest florist is twenty kilometers away. She used to phone them; now she asks Jules to order the flowers online. He just has to click on "Delivery bereavement flowers," and choose between "funeral bouquet, casket spray, or condolence arrangement."

Every October 6th, she leaves the house at eight in the morning, flowers under arm and stick in hand. She limps along for about three-quarters of an hour to reach the tree, places her wreath, wraps a ribbon which she gets specially embroidered around it, and then goes back home.

Gramps has never wanted to accompany her, never wanted to drive her to the tree, Gramps has always hated that ritual.

Gran has always refused to let Jules or me accompany her. As children, we had no choice about going to cemetery, but she spared us the wreath of flowers in the ditch. Even if someone pulls up alongside her, offering to take her there, she declines.

Every Saturday of that month, when I'm not on night duty, Jules and I pass the wreath on our way to the Paradise club. For the first couple of weeks, the flowers do their best to look like flowers, but by the end of the month, they've lost all their color. In November, the wreath is nothing but a brown heap, which, if you drive by fast, you might take for an animal or clothing thrown into the ditch.

At the first fall of snow, someone removes it. For a long

time, we thought it was the road-maintenance man, but when Jules was around fifteen, he discovered, by chance, that it was Gramps.

Last winter, Gramps left it to rot away. By spring, all that remained was the white ribbon on which you could still, just about, read these words: "Forgive me."

## 70

*Hélène died in the late afternoon.*
*She departed leaving her fable behind her: there are as*
*many birds as humans on this earth. And love is when*
*several people share the same bird.*

\* \* \*

*Rose asked Claude if he would like something to remember*
*her by: a dress, a headscarf, or anything else. He replied, The*
*photo of Janet Gaynor.*

# 71

Between five and six in the morning, while that bastard pretended to sleep, there, right beside her, in their bed, she had been thinking.

After she had hurled insults at him, with her heart pounding harder than it ever had, even on the day she'd delivered the twins, Eugénie had considered firing a bullet into both his knees while he slept, so he'd be stuck in a wheelchair forever. But that wasn't painful enough. He'd have carried on eating, drinking, sleeping like before. And he'd be taken for a victim. No, nothing should remain as it was before. And anyhow, she couldn't have tolerated going to prison. No one would force her to leave her house, and definitely not him, that scum who was having it off with his daughter-in-law, that scum for whom she'd sacrificed her life. That scum who'd humiliated her in the worst way possible, by sleeping with the wife of his son, of *their* son.

She had to find a way of making him have nightmares in this bed, until his very last breath. And that's when she decided to eliminate him from the surface of the earth. Not physically. No, not in one go: he had to suffer. Dying straight away would have been too easy; he had to be tortured until it killed him. She had to find a way for him to die slowly but surely, an agony that would go on and on. To find a hell for him. A hell that was personal to him. To trap him alive, behind invisible walls, the walls of shame, of guilt.

She had read that the Nazis had done experiments, in both

physical and mental pain, on prisoners by torturing a relative or other loved one. She had read that, to do harm to someone, terrible harm, unbearable harm, you shouldn't lay into that person directly, but rather lay into the person they loved most in the world. That's how the idea for the harm entered her head. The source of the harm.

Harming Annette to destroy him.

The alarm clock showed 6:00 A.M. She had to move fast.

Eugénie went out into the street. It was cold and dark. She had on the mohair dressing gown that that scum had given her last Christmas. Armand's car was parked on the sidewalk opposite, as usual.

She took off a wheel in a few minutes. She knew her stuff in mechanics. At the farm, it was she who always changed the tractor's oil. Her brothers were even jealous. No vehicle held any secrets for her. Her father had taught her everything. Even Armand didn't know that, and she'd liked the fact that no one knew she'd been a tomboy. She started to scrape the brake cables with a paring knife, that little vegetable peeler she'd used all through the twins' childhood to peel the potatoes. She'd never given them frozen fries. Always Charlotte potatoes that she selected carefully, peeled, and then sliced into long, fine pieces. As she scraped away the top layer of rubber, she thought of Armand's body when he had come back to bed, his body with the smell of another woman's cunt on it.

That body that had deflowered her. That body to which she'd given her life and two children. That body that had scared her, hurt her, and that she'd ended up adoring. That body that had crushed her, rubbed itself, shuddering, against her for more than thirty years. The scent of it that clung to his shirts and that she'd secretly breathe in before washing them. She'd tended to its blisters, put Band-Aids on its grazes, buffed its fingernails, shaved its nape, applied heat treatment to its aches and pains, given it cough syrup.

While she was tampering with the brakes, she was sweating,

hatred welling up with every hot flash. Her hands weren't shaking. Her life had had it. Like the washing machine. She'd known that machine had had it well before Marcel checked "one last thing." And when life's had it, you don't shake anymore, you don't cry anymore, you hate.

She screwed the nuts back onto the second wheel and removed the jack, which she returned to its place in the garden shed with all the other tools and products. Weed killer, wood glue, drill, screwing machine, hammer, sander, monkey wrench, screwdriver. Those tools she'd pretended to be unfamiliar with, while, on the quiet, she'd repaired everything in the house, even the toilets, forever getting blocked because the evacuation pipe was too narrow.

"That one" had never asked himself any questions when he breezed in from his factory. Never a blocked U-bend, never a creaking door hinge, never a nail to hammer in, never a strip of wallpaper peeling off, never any furniture to assemble, never any mold, never a lick of paint needed, never a light bulb to change, never a broken-down boiler, never a plank to be nailed, never a screw coming loose, never any cracks in the walls, never a spot of rust appearing.

She went into her kitchen. It had taken her just fifteen minutes. She washed the peeler, the water scalding her fingers. She put it away with the other cutlery.

As she went back upstairs to bed, she gave thanks to Armand: at last she felt something strongly. At last she was moved by a powerful emotion, even if it was hatred. She had read that there's but one step between hatred and love.

## 72

In the late afternoon, Lucien arrived, swimming. He emerged from the Mediterranean, breathless.

There were still people on the beach and in the water. The sun was already low, but it was still hot. The sand, crisscrossed with footprints, was warm. The air smelt of the sugar from the donuts, the salt from the fries stalls, and the wind carried the laughter and joyful cries skywards, a symphony only the sea can get children to play on a vacation evening.

Hélène was stretched out on her towel, under a parasol. She was reading a novel and wearing an orange two-piece swimsuit. He lay down beside her, on the towel his dry clothes had been rolled up on for thirty-five years. He dried himself and slipped on his creased shirt. She smiled at him. She had sand in her navel; he brushed it away with his fingertips. Her skin was hot and slightly sticky, a mix of suntan oil and perspiration. She shivered and said to him, I can read now, listen. He replied, I'll listen to you, and afterwards we'll set off again together. She nodded yes. She licked her index finger, turned several pages, chose a passage in the novel, and began to read.

73

Sunday, October 6, 1996

At around seven in the morning, Annette must have gone downstairs very carefully so as not to make a noise, not to wake anyone. She must have warmed up some milk, drunk it from the mug with her name on it—a birthday present from Eugénie when Annette was "seeing" Alain. "Seeing" being the word used in Eugénie's family for a couple before marriage.

Annette must have put on her parka, her trainers, taken the keys to Armand's car from the nail in the hall, left the house, driven off, done the nine kilometers to the old chapel on Mont Chavanes—a place that looked like Canada in the middle of Burgundy—to go for her jog.

It was the same ritual every time. On arrival, she'd park down below, walk up to the little chapel, with its permanently open door, to admire daybreak through a 16th-century stained-glass window depicting Mary Magdalene's burial. No more candles or pews, just the walls, the dusty floor, and this miraculously preserved window that so fascinated the Swedish girl.

She'd return home an hour later, take a shower, feed Jules, and then, over breakfast, wear them all out with this Mary Magdalene. This woman who could have been Jesus's mistress, the mother of his children, or merely a loyal friend—no one knew. A kind of whore, exactly like her. A whore, whore, whore, whore, whore, whore, whore, whore, whore. Eugénie never said bad words, she thought them.

According to Eugénie's calculations, Annette must have

sailed through the first junction without braking because, that early in the morning, there was no one around; she must have driven along the river until the grade crossing, some two kilometers from the house, where a nasty bend would, inevitably, have forced her to brake, and . . . boom. Her pretty little face up in smoke.

From time to time, Eugénie would glance over at "that one," who was still pretending to sleep with his back turned to her. Lying in her bed and staring at the ceiling streaked with light from the streetlamp, filtering through the shutters, she had gone through Annette's journey from the house to the chapel at least a dozen times.

She got up to prepare the children's breakfast. Who would come to tell them about Annette's accident? Annette disfigured, Annette seriously injured, Annette dead, Annette reduced to dust. Who?

They would organize a fine funeral for her, among some glorious stained-glass windows. They would place white roses on her coffin. Armand would never get over it. Alain would start over, and she, Eugénie, would look after Jules in the meantime. No way was the little one going over there, to those wretched Swedes.

When Annette walked into the kitchen, deathly pale and red-eyed, with Jules in her arms, Eugénie just looked down, said nothing. Not even hello. Annette prepared the little one's bottle and then left the kitchen.

It was the first time Annette hadn't set off for her jog on a Sunday morning in Armand's car. She never took the twins' car to drive to the chapel. Armand's car handled the hills better for getting up there. Well, that's what she believed until last night. She had just realized that Annette liked to take Armand's car because it was Armand's. Even on rainy and snowy days, she would go up there, as though some invisible hand were forcing her to.

Eugénie looked out of the window: the car hadn't moved. She noticed, too, that the two cars were parked one behind the other. Armand's Peugeot and the twins' Renault. That had never happened before, either. The boys always parked the Clio on the dip in the sidewalk that Armand had got made for them, just opposite the garden. A space that remained empty when the twins weren't there. Where she'd even pull up the weeds that sprouted through the concrete when they were away for too long. Because their car no longer cast a shadow on the sidewalk. Something must have been in their way last night.

Eugénie remembered Marcel's van . . . He'd had a drink after trying to repair the washing machine. Eugénie went out into the street and punctured the front left tire of Armand's Peugeot so that no one could use it today. She told herself she'd fix the brake cables tomorrow.

She hurried back into the house, wanting to check that Annette and Alain weren't taking Jules to that confounded baptism. She was too scared that a row might erupt between them.

And in any case, there's drinking at baptisms; it was too dangerous.

## 74

R oman said to me:
"I hate Sundays."
"You could always come and see me."
I said that to my feet because, this morning, I found looking him in the eye impossible again. Hélène's death had taken me back to square one where his eyes were concerned.

"Will you be staying in the area?"

"Where else do you expect me to go?"

"Well, regarding that, I have a present for you."

He said it to the beer he was drinking. Because something about me must have been impossible to look at too.

We were on the cold, impersonal concourse of the TGV railway station, the one that's a forty-minute drive from Milly. A few bistro-style tables had been put there, in a corner, beside a makeshift bar on which three travelers leaned, sipping their coffees. We were sitting close to an automatic exit door that kept opening and closing without anyone ever walking through it. Every so often, our conversation was interrupted by the almighty roar of a train speeding towards Lyon, Marseille, or Paris.

That morning, Roman had phoned me at The Hydrangeas to tell me that he wanted to see me, but not there. For now, he just couldn't bear to be back there, at The Hydrangeas, again. He handed me an envelope. A large envelope.

"You can open it once I've gone."

He said that to my eyes, because this time, we did look at each other. At the same time.

"OK. I have something for you, too."

I leant down to my bag, which was on the floor. Jo always says you mustn't put your bag on the floor, it brings bad luck, and you'll never have any money if you do so. I thought of Jo's love for Patrick as I handed the blue notebook to Roman.

"It's your grandparents' story. I've finished writing it."

"Thank you."

He stroked the cover of the blue notebook as though it were a woman's skin. And, without looking at me, as he inhaled the paper of some random pages, he murmured:

"The day I asked you to write down Hélène's story, you had an eyelash on your cheek . . . I asked you to make a wish."

"Yes, I remember."

"And . . . did you make your wish?"

"Yes. That's it."

I indicated the blue notebook to him. "My wish was to write it to the very end, not give up halfway."

There was a great silence, a general strike, no TGV for several minutes. He drank some beer. Stroked the blue cover with his girl's fingers. And then said:

"It's a fine title, *The Lady of the Beach*."

"Where are Hélène's ashes?" I asked.

"My mother scattered them into the Mediterranean."

"Hélène called it her blue suitcase."

He finished off his beer.

"And Edna?"

"Edna lives in London, at her youngest daughter's. She'll be ninety-four next month. She had two children after . . . Rose."

"Do you see her?"

"Occasionally."

A woman's voice joined our table, the one announcing his imminent departure. He stood up, took hold of my hands, kissed them, and headed for the platform.

His departure floored me.

I did what they do in films, I ordered a whiskey. A drink I loathe, but I so wanted to be in someone else's film. I downed my whiskey in one. It burnt me inside. My head began to swim a little. I thought of Hélène and Lucien. And I saw the two of them there, behind the bar. They'd changed bistro. I even saw Louve, asleep on the sawdust.

I thought of the Mediterranean. I thought of the seagull. I thought of afterwards, of Gramps and Annette.

The envelope Roman had given me was still on the table. It was just a brown envelope, but surely contained more than just a postcard. I opened it. Inside, there were some documents. The most serious-looking kind. Those that, all your life, you put away in a drawer so as not to lose them. They were the deeds to a property.

I went over them several times because my full name kept cropping up, but was still none the wiser. It was all written in Italian.

I almost ordered another whiskey, but then I spotted the other envelope, smaller and paler, tucked in the middle. With "Justine" written in fountain pen on it, as beautifully as it had been on the flyleaf of *From the Land of the Moon*.

Inside the envelope, I found a note. Still in Roman's handwriting: "Justine, the Sardinian house is yours. My family and I bequeath it to you."

I gazed all around me. I pinched my own arm. I stood up.

I was about to leave the station concourse when the barman caught hold of my arm. The one I'd just pinched.

"Mademoiselle, you've forgotten that."

He pointed at a huge parcel placed against the lowered shutter of a newsstand.

"It's not mine."

"It is. The man you were with told me it was for you. And even that it weighs a ton."

On the parcel, that same "Justine" again, written in blue ink.

I asked the barman for some scissors. He didn't have any. But he took a little knife out of his pocket. He cut the strings carefully, repeating three times, *If you ask me, it's something valuable.* It's true that it did look like a carefully wrapped painting, straight out of a museum. A painting I wouldn't be able to carry on my own, it was so large and heavy. It would never fit into Gramps's car.

While the barman was unwrapping the mysterious object, I kept looking inside my bag to check the two envelopes were really there. That they hadn't flown away. That the whole thing wasn't a dream. Even though it was one. I, Justine Neige, orphan, twenty-one, nearly twenty-two, was the owner of a house because I'd listened to a woman telling me her story.

The four travelers now leaning on the bar came over to us. When the barman had finally removed the many bits of cardboard and wrapping paper protecting the object, I discovered that it wasn't a painting, but a huge black-and-white photograph under glass.

Initially, I recoiled. Someone had followed me without my knowledge.

On the photograph, Hélène's seagull was in the foreground. I was sure it was hers, I'd have known it anywhere. It was flying behind me, against the light, in the lane where I feed the fat cat.

The photograph was breathtakingly beautiful.

The four travelers murmured how marvelous it was. The barman couldn't tear his eyes away from it. He swiveled it around. On the back, it was signed by Roman, and there was a title and a date: "Justine and the bird, January 19, 2014."

Three days after Hélène's death, the seagull had come to bid me farewell. And Roman had captured that moment forever.

## 75

In room 19, the new resident is called Yvan Géant. He's eighty-two years old. He bust his hip. He's a man with kind eyes, adored by all the nursing staff. From time to time, he silently wipes away a tear with the back of his hand. He can't bear living here. He often says to me, *Justine, I never would have imagined that I'd end my life in such a place.*

To take his mind off things, and mine, I get him to talk. As soon as he starts to tell stories, his face changes. It made me feel like carrying on with my writing. And yet Monsieur Géant doesn't have a grandson with blue eyes.

I went to old Prost's store to buy a new notebook.

I jot down what Monsieur Géant tells me in my new notebook. Sometimes, I read it back to him. It makes him laugh. He tells me that it's as if he were listening to someone else's story, that my words are finer than his life. Since I'm always being told that when an old person dies a library burns to the ground, I'm saving a little of the ashes.

When I've finished my day's work, Monsieur Géant talks to me, and I write:

*The first time I went to spend a month at my Aunt Aline's and Uncle Gabriel's house, I was six years old. It was wintertime. I'd broken my arm, and my parents, who worked all day at the tannery, didn't want to leave me alone at home. Aline and Gabriel had a rather isolated farm in the Vosges mountains, above Le Thillot.*

*I used to sleep with my aunt, and my uncle slept above us, in another room. It was so cold at night that we'd sleep wearing balaclavas. I loved that chill all around us. I fell in love with my aunt and with the life over there. I kept returning to their house until I was fifteen, during my summer vacation, all my summer vacations, and every Sunday.*

*Aline was like my second mother. She'd never had children, and I don't know why. At home, there were four of us, and my parents didn't have time to look after us. At my aunt's, I became an only son.*

*My Uncle Gabriel had a son from a first marriage called Adrien, but he was twenty years older than me. Probably the same age as my Aunt Aline, but at the time, I didn't realize that. When you're small, all grown-ups are old folk.*

*Over there, I spent my life in the mountains. I never worked for my uncle and aunt. All they asked of me was to load the hay into the loft at the end of summer. We'd take two large sheets, knot the four corners, throw the hay inside. It smelt good.*

*Aline, she was an angel. What remains to me of her is an aroma, that of the fir-tree branches I used to burn in the stove. All my life, I've thanked God for the day I broke my arm.*

## 76

October 6, 1996

10:00 P.M. Armand has just got back from being at the morgue with the police officers. He pretended to identify the bodies, turning his back on the coroner and closing his eyes.

He said, *It's them*. He'd only identified the shoes Alain was wearing.

Armand said nothing to Eugénie. In his silence, she heard that it was them. That it was over. That they were dead. All four of them.

Eugénie Martin, married name Neige, is huddled up on the sofa. She's incapable of crying for her sons, of screaming, of banging her head on the walls, of losing consciousness, of letting herself die. A single thought obsesses her, consumes her grief, paralyzes her, prevents any kind of mourning: she wonders whether she didn't tamper with the wrong car.

She retraces her actions in her mind, comes out into the cold, dark street wrapped in her mohair dressing gown, jack in hand. Squats beside the car, removes the wheel, takes the peeler out of her pocket and scrapes the brake cables while still smelling her daughter-in-law on her husband's fingers.

What if hatred and panic had made her make a fatal error, confuse two black cars, a Peugeot 206 and a Renault Clio? It must just be a coincidence, a horrendous coincidence, that she tampered with the Peugeot, and it's in the Renault that they killed themselves.

It's an accident, just an accident. And yet, every time she goes over her actions that morning, she's no longer entirely sure.

Sometimes she takes the wheel off the Peugeot, sometimes off the Renault. All she'd need to do is go out into the street and crouch down to know. All she'd need to do.

Never before had Christian or Alain *not* parked in their place. Never. For them, places were sacred. Each had his place on the coat rack, at the kitchen table, at the dining-room table, on the sofa in the sitting room, in his bed, for parking his car. Each his own place.

Why had Marcel parked his van where the twins always parked? Since the day they'd had their driving licenses? Why had the washing machine broken down? Why hadn't Annette driven up to see Mary Magdalene on the Mont Chavanes?

All she'd have needed to do . . .

\* \* \*

October 6, 1996

11:00 P.M. They're dead. All four of them. Must update family record file, forehead against window pane, staring into the night, into depths of the night, legs pressed to radiator, balls scorched, acid tears, morgue smell on shirt, head freezing cold, he sees her going out onto the street, in a trance, seems broken, Eugénie smashed to pieces like the car, in the same state, tottering, confused, leaning on a tree, Eugénie, her silhouette, grief that turns you crazy, distorts your vision, impossible, impossible, the silhouette of his wife on the sidewalk, impossible, like a thief, inheritance, coffins, plaques, funerals, his wife in the street, regrets, wan light from streetlamp on her hair, the mortician's, town hall, register deaths, tomorrow morning, health insurance, bank, close accounts, hallucination, life assurance, standing beside the car, his wife standing beside the car, for ages, a ghost, burial, change of address, she crouches, looks for something, inhuman, removes hub cap in one go, songs, religious ceremony, the nut, winds the jack clockwise, his wife like a man, lock of blond hair, Treasury Department, the car levitating, his car, my car, holding a wheel, his wife, my wife, a wheel, stops still, turn off meters, inform energy, water, gas, electricity suppliers, she, kneeling, turns around, looks up at the bedroom window, condolences, looks at me, inhuman, her eyes, inhuman, a torture victim, the stained-glass windows, Annette's skin, that's them, the shoes, winds anticlockwise, the opposite direction, deceased, goes back into the house, collection of the bodies, his wife in the street, obituaries, now she's back in the house, returned to the house, wheel, put wheel back on, before coming back in, death certificates, declare income of the deceased in year of their deaths, burn the two fruit trees, why his wife, why Eugénie in the street, kneeling beside his car, the car, my car, flat tire this morning, this morning, Marcel, washing machine, it's had it.

## 77

I'm the sort that stays. The sort that doesn't plan to leave. The others, the girls and boys from my class, those who'll return to this hole once a year to visit parents, will come across me and say, *Justine, you never change.*

I'm the sort that the passing years will barely change, a bit like those statues, familiar figures that you find outside churches or town halls and can no longer remember whom they portray.

The sort that keeps their childhood home to turn it, one day, into their adult home.

I will never leave Milly to live somewhere else.

I will never live very far from my grandparents, or from my parents' grave.

I still set Gran's hair once a week. And when I touch her head to separate strands of her hair with my comb, I avoid thinking about the source of the harm.

Gramps sits beside us. He watches us, reads *Paris Match*, makes a few comments, which he'd never do before. Before we found ourselves in the car on Christmas Eve. Before "she loved me."

I've never spoken about Annette again with him. I never will. I've never spoken about October 6th again with Gran. I never will.

I feel like a child who discovers that one of her parents is a war criminal, and keeps silent. Keep silent for Jules.

Jules, who has just passed his bac. He left Milly for Paris last August 27th. At first, when I went past the door to his dark room, I felt as if he were dead. Now, I'm getting used to it. Jules will never return to Milly. Except for Christmas, Easter, and the August long weekend.

During school vacations, Jules will go to my Sardinian house. I've given him the keys.

Last summer, I was with Jules when I slipped the key into the lock of my house. It's him who held my hand as I wept tears of joy. They were the first I had wept. I couldn't even see the sea through the windows.

Jules fell madly in love with the people of Muravera, particularly the brunettes. The island is so beautiful, it seems like another planet. Indeed, over there, the sea is called the Tyrrhenian.

The house is attached to another house. The neighbors, Silvana and Arna, are two sisters, two widows who resemble the grandmother of Milena Agus, the author of *From the Land of the Moon*. Their long curly hair is white.

When Jules is over there, Silvana and Arna look after him. They give him tuna *bottarga* and flat bread. Jules is the son they never had. Jules is the son of a good many people. He still thinks he's living on his inheritance from Uncle Alain, who still smiles beside his wife and his brother on his grave. I want to let him believe that. Because believers are stronger than the rest. So the priest at The Hydrangeas says.

After the TGV station, Roman sent me a postcard to The Hydrangeas. It's Starsky who brought it to me, and I could tell he'd read it by the way he looked at me. It felt like a violation, him having set eyes on Roman's words.

*Dearest Justine,*
*Thinking of you, lots, here in Corsica.*
*Blue notebook read and reread, in my sweater.*
*If I'd read it before, it's not a house I'd have given you, but the empire of the birds.*
*Fondest,*

*Roman*

*PS: Carry on writing . . .*

I know it off by heart. Fifty-three syllables, a hundred and one consonants, seventy-one vowels. I've pinned it below one of the windows of my Muravera house. To make an extra window.

I think often of Hélène, of Lucien, of their seagull. I miss them. I miss their love story. Sometimes, I think Roman gave me the Muravera house so I'd see them swimming.

At The Hydrangeas, we've had a victory: a small mongrel with the silly name of Titi. He weighs five kilos, comes from the animal shelter, and all the residents are nuts about him, as am I. Titi has changed the life of Yvan Géant, the gentleman in room 19. He thinks of only one thing, walking Titi in The Hydrangeas' gardens. In the end, dogs are like fine weather, they take your mind off things.

The anonymous caller has resurfaced. There were three calls last week from room 29. The staff are under surveillance. Starsky and Hutch are still on the case, but it's of no interest anymore to the papers or TV. Old people are newsworthy during heat waves, but afterwards, they're forgotten.

Starsky and Hutch will soon be retiring, and the Municipal and Public Space Department building is about to close. All the archives have already been moved to Mâcon, including those relating to my parents' accident.

In a few years' time, maybe Starsky and Hutch will become residents at The Hydrangeas. Will the anonymous caller, whom they'll never catch, call their families if they're forgotten on Sundays?

I gave in. I showed the lines on my palm to Jo. One evening when Maria and I had supper at hers. Patrick wasn't there. We'd drunk quite a bit and I finally held my hand out to her. She told me I'd have a lovely life and two children. A boy and a girl.

A fifty-fifty chance of not ending up forgotten on Sundays myself.

## 78

Yesterday evening, I discovered who the anonymous caller is.

All the residents were sleeping. Even Madame Gentil, whose hand I'd had to hold because she was anxious about the "bombings."

Before dozing off, Madame Gentil told me what she's been telling Jo, Maria, and me for months. It's always the same story: she was born in 1941; her family lived down in the cellar of their house to shelter from the bombs. She would hear the sirens, and the planes as they flew overhead. One morning, she woke up in a strange room. There were flowers on the wallpaper and big windows that let the sunshine in. She thought that she was dead, that she'd gone to heaven. In reality, the war was over and her parents had carried her upstairs while she slept.

So, I was in the office, and it must have been around eleven o'clock. There wasn't a sound, apart from Titi snoring in his basket. Someone activated the emergency alarm from Monsieur Paul's room. I rushed there because the nurse was on the third floor.

Between the office and room 29, I thought again about the anonymous caller. My imagination ran wild over his identity. Like in the Claude Sautet film, *Les Choses de la vie*, I saw again the faces of Gramps, Gran, Jules, Roman, Maria, Jo, Patrick, Starsky, Rose, Madame Le Camus, the priest, the physiotherapist, and my own face. I imagined all those faces calling the families of those forgotten on Sunday from Monsieur Paul's room.

I opened the door to room 29 and caught sight of my

reflection in the mirror. My double. My twin. Maybe I had an evil twin? Considering what I'd just discovered about my family, nothing else could surprise me. Or perhaps I had a split personality, with one side dominating the other.

Monsieur Paul was sleeping peacefully, all was well. I deactivated the alarm.

Beside my reflection stood the anonymous caller, close to the bed. He was deep in conversation with the son of Madame Gentil, that poor Madame Gentil whom I'd had to reassure twenty-five minutes earlier about the bombings.

"Good evening, sir, it's The Hydrangeas here, in Milly, I regret to inform you of the death of Madame Léonore Gentil. Yes. No. She has just passed away. She had a cardiac arrest. She didn't suffer. No, not now, the morgue is closed. Come to reception tomorrow morning, at 8:00 A.M. Yes. I'm truly sorry. The entire nursing team at The Hydrangeas joins me in offering you our sincere condolences. Goodnight, sir."

I sat down on the bed. My legs couldn't carry me anymore. The anonymous caller had activated the emergency alarm because he knew it was me in the office. Me on night duty. Me who would be in room 29 when he called the son of Madame Gentil. He wanted me to know who he was.

He removed the voice modifier he'd placed over the receiver and hung up.

He moved closer to me. I stroked his face as if seeing him for the first time. In fact, I was seeing him for the first time. I was seeing him as he was, and not how I wanted him to be. He smiled. I put my fingers into the dimples in his cheeks.

When I was telling him about those forgotten on Sundays, I never thought he was listening to me. I just thought he was hearing me. And it was after the Paradise club, too. I was hammered, and the following morning I couldn't remember much. Just snatches of sentences. He'd remembered for me.

He still hadn't said a word to me. And I'd said nothing, either.

He was wearing a stripy sweater that didn't remotely go with his Prince of Wales check slacks. As usual. I thought, I'm going to have teach him how to coordinate colors.

It was the first time I was making a plan while thinking of someone who actually exists.

He took the seagull pendant between his fingers and kissed my hair. Like on the day he took me to Saint-Exupéry airport.

"Have you been making anonymous calls for a long time?"

He smiled.

"Since I've known you."

"And have we known each other long?"

He didn't answer me. He stroked Monsieur Paul's cheek and whispered, *He's my grandfather.*

I closed my eyes and said to him:

"What's your name?"

# ACKNOWLEDGMENTS

Thank you to my grandparents, Lucien Perrin, Marie Géant, Hugues Foppa, and Marthe Hel.

Thank you to Eloïse Cardine, a geriatrics nursing assistant, who gave me EVERYTHING.

Thank you to my personal reading committee, so essential, vital, precious: Arlette, Catherine, Maman, Papa, Pauline, Salomé, Sarah, Vincent, Tess, Yannick.

Thank you to Maëlle Guillaud.

And finally, I give thanks to Claude Lelouch for a thousand and thirteen reasons.